Like a Child to Home

Bill Engleson

Copyright © 2013 by Bill Engleson
First Edition – July 2013

ISBN
978-1-4602-1929-4 (Hardcover)
978-1-4602-1928-7 (Paperback)
978-1-4602-1930-0 (eBook)

All rights reserved.

No part of this publication may be reproduced in any form, or by any means, electronic or mechanical, including photocopying, recording, or any information browsing, storage, or retrieval system, without permission in writing from the publisher.

This is a work of fiction. Names, characters, places and incidents are products of the author's imagination or are used fictitiously and are not to be construed as real. Any resemblance to actual events, locales, organizations, or persons, living or dead, is entirely coincidental.

Produced by.

FriesenPress

Suite 300 – 852 Fort Street
Victoria, BC, Canada V8W 1H8

www.friesenpress.com

Distributed to the trade by The Ingram Book Company

> "In the course of time, legislation and regulation become more important than ethics, and at that point we are lost."
>
> JOHN FREDERIC GIBSON, *A SMALL AND CHARMING WORLD*

> "A writer is congenitally unable to tell the truth and that is why we call what he writes fiction."
>
> WILLIAM FAULKNER

> "Is it my fault that my kind
> Are always drawn towards the sun
> Like a child to home
> Whenever dark is done."
>
> STAN ROGERS, 'CALIFORNIA'

Acknowledgements

As *Like a Child to Home* was coming into its own, I read a fledgling chapter or two at a Denman Island writers group I had been invited to join after exposing my weakness for fabrication in the monthly Denman journal, The Flagstone. The writers group was a new and helpful initiation for me to sorting out the complexity of planning a novel as well as in sharing the love and the labour of writing with others. I would like to thank Diane Davis especially, who organized that group and kept it humming for as long as possible.

In the novel's infancy, Dr. Mike Webster took one early chapter on a flight to Australia. He reports he slept well on the flight.

Helen Blum read much of the pre-edited version a few months before I concluded the work and furnished very helpful direction.

Jean Cockburn, DD Fuchs, Moira Webster, and Butch Leslie, each bringing their respective acumen and life experience, read the pre-edited work and offered very valued observations.

I would like to thank my partner, Sharon Clarke, not only for the precision of her 2nd proof edits but for initially creating a tiny writing nook in the basement to park me. Without this cubbyhole, I would have been spread out all over the house.

Ricki Ewings professionally edited my novel and brought a great level of knowledge and curiosity to the work.

Photographer and multi-talented artist Reilly Leivers (http://www.jerkwithacamera.com/) provided the image selected which, I hope, captures the atmosphere of much of the novel, except for, of course, the funny bits.

And finally, to all the youth, their families, my professional family and anyone else I encountered in the trenches over my 30 year career, thank you for letting me perform a job that I loved, even when, on a relatively few occasions, I didn't. I hope this novel shines a bit of a beacon on the work.

Chapter 1

Wallace Rose
Monday, November 19

It was still dark when I arrived at my office. It was always dark when I went to work in early winter. Though my commute took less than 20 minutes, the winter ride seemed endless. The West Coast rain clanged down like sheets of aluminum, drowning all the hope out of the city. Streets were flooded; the stripped leaves of deep November were swept into a saturated system of gutters.

I parked in my usual spot at the back of our one-story office building, grabbed my briefcase, and bailed out of the car. The slight overhang gave me some protection from the fierce little storm while I found my office key, entered, and shut off the alarm. I went to my cell, hung up my coat, treated the computer with a wakeup call, and checked my e-mail. There was little that interested me. I read a couple of communiqués from Victoria about the good effort we had all made to celebrate Diversity Day. Apparently the minister was pleased. That certainly made my day. Everything else was bound to be downhill.

I took a peek at the list of after-hours memos. After-hours workers troubleshoot child welfare concerns between 1630 hours and 830 hours, and on weekends. They do what is essential and pass everything back to the district office. There were memos for me and each of the two other social workers in the office. There was also a fresh catastrophe alert for the intake worker. That was me today. Doreen Walker, the administrative assistant, would have to call up the information when she came in.

I grabbed the morning papers from the front hall, made my way back to the lunchroom, and assembled a strong pot of coffee. I have always needed some time in the morning to wind myself up. In this work, where decisions of importance are made daily, you have to be able to manage cases from a number of directions simultaneously. This may sound tangled, but I never take situations at face value. They are always complex, because people are the key ingredient in the mix. And the way some people are wired is inevitably, incontrovertibly nightmarish.

As I waited for my coffee and browsed the sports section, the staff entrance door opened, and soft footsteps fell on the muted-grey carpet. Roberta, office manager and mistress puppeteer of our tiny work enclave, rounded the corner and sang out, "Morning, Wally. Good weekend?"

"Too short by a dog's breadth," I replied. "And you?"

"The same." She began her morning routine, which included depositing her lunch in the staff fridge, putting the kettle on for tea, and whisking away to her office.

Roberta is the last of a long line of talented office managers I have had the good fortune to work with. They are the paper queens, women generally, who bring a sense of order, routine, and competence to the world of child welfare.

What a world of tumult it is! It is a paper and electronic prison to those who work in it and those who are trapped in its web. It wasn't always so administratively constricted. In an earlier time, it was all about the people, all about doing for others.

The staff entrance door opened again. Likely it was Cathy Baker, one of my peers. An eager young woman, Cathy is almost as punctual as I am.

"Hey, Wally!"

"Catherine, good morning," I said, barely looking up at her. "You're sounding incredibly chipper for a Monday morning."

I gave her a glance to underscore my staggeringly simple observation. She looked sparkling. I had worked with her for two years, mentoring her in this, her first social-work job. I had fallen into the role easily, partially because mentoring had always been one of my natural worksite functions but in Cathy's case, her youth and her warmth simply captured me. Given my advanced years, I was aware that I was ever ripe to be ensnared by the glow of youthful vigour. Nonetheless, I was able to cap my vulnerability and remain moderately professional.

"Thank you. If I am chipper, it must be because I had the dullest weekend."

"Sorry to hear that," I consoled. Dredging my Friday memory, I asked, "Weren't you going up to Whistler with…what's her name?"

"Laney."

"Right. Laney."

"She cancelled. And it was her boss who had the condo. *C'est la vie*. What about you? Did you have anything exciting going on?"

"Just anticipating Monday morning in the salt mines," I lamented.

"You poor sad sack. No personal life at all, eh?" she smilingly replied.

"Look who's calling the kettle an old pot," I hurriedly interjected, hoping to move on to something less banal and banter-like.

"Actually, I was relieved the Whistler thing didn't happen. After Friday, I wasn't much in the mood for frivolous relaxation."

"Sorry, kid, but it's just after days like that that you need to cut loose."

"And you practise what you seem to be preaching, I suppose?"

"Sometimes," I sheepishly admitted. "Not this time, but I was uninspired, and besides, Jake and I spent some time together for the first time in a long time."

Jake is my son, and we didn't often get the chance to hang out. He lives on Vancouver Island and attends university there. His mother and I had parted ways quite early on in his life and she had moved to Victoria. I had proven a bit of a bust as a long-distance dad, even though I was thankful Jeanne hadn't moved to the other side of the continent.

"Jake came over to see you?" Cathy inquired.

"Well, not just me. Yours truly was a bit of an add-on. They mostly came to visit the parents of his girlfriend; we all met up for coffee Saturday afternoon."

"That's nice."

Nice. That's exactly what it had been. A nice, soft-focused, innocuous, gentle passing of time between a lout of a dad, a somewhat standoffish son, the son's potential in-laws, and the girlfriend. I hadn't seen Jake since the summer. Jeanne, his mother, my long ago wife, had invited me over to the Island for a barbecue. She and I hadn't spoken in a couple of years, not since I had attended Jake's high school grad. Jeanne had married Charlie Oliphant a few months after we legally became separate entities. Seven months later, she had twin girls, reinforcing my sense of serious abandonment. I like to sound bitter about that, but the truth is that Jeanne was a pain in the ass, an upwardly mobile, highly unimaginative schoolteacher. They do their best work conceptualizing with one of their own kind. Charlie taught in the same school as Jeanne. They were a perfect match.

Jeanne's cunning way of preparing me for the possible nuptials of Jake and his girlfriend Heather had been to send the barbecue invitation. More to the point, she wanted to see if I could contribute to the gift she and Charlie were thinking of for the young couple. Jeanne had had to wait until she was in her mid-thirties to travel to Europe and deeply resented that we had only headed south to the beaches of Mexico in our brief heyday, when it was perfectly evident that Europe was where young people should go. She wanted me to split the cost of a year's touring in Europe for the newlyweds.

"Paris, Wally. If we'd gone to Paris, it's possible we would have stayed together," she whispered to me, three sheets to the wind, leaning awkwardly against her backyard's dying cherry tree.

"They look perfect for each other…but Paris would cement it," she added.

It was a trap. Refusal to pony up and she could accuse me of not investing in their chance for marital durability.

"What do you think the cost will be, Jeanne?" I asked, trying to sound the pauper I often believe myself to be.

"It's not that 'spensive," she slurred.

At that point, I hailed Charlie over. He put Jeanne to bed, and I escaped without liquidating my indifferent assets.

This past weekend, I'd finally met the prospective in-laws and had had to face the fact that the son I barely knew was about to become even more distant; and, more frighteningly, probably produce grandchildren for me to ignore.

Heather's parents, Grace and Leonard Cawkwell, were pleasant accountants both, one working for a year-round tax preparation company and the other, Len, ("Call me Lenny, Wally"), for the telephone conglomerate. Heather herself was a dark-haired, slim wisp of a girl, with a loud voice and a sparkling set of teeth that spoke to either successful parents or excellent genes. She was a happy young college kid, and I couldn't understand why she and my offspring were hell-bent on getting hitched. I had thought this latest generation had grave doubts about some of the more traditional customs that circumscribed marriage. This weekend, listening to Jake and Heather babble with optimism that they would beat the marital odds of divorce through sheer willpower, I just bit my tongue and wished them the best. I clearly knew little about the aspirations of their generation.

To seal my part of the bargain, I called Jeanne that night, reminded her that Charlie had packed her off to bed before we had discussed the cost-splitting honeymoon-to-Paris idea and said, "Okay Jeanne, I'll try and pick up my share. I may have to move into your basement when I retire but we'll send these lovebirds to Paris."

I had left her speechless, a first for both of us.

"Yeah," I said to Cathy, "It was nice. But on another note, I think we should discuss the Prentice case." As I said that, I could see Cathy wilt. I paused a second and then said, "Let's go to my office." She nodded, and I followed her down the hallway to my little office cell.

It remained as messy and disorganized as it had last week. And all the weeks before. I was fairly sure that I was sufficiently systematic in my job, that all the paperwork that needed to get done got done. Over the years, fellow workers and an assortment of supervisors had barely been able to conceal their astonishment not only that I was able to keep up with case notes, file recordings, and the like, but that I was consistently ahead of the game.

Like a lot of old-time social workers, I had fallen into the job between less productive engagements. Because I came from the outside, I was forced to learn the job quickly, thoroughly and, most importantly, to scope out what was essential to do to keep the suits off my back.

The suits exist in every human endeavour. They are the hungry ones, the ones who clutch and grab their way to the top of whatever heap they find themselves. They are just a bit slicker than anyone else, just a bit keener and slimier. You can't kick back with the suits, even if they had once been in your social set. They have different agendas. You won't find them dissing the system. In fact, extracting an opinion out of them is as difficult as blowing up stumps with firecrackers. And the really, really frustrating thing about these corporate leeches is that they attach themselves in such a way that you are usually compelled to stay unnaturally close to their available flank to get done the vital things you need to do. You never feel clean about it.

Cathy and I settled in to my little cubbyhole.

"Sorry, I should have been a little more tactful," I apologized.

"Hey, I'm just a little raw about it," she replied. We sat quietly. Roberta buzzed by, waved at us, and went to fetch her tea. In this business— the business of injecting ourselves into the lives of traumatized people—every day, every week, every blessed minute holds the possibility of having our emotional skin scraped by the grater of someone's pain.

The lives of Carla Prentice and her daughter, Skylark, had come our way last Tuesday. Cathy had taken the call from Mrs. Prentice and asked me to buddy up with her. We rarely have the human resources to partner up, but if fellow workers want the assistance, we scramble to find a way. That usually means juggling something else that will likely only get done later then we might want.

Carla Prentice had called the office the previous Tuesday morning, November 13. According to Cathy, Mrs. Prentice came across over the phone as a bit of a basket case. Skylark, her 14-year-old daughter, hadn't been home in five days and was running with some rough people, she thought. The police had accepted the missing persons report, "for all the good that did," and had recommended she call us, as they usually do in such cases.

We meet regularly as a team on Wednesday mornings. Kate Morris is our clinical supervisor, and Chimera Walters is the third social worker. The larger team also consisted of a host of other workers doing related but slightly different work. We had three resident probation officers, a resource worker, a specialized immigrant youth team (primarily addressing Asian boat refugees), and a manager of the whole kit and caboodle (who was perpetually away at some meeting). While not visibly a suit, he was required to seem as if he was when in their presence. The office also had three administrative-support office workers, led by Roberta; they kept everything moving and at least some of us, especially me, from sinking.

But, sadly, I was tumbling into a bottomless lake, up to my floppy ears in administrative alligators. As Cathy and I sat in my office Monday morning, I was consumed by the overwhelming toll last week had taken on me. My legs and arms dragged me down in my chair, and I felt immobilized. If I'd had any sense, I would have taken the week off and flown to Cuba or some similarly warm and distant place.

The thing was that last week was no different from any of our work weeks. Each and every day is like an expedition to the escarpment. Along the way it gets hairier and hairier; supplies, resources, and personnel fall away. Giant apes throw rocks at you. Friends and fellow workers plummet into the deep canyon. Some scream; others simply plunge in resigned silence. You scramble up the cliff, clinging precariously to the stone by your bloodied fingertips, hoping the emotional pitons don't pull loose. The demands of each day remain, heavy, as constant as a hard, thick, endlessly squalling West Coast rain. That's the way of a rain forest; a damp union of souls and squalls.

Chapter 2

Carla Prentice
Wednesday, November 14

At the team meeting on the fourteenth, we prioritized new cases, reviewed current cases, kibitzed some, planned whatever training we thought we might need over the next while, discussed having a Christmas party (although we had left it quite late), and discussed youth and related community issues with the variety of community workers who attend our meetings.

Towards the end of the morning, Cathy raised the issue of the Prentice family.

"Kate, I'd like Wally to go out on this with me."

"Wally, do you have the time? It sounds pretty Mickey Mouse to me. Without-what's her name again?"

"Skylark," Cathy answered.

"Without Skylark, we've got nothing to offer. Nothing to do really. It shouldn't take two workers to do nothing."

"Right now, maybe. I don't know, Kate," Cathy searched for the right words. "I've heard Skylark's name mentioned before." Turning to Drusilla Janes, an outreach worker who had close contact with street and curb youth, Cathy said, "Dru, we've heard that name before, haven't we?"

Drusilla Janes was a tall, muscular woman, with short, bright-yellow hair, who was usually bedecked in dark clothes and reams of cheap, gaudy, delightful jewellery. She was much respected by most of the tough, lonely youth she worked with. She worked late afternoons and evenings usually and, like many of her breed, was only a pager away from the dispossessed, wounded children she ministered to. Often, in the calamity of her days, she encountered the pre-dispossessed, those children hanging on to a semblance of family life, those children who perpetually redefined the events of their lives to make things seem balanced and understandable.

"There's a Skylark who was tight with Corinne Bailey," Dru offered. "If she's the same one, she spent some time at Cori's dad's place in the summer. Dark hair, petite, and a nose ring, I think. I met her once when I picked Cori up for court, sleeping on their couch. She woke up and said hello as we were leaving. Likely the same girl. How many Skylarks can there be?"

With that tiny piece of recall, coupled with a search of our electronic records (which revealed a closed family-service file at Records Management Unit, our central, closed-file storage depot), Cathy called Mrs. Prentice and arranged a 2:00 p.m. home visit. She had already requested the closed file, but the earliest it would arrive via house mail would be tomorrow. Any pertinent information in the file would have to wait upon its arrival. The staff at RMU are clerks for the most part and are not allowed to take, nor comfortable with taking, a peek into these highly confidential and personal files. Only in extreme emergencies would I badger them to peruse the material for me. This case wasn't shaping up to be much of anything. The closed file was over five years old, and sometimes it's better to come at a family cold, without any preconceptions. There are so many caveats to that bendable rule of thumb that sometimes it is just dumb luck that keeps your sorry butt out of the frying pan. We were mitigating fallout by planning to go in tandem.

Cathy ate her bag lunch in the office lunchroom, and I grabbed a sandwich at a local deli. We both then did paperwork and other assorted, accumulating tasks until 1:45, when we convoyed to the Prentice home.

Carla Prentice lived in a portion of the main floor of a nondescript, basement-shy box— what was once called a "west-coast special." The street was pockmarked with small potholes, pit holes really, that telegraphed the sort of care this older neighbourhood could expect from the city. Many, if not all, of the owners on this street had either built or bought at least two decades earlier. It was likely that they had moved on by now and were subsidizing whatever their lives had become from the sale of this primary investment or by renting out these abandoned warehouses to as many people as they could cram into the available space. The Prentice suite was entered through a door off of the cluttered carport. The carport contained an assortment of garbage, some in plastic or metal trash cans, and some in green bags. An old, green Plymouth

Duster with expired plates and at least one flat tire took up most of the space. A relatively new, unlocked, ten-speed bike leaned against one of the walls.

Cathy tightened her right hand into a knocking fist and ra-ta-tat-tatted on the door. It was a door knock I could easily admire. It sounded of authority, confidence and efficiency. It had a no-nonsense quality to it which, while it might initially alarm those on the receiving side of the door, might also bring them a perverse comfort. They might instinctively know that whoever was seeking entry in such a brusque manner not only knew who they were, but also knew exactly what they were doing. Cathy had learned this technique from me. It may seem a small point, a nebulous skill to some, but most of what social workers do involves interaction. The stage has to be set. Protection workers not only need to know how to set a scene in someone else's theatre, they must also have the capacity to safely direct, or, at least guide the drama.

As in control as we needed to be, we also had to be able to gain trust, real trust, not by intimidation, but by force of character, painfully coupled with whatever legitimacy our function gave us.

A voice behind the Prentice family door whispered, "Who is it?"

"It's Cathy Baker, Mrs. Prentice, from children's services. My colleague Wally Rose is with me. I called before lunch."

The door was weather-beaten and had a large indentation near the knob. A boot, lashed out in anger, might have met this door sometime earlier. Perhaps before the Prentices had lived here, perhaps not.

The door opened, and we were ushered in.

"Please come in, Ms. Baker. The place is a bit of a mess, I'm afraid. I've been working double shifts because of Christmas coming, and I haven't had much spare time."

"Shoes off?" I asked. While it may not be the smartest thing to do to take off your shoes in a stranger's house, I like to ask. For a number of reasons there is a rule of thumb that professionals entering a location they are not familiar with should keep their footwear on their feet. Safety concerns (broken glass, rusting metal, and casually strewn hypodermics for example), and the ever-present potential need to move quickly out of harm's way or go after someone who has bolted are but two. I had already concluded that Carla Prentice was sufficiently concerned about the state of her home that she would grant us the freedom to keep our feet covered.

"Keep them on, please, if you'd like. I've been too busy to vacuum anyway."

We followed her into her living quarters. The curtains, worn red velvet, were drawn, and the only light available, other than the fading winter glimmer coming in from a small window over her sink, was from two small lamps on either side of a cloth-covered couch of indeterminate vintage. The coffee table was littered with playing cards and a large glass bowl overflowing with the remains of many cigarettes. A door to the right led to a bedroom, I supposed and the bathroom was likely off to the left. Three rooms; little space. How on earth would I ever be able to live in such restricted space? This thought was never far away. Most of the homes I visited were small. I could feel the walls closing in on me. Some would say I am a bit overweight, and that, added to my over six-foot frame, causes me to fill up a room more than others are sometimes comfortable with. Stuck in my own skin, I am aware that I crave large space around me. I've always assumed that it's some pre-coffin phobia. It only goes away when I'm hiking in the mountains or on those very rare times when I visit a place like New Mexico or Utah.

"Please sit down," I heard Carla Prentice say. "Can I offer you anything? Tea? Coffee?"

"Tea would be nice," Cathy replied.

"I'm fine," I added. "But thanks."

Carla Prentice went to her stove, picked up the kettle, turned 90 degrees to the left to fill it, placed it on the stove, and turned on the electric element.

My eyes had adjusted to the pale light of the room, and I was able to have a better look at her. Carla Prentice was about five foot five. She was wearing a baby-blue tracksuit and grey wool socks. The room was chilly and I quickly scanned it to see the thermostat. The multi-purpose room didn't appear to have one.

Her face was angular, slightly drawn, with high cheekbones, pale lips, and tired, blue-green eyes. She had a good nose, straight, not overly large. Her red hair was held by what looked like a rubber band into a shoulder-blade-length pony tail. She looked over 40, but I knew from our records that she was half a decade younger.

"Mrs. Prentice," Cathy intoned, deciding to get down to business, "as I said when I called you back, there's not much we can do until your daughter returns."

"Carla. Please call me Carla."

"Carla, regardless of what little we can do, we would like to know a little more about why Skylark left home. Has she done it before?"

She turned away from the stove and sat down in a wicker chair opposite where we were on the couch.

"It's been five days. My god! Five days! She's never been away this long from me before."

"Is it just the two of you?" I asked.

"Now? Yes. Now it is."

"You have other children?" I enquired.

"One. My son, Jordan."

"And where is he?" Cathy asked. Although she had the lead on this case, it appeared to me that neither of us had found the intimate rhythm that ideally occurs between client and worker. Once we had some sense of that harmonious engagement, the other would withdraw from asking questions and focus on taking notes. Until then, we each relied on memory and a post interview debriefing, time permitting.

"Jordan? He lives in the city."

"How old is he?"

The closed file had told us that Jordan was currently about 20 years old.

"He turned 20 in July. He's lived away from home since he was, I don't know, 16."

"That's pretty young to be on your own," Cathy offered.

"I wanted him to stay. But he wanted to try living on his own."

"Raising kids today is difficult," I volunteered.

"Do you have children?" she queried, looking at me.

"I do. A boy. Actually a young man now. Do you see your son often?" I asked, attempting to reroute the discussion back to her family.

"Life gets so busy," she lamented. Weariness seemed to overwhelm her. The kettle shrieked. Startled out of her thoughts, she rose quickly from her chair to curb the siren. She poured the hot water into a Brown Betty (or rather a bright-blue Betty) teapot and added two teabags almost as an afterthought.

"Black or milk?" she asked.

"Milk," I said, not wanting to derail her graciousness.

"Milk for me as well," added Cathy.

Once the teapot, cups, and milk were placed on the coffee table, we attempted to pick up where we had left off.

"Carla, Wally was asking how frequently you saw Jordan. I'd also like to ask how Skylark and Jordan get along. Is it possible she has gone to stay with him?"

"He doesn't have a phone as far as I know. And to be honest he's pretty mobile. He's never been all that open with me about where he lives. I stopped pressing. You know, nosy mother questions. I haven't seen him in a couple of weeks. Since Thanksgiving. I don't think he really knows much about her life I'm afraid. They don't see each other all that often." After a brief pause she continued.

"Skylark was ten when Jordan left. She adored him when she was younger. He enjoyed her adoration. Really seemed to thrive on it. He was such a fun-loving kid for quite a few years. Then it sort of started a long slide. Before he left home, we had words."

"Words? What sort of words?" Cathy inquired.

It wasn't a bad question, but Carla's meaning seemed obvious to me, and I could tell she was in enough distress as it was.

"Painful, hurtful, angry words," she said, quite sorrowfully. "He'd stopped going to school, was sleeping all day and up and out all night. He'd allow others…he'd bring home all sorts of people to hang out and smoke and do drugs; occasionally there were young girls. It was an ugly time."

"I needed him to watch Skylark, but…he usually refused. And I couldn't trust him to keep her safe. Some of his friends were…simply awful. And then we'd get into these terrible endless screaming matches. I made so many mistakes. And Skye got caught in the middle. She loved us both and…I didn't handle it well. Any of it, really."

"Is there anyone else you can think of who she might have gone to?" Cathy asked.

"There's my mom and stepdad, but they haven't seen her as far as I know. We don't have much contact with the rest of the family. That's another thing I regret."

"Carla," I interjected, "are you concerned that Skye had some of the same issues your son had? Drugs for instance?"

"Of course I'm worried about all of that. I wish I wasn't, but…I don't know… Skye has her share of mood swings. At least, I thought they might be mood swings. How can a parent of a teenager tell? Some days I'd just have to pussy-foot around the house…afraid I'd say the wrong thing to her…or look at her in a way that might set her off."

We were silent for a few minutes, sipping tea and, perhaps, giving some thought to all those families, our own included, who had suffered from years of estrangement, years of things said and unsaid. As accomplished as we humans had become at developing technology to make our lives easier, we still had some distance to go to repair the lives of people beaten and busted up by familial discord. Whether rich or poor, none of us had any exceptional capacity to fix those wounds. The rich, at least, could soothe their domestic wounds with the comforts of the wealthy. The poor were left to their own undernourished resources. Carla Prentice's tale, at least as much of it as we had thus far been privy to, was almost an everyday occurrence for far too many families.

"Carla, whatever supports we can offer, counselling and the like, the hard truth is that we need all the participants available. Have you tried counselling before?"

"When Jordan left, the police referred me to…a street worker, I believe."

"Do you remember the name?" I asked.

"Manuel…Miguel. I'm sorry; it was a long time ago. I spoke to him once or twice and sent him a photo of Jordan, but I don't think he ever had any contact with him. Jordan stayed out of contact with me for almost a year. A whole year! Then the police found him panhandling downtown and brought him home. But by then, he was…almost feral. That's awful, I know, but that's how I came to think of him. Of what he'd become. I couldn't have him live with us after how he must have been surviving. Squats, sordid places like that. He told me some of it one night after he'd been home a week or so. He actually looked…caged. He seemed to know he had to leave. And he did. Quietly, as if…as if it was his gift to us."

"So," Cathy resumed, "apart from the street worker's involvement, whatever that might have been, there was no counselling?"

"No, none. That was a mistake, I guess. I'd do almost anything not to have…what happened between Jordan and me…I don't know what to call it really…whatever it was…I don't want Skylark and me to fail like that."

"With your permission," Cathy offered, "I will open a file and make an anticipatory referral for counselling with an agency we use. It's called Family Link. They have a bit of a waitlist, so the sooner the referral is in, the better. They have good people. Very experienced."

"Of course you have my permission. I can't say what Skye will say about it."

"Let's cross that bridge when we need to," Cathy suggested.

The offer of counselling was likely minimal comfort to Carla Prentice. Still, there was something almost tangible about the offer, and it gave some hope that Skylark would return and that when she did, there was a possible safe step that could be taken.

"I have a couple of wrap-up questions, Carla," I added. "You've made the missing persons report to the police?"

"Yes, I've done that."

"Do you have the report number?"

"I wrote it down. There by the phone next to you."

I looked at a message pad near the phone, which was to my right next to a lamp. I picked up the pad and made a note of the police report number.

"Two other things. Three, really. Do you have a recent photograph of Skye?"

"Yes, we took some pictures at Thanksgiving. I'll get one for you."

"Thanks. And I meant to ask, do you know some of her friends? People she might go to?"

"This past year, I've lost…I don't know…whatever connection we had. She has a couple of close friends…Deidre Chang and Sue Gainsborough. I'll write down their numbers. I called their parents the day before yesterday, but neither girl had seen Skye. At least that's what they said."

She wrote down the numbers and passed the sheet to Cathy. We got up and made our way to the door.

"One last thing," I started to ask, when the phone rang.

"Excuse me," she said and rushed to the phone. We hovered at the door, not quite ready to leave.

"Oh, hi, Dad," we heard her say. "Yes, the social workers have been here. They're just leaving." Carla was silent, listening to the person on the other end of the phone, who I assumed was her stepfather.

"You don't have to yell. They were helpful. I won't listen to you swear, Dad. I won't put up with it."

Twenty feet across the room, I could make out the swelling, audible anger of the male on the other end of the connection. Cathy's grimace let me know clearly that her auditory skills were as good as mine.

"CALL BACK WHEN YOU CAN BEHAVE, BRIAN," screamed Carla into the phone. She slammed it down. Tears welled up into her eyes. Her face was flushed, her anguish palpable.

"I'm sorry. He...he can be such a bastard at times." And, after a pause, she added, "I've never hung up on him before."

"Are you going to be okay?" Cathy asked.

"It's nothing new. Since he's retired, he's got lots of strong opinions on my parenting. Who's to say he's not right?"

Though Cathy's question had been directed at Carla Prentice, wanting to elicit how she was faring after the exchange with her father, Carla's response seemed to indicate that she was more concerned about him and his reactions. I found that somewhat worrying but the interview had reached its conclusion.

"We'll be going," I said. "One last question...probably means nothing. Does the name Corinne ring a bell? Maybe a friend of Skye's from the summer?"

"I...I don't think I know any of her friends with that name. She was pretty wild last summer. One time that I know of she stayed out overnight. At least one night. I had decided to live and let live, not nag her like I'd nagged Jordan."

"I'll make the referral and let you know when it's been accepted," said Cathy. "Here's my card. Feel free to call for whatever reason, Carla. By the way, just for the record, could you write down the last address you had for Jordan?"

Cathy handed Carla the same piece of paper on which she'd written the names and phone numbers of Skye's two friends. Carla wrote the address down and handed the sheet back to Cathy.

We walked out into the retreating winter light. It was a little after three. I had a four o'clock appointment at the office, and Cathy had a home visit.

"You want to debrief later?" I asked, rather hopefully. Over the years I'd worked in a variety of offices. After-work drinking wasn't all that popular or prevalent in our sector. But, sometimes, the day just demanded some professional company and a glass of wine.

"What time do you figure?" she asked.

"I've got my four o'clock with Ryan. Shall we say 5:30 at the Out Inn?"

"Such a lovely little alternative pub," she laughed. "I'll meet you there before six. My visit with Tessa might run over by a bit, but not by much."

Cathy was paying her first visit to her client Tessa Mallory's new independent-living apartment. A large measure of our specialized youth team work involves assessing and preparing government wards, that is, teens in the legal care of the state, for what is called independent living. Independent living is the final preparatory push for youth in state care, youth who have reached the ass-end of that care and are quickly moving towards the age of majority which means they are about to turn nineteen. Youth in state care can have an amazingly diverse set of experiences on their journey to adulthood. The lucky few have family life replicated as painlessly as possible for them. As you might imagine, matching youth with those rare and exceptional families is often as much dumb luck as it is good planning. Tessa was one of Cathy's favourite youth, favourite because she was a relatively accessible young woman, open to support and advice; favourite because that very openness allowed Cathy to stretch the capacity of our penurious system of care to allow Tessa to have at least some of the advantages that a kid raised in an intact middle-to-upper-middleclass home might have. Often, the young people we were mandated to serve were victims of their own stunted imaginations and one of our roles was to stimulate their dreams if possible. Kids like Tessa still knew how to fantasize a better life.

As we walked to our cars, I muttered, "Damn, I meant to ask her about that door."

"It'll keep. We grilled her enough, I think. See you in a while."

In moments, we were both out of there.

Chapter 3

Gord Lafferty
Late afternoon, November 14

I headed back to the office to keep my four o'clock appointment with 18-year-old ward Ryan Conway. I had been Ryan's social worker for the past two years. He had been midway through his sixteenth year when he became a permanent ward of the state. That was unique at the time. The trend in the past few years had been to seek alternatives to state care for older teens. Cost was one factor, though the suits denied it at every turn. A more germane reason, one that offered some solace to those of us on the front lines, was the realization that state care was singularly incompetent most of the time in the management of older youth. The long and the short of it was that we simply weren't able to bring any noticeable change to the lives of these older young people. Whatever round-holed experience they'd had in their lives, our square-pegged solutions held short sway for most of them. At least, that was my informed professional perception.

There was one thing we could do, however, one small practical bit of assistance we could provide—if we were so inclined, if we could find the time, if the kid chose to make use of it. Lots of ifs. That one thing was the classic friendly ear coupled with well-chosen words and money.

In Ryan's case, we had taken that rare extra step and assumed legal responsibility for him. That mostly entailed providing him with rent and food money and encouragement to get a job, get some training, and now, as he precariously, inevitably, wobbled on the precipice of the age of majority, prepare him as best we could for living on his own hook.

I made it back to the office with 15 minutes to spare. I parked in front of the office and went in through the public access portal.

Denise Shields, a relatively new office worker, buzzed me through.

"How's the afternoon gone here, Denise?" I asked, hoping that it had been peaceful. I was on intake, and no one had paged me— generally a sign of tranquility.

"Nothing for intake," she replied intuitively. "Is that what you were asking?"

"Am I that easy to read?"

"Apparently. Anyways, no intake calls on my watch. Mr. Lafferty did ask to be notified when you return. He wants to see you."

"A manager…actually in the building. I'm flabbergasted! I've got a few minutes I could give him. Ryan Conway should be here shortly for a meeting with me. Get me from Gordon's office, will you?"

"Will do, Wally."

Gordon Lafferty was our area manager. On a good day, he was our buffer from the excess machinations of the policy-mad, budget-brained suits who guided our world. On a good day, he would approve our outrageous requests for additional funds to improve the lives of our wards. On a bad day, he was the hammer, the messenger of denial and detailer of infractions, the heavy who pounced, the one who said no, the one who ultimately could sack the weakest or the unluckiest of us. We both feared and loved him. He was our check and our balance.

Over the years, I'd had multiple dealings with Gord Lafferty. As union steward, as an aggressive union steward, I had represented a number of employees who had found themselves accused of committing mostly small demonstrations of human failing in the course of doing their job. Often Gord was the management rep. On the surface, his job was to investigate the alleged delinquency and take appropriate action. On the surface, my job as steward was to represent the member's interest and process any grievance the employee might choose to submit after the employer's rep had issued his findings. In reality, at least my take on reality, Gord frequently went over the top in affixing guilt, and this harsh response in turn necessitated that I aggressively speak up. We had butted heads often, and I liked to think that we shared a similar number of headaches as a result.

Gord Lafferty occupied the largest office in our little outpost, even though he used it no more than once a week and often less than that. It was a corner office with large windows on two walls. The centrepiece of the office was a sparklingly neat, sort of unlived-in-looking desk, a manicured sort of desk with a photo of family in a gold picture frame on the right side of the desk, an immaculate desk blotter dead centre, a phone and monogrammed notepad on the left side. That was it for the desk. Absolutely an unlived-in desk in my view, like an apartment rented for trysting alone.

Gord's office was big enough that he had squeezed in two government-issue loveseats and a small, round coffee table. Because most of our offices could comfortably hold no more than three people at a time, we regularly commandeered Gord's office for meeting with larger groups. We did this so frequently that we had considered requisitioning the space for meetings full-time. Actually, I had considered it, but there was always the fear that if there was an acknowledgement that Gord was rarely in the office, he might be compelled to spend more time. Nobody, least of all me, wanted that. So the issue simmered just below the surface, where it rightfully belonged.

Gord's door was open, and he was on the phone. He was a pleasant-looking sort of fellow, a couple of inches short of six feet, with an athlete's build; with thin, almost disappearing, dirty blonde hair; and a face graced with a broad, toothy smile like a happy-go-lucky sportsman who'd just downed one too many brews. In his private world he was a sportsman, a team player, one of the boys. And, like many a successful suit, he used those skills of buddydom, nurtured through a lifetime of camaraderie and competition, to deke his way up the ladder.

I stood in his doorway for a couple of minutes. Eventually, he looked up, continued talking, beckoned me in, and gestured that I should take a seat opposite him. I took the proffered seat and waited for him to complete his telephone conversation. "He's here now. Uh huh. No, I haven't discussed it with him. Well, I intend to. That's pretty drastic, Ted. Look, let me call you back. Yeah, before five, Ted. Ciao."

"Sorry about that, Wally. I should have closed the door."

"What's up, Gord? You wanted to see me?"

Gord opened up a file folder in front of him. He twitched a tad, displaying a facial wriggle. He had a moderately constipated look, one that often precedes something unpleasant. Or I might have been reading too much into his facial tics.

"Look, Wally, a serious situation has come to our attention. No way around it, so we might as well hold our noses and jump right in. It's got to be done. And I've got to do it."

Then he paused, perhaps stymied by the magnitude of his unenviable task. This surprised me, because he wasn't usually a pussyfooter. Too many times I had wanted him to preface his blunt style with some softer peddling.

"We've had a complaint about you, Wally. I really want to deal with it as quickly as possible, but you need to get a steward before I do. Unless you want to waive that right, of course. Then I'd be prepared to deal with it here and now."

I silently sucked in some of the windowless air that passes for oxygen in the sealed containers we toil in. A complaint. Not unheard of in our line of work. Whenever you are engaged in intruding into the private lives of adults and youth, you expect backlash. Agents of social control not only expect repercussions from those they encounter and their posse of advocates, we are expected to encourage it. Many, not all by any means, but many of the people we inspect and detect and afflict with our state-sanctioned presence are lifelong victims not only of their own weak sense of selves but of state diminishment. Many times, out of the painful frustration of being constantly scrutinized by officials of oversight, they have to strike back.

I had led a charmed professional life up to this moment. But now I was in the soup. As curious as I was, I was not going to weaken my position by waiving any rights of process. And Gord Lafferty knew that I would be foolish to accept his modest offer to babble right there and then. It made no sense to me that he had tried to subvert the way these issues are addressed.

"Look Gord, let's not waste each other's time. Let's set a meeting time, and I'll try and get a steward. Happy with that?" I asked, just a shade more angrily than I intended.

"This is a serious complaint, Wally. I'm tempted to suspend you pending disposition."

"Then let me know what the hell it's about," I insisted, barely hanging on to my self-control.

While I tried to contain my shock, I would never, even for a millisecond, expect that I or anyone would receive any spontaneous decision from Gord Lafferty. Whatever was going on, he would have cleared it with a superior. The last thing I wanted was a suspension. Invariably, in our anally constricted organization, suspension meant no pay. Nada. Not only did they kick you when you were down, they made sure you stayed down by cutting off their contribution to your financial resources. In other organizations, the police for example, cops who were suspended were not usually suspended without pay, even if they had allegedly shot some innocent twerp or beaten some out-of-it stoner. Whatever the allegation, cops were afforded the fiscal legs to keep their heads above the sludge until the complaint was resolved. Teachers also were often accorded similar treatment, even if they were accused of sexually abusing their students or teaching creationism.

In the past, when I had represented comrades who had been suspended without pay, the ones who invariably held up best were those with working partners. The singles, the ones who lived paycheque to paycheque, typically didn't last more than a couple of months. No matter how righteous their defence was, they folded, swallowed whatever bitter pill was being shoved down their throat by the employer, and drifted away into another life.

That might be my fate, single loner that I was.

"Gord," I said, putting the brakes to my impatient reverie, "I'll call the union and try to get back to you by end of day. Noon tomorrow at the latest."

"No later than noon, Wally. This can't wait."

I let him have the last word, fearful of what mine might be.

Denise came up to me and handed me a note that told me Ryan was here for our appointment.

"Denise, could you ask him to give me five minutes? I need to make a call," I whispered.

I scurried to my office and dialled the union. I wanted to speak to Millie Hunt, my union local's staff representative.

I got through to Millie and confirmed that she could represent me at a meeting with Lafferty. Noon tomorrow would work for her. As we were flying blind, there would be no point in meeting ahead to caucus. I knew enough to keep my lips sealed and wait to hear what the poison pen letter was being delivered my management. I e-mailed a note to Lafferty, copying Millie, confirming noon the next day for the inquisition.

With that annoying diversion out of the way, I collected my thoughts and went out to get Ryan Conway.

Chapter 4

Ryan and Erin
Wednesday, November, 14

Ryan was a tall, shaggy, worn-down young man. His clothes always looked slept in—likely were; and that, combined with a one-or two-day growth of light blond beard, seemed to add to the urgency he displayed in getting his needs satisfied. A quick response was never quite fast enough.

Housing was an interminable issue for him. The little money we gave youth like him for housing invariably meant that they would have to share space. Most of the youth I encountered simply didn't have the social skills, the common sense, to live on their own, let alone share an apartment with one or two peers. Ryan had great difficulty sharing anything.

As I approached Ryan in the waiting room, he was smiling and chatting to a thin young woman I didn't recognize. She had fine facial features, the delicate jaw of Audrey Hepburn with the same slinky, contained body. Her nose was pierced, and her thin, short coat did not attempt to cover a belly ring and the tip of what I briefly imagined was a dark, red flower that suggestively blossomed above her belt line.

"Ryan, how are you?" I asked, reaching out to shake his hand just as he moved to high-five me. Not wanting to appear to be the social klutz that I sometimes am, I limberly readjusted the direction of my hand and contrived a reasonably capable salute to match his.

"Fuck, man, I've been better."

"Come in to my office," I suggested. "Coffee or anything?"

"Any juice?"

"I'll check," I said. We usually try to keep juice packs and a few portable foodstuffs available for youth in need who come our way.

"Orange juice, man, if you got it. I'm running low on my vitamin C."

"Right," I muttered.

As we began to walk through the security door, he tugged the sleeve of the young Hepburn look-alike and said, "This is Erin, Wally." He gestured to the girl. "I'd like her to come along."

"By all means. Juice or coffee, Erin?" I asked.

"A cup of coffee would be great. Is it fair trade?" she queried, with the assertive poise of an anti-global activist.

"I don't know," I replied, wishing I did, knowing I should pay more attention to food sources. Offices are complex communities. Chores need to be done by shanghaied volunteers. Who did buy the coffee these days, I wondered? What were the odds our meagre coffee fund helped support small organic farmers in Bolivia, farmers who didn't clear-cut trees, who kept the forest to provide sufficient shade for their coffee bean crop? Who did I work with who might have articulated such a position? The truth, the pathetic, unvarnished truth, was that whoever bought the coffee likely bought a huge bag of beans at some bulk food store as an afterthought when they were out shopping for their at-home family.

"I can't guarantee the origin of the beans," I woefully confessed. "And, at this time of day, whatever coffee's left may be at best a bit sludgy, regardless of pedigree. Still, want some?"

"I'll risk it. Life on the edge—that's for me," she said, beaming with a gloriously warm smile. I knew the odds were I'd come to like this young woman if she stayed in Ryan's world. Whatever her life had been, she seemed to have juggled it well. I came across too few like her. Youth like Ryan were all too prevalent. Life had kicked them in the teeth, and they were forever spitting out enamel chunks. Nothing ever worked for them. They almost never had the inclination or the ability to examine themselves and the part they played in their own defeats.

I parked Ryan and Erin in my office, got two coffees and one OJ, and sat down.

Ryan had made the appointment last week without telling me what the issue was.

"It's your meeting, Ryan. What's on the agenda?"

He stared down at his black-booted feet. That in itself let me know his footwear was on its last legs. There was a wide split on the instep of the right boot that didn't look repairable.

"Fuck, man, my old man fucked me."

"What do you mean, fucked you?" I asked in my professionally logical voice. I knew Ryan's father had little to do with him. Their history was a cheerless tale, not all that untypical of youth in care. When Ryan was ten, his drunken dad cracked up the family car. His sister and cousin were killed in the crash, and dad did two years for driving while intoxicated. Ryan came out of the crash with some broken bones and his mother had suffered serious head injuries. No one on his mom or dad's side came forward to offer themselves as interim parents while his mom mended, so Ryan spent some time in care until his mother healed sufficiently to resume his care.

However, she developed a dependency on pain killers; from then on they lived as close to the periphery as a family can in our country. Ryan basically raised himself. They had to move often; his mother couldn't manage her small disability income. She certainly couldn't manage him. His behaviour deteriorated. He and his mom were evicted regularly, even from subsidized housing. It was all terribly bleak.

Once his father was released from jail, he'd hooked up with an old girlfriend and refused to have anything to do with Ryan. Whether it was guilt or that he was pretty much an asshole, the end result was the same. Ryan wouldn't have admitted it, but what he really wanted was for his father to reclaim him, to love him and undo the past. Ryan's mom was extremely bitter about his dad and the poison permeated all of their interactions. In the end, after years of yo-yoing in and out of care, he'd finally come back, on a permanent basis, shortly after I took over his file.

"My grandfather died and left me some money. My old man spent it all."

"How do you know?" I asked.

"My old lady got a call from my gram. She'd given my dad $2,000 to give to me and she wanted to know if I'd got it. Jesus, she's old and gimped up. She knew he'd just take it himself. She hated that my granddad wanted to leave anything for me. Hated it!"

As Ryan escalated in pain, I tried to think of a way to interject something that would comfort him somewhat. Erin had moved closer to him, but wisely, I thought, refrained from reaching out in a consoling gesture. I had seen him in this sort of spiraling out of control state before on many occasions. I was convinced that he almost preferred this frenetically intense condition of agitation. I also knew that his 'gram' was a bitter old woman and quite likely had intended to fan the flame of familial discord, first by giving her alcoholic son the money that should have gone directly to Ryan, and second, by calling Ryan's tortured mother to make sure Ryan and his mother were aware of the fiscal betrayal by his father.

It seemed pointless to share with Ryan that any and all bequests that come to wards of the government are kept in safe keeping by the Public Trustee until they age out at 19. At least that's the rule, one I've ignored on occasion to lessen the provocation of the bureaucracy on the youth under my guardian wing.

"Ryan, Ryan!" I finally interjected. "Time out. Do you think you might want to go out back for a smoke?"

He collected himself a bit and said, "No smokes, Wally. I'm tapped out."

"Erin, do you smoke?" I asked, suspecting that she didn't.

"Uh huh, but I'm out," She replied. My ESP had failed again.

"Let me see if I can scrounge up a couple," I said, plainly showing little concern for the health and welfare of my ward and his friend.

The office was down to two smokers. Luckily, I found a partial pack in the empty office of our transient foster-home worker who was forever on the road. I lifted two of the smokes and promised myself to leave a confessional note.

Cancer sticks in hand, Ryan and Erin went outside for their ceremonial, if somewhat stale, smoke. I checked my e-mail and saw that Gord had read my note and confirmed the time of our meeting. I sat back, planning how to get Ryan away from the topic of his irretrievable losses and discuss other, more timely matters.

He and Erin returned. He was much calmer. That might last for a couple of minutes, I thought. I tried to enjoy the essence of cigarette smoke that clung to them like invisible, rancid confetti. I was still drawn to the memory of lingering cigarette smoke. Decades after I had last smoked a cigarette, I had yet to join the vociferous reformed-smoker brigade. I chalked it up to a strong sense of loyalty to lost causes; the political left, the cultural benefits of television, and the drop-dead gorgeous, albeit deadly, addiction of tobacco.

"Look," I started, "if you want, I can try and talk to your dad. Find out about the money."

"It would be useless," he said. "He hates social workers, always has. It would just make it worse."

Ryan wobbled his head and squirmed an inarticulate shudder. His scrunched-up expression told with certainty how much worse he believed it would be if I contacted his dad. It was your everyday celebrated fear of the unknown.

"Have it your way. The offer's there. You just have to ask if you change your mind. Let's change the subject, okay?"

"Sure," he replied. "Whatever."

"Good. You wanted to talk to me about housing too. What in particular?"

"Jesus, Wally, you musta guessed. Scotty evicted me."

I wasn't surprised. Ryan had had a whole range of places that he'd moved into and subsequently gotten the boot from. This latest was in a basement suite of a nodding acquaintance's father. The suite had a six-foot ceiling; Ryan was almost as tall. The whole Scott clan lived upstairs, and Ryan had one room in the basement with a couch and hotplate. He shared the bathroom with three or four young Scott males, including his nodding acquaintance.

"Why were you asked to leave?"

"They didn't want me to have Jeanette over."

Jeanette was Ryan's recent girlfriend.

"That doesn't seem all that reasonable."

"Well it seemed bloody reasonable to Mr. Scott. Anyway, his house, his rules, right?"

"Can I ask why they don't want Jeanette around?"

"It's personal, Wally," he said, glancing at Erin. Erin looked like she knew what the Scott family had against Jeanette but was sworn to secrecy on pain of death. I couldn't imagine what it was. I had met Jeanette a couple of times. She was pretty, seemingly respectful, and more or less presentable.

I was chauvinistic enough to know that many young men on the rough edge of society were smartened up by the presence of the right young woman. Girls, women like Jeanette, brought a slightly stronger sense of maturity to the relationship. Just that topping up seemed to pull young men back from the abyss. Sometimes. With luck. Not often enough, however.

Still, if the Scott's didn't like her, sensed something unsettling about her, there had to be something seriously off about her. Families like the Scott's were feral in their capacity to survive. They seemed to risk little that would jeopardize their way of life. Providing a space for Ryan was a low-risk activity for them, given the rugged way they lived. Mr. Scott was a long distance hauler, and all his sons were also involved in driving/vehicular occupations or pastimes. Mrs. Scott allowed her house to be used as a social centre if for no other reason than to maintain control over her brood and their set. Ryan was simply one more hanger-on, a source of short-term, easy money. Even before he had moved into their basement, his time was doomed to be up there. There would be something that he would do wrong. He knew it, the Scott's knew it, and, for sure, I knew it.

"So, yes, it's personal and none of my business. Can I ask if whatever it is might impact your next living arrangement?"

"Christ, it might. It's still personal, right? I don't want to talk about it. All right?"

I didn't mind touching the occasional sensitive nerve.

Frequently I found myself struggling with Ryan. It often felt like everything I said was bound to ignite him.

"Does Sadie know you need to move?" Sadie Cohen was Ryan's probation officer. He was on one year's probation for assaulting a group-home worker. He'd never truly accepted his responsibility for the assault, even though he pled guilty eventually. There were always tensions in group living environments, much like any home, but they were, on average, significantly more intense in the artificial confines of group homes. The primary differences were the constantly changing staff and kids, the small nuances of meaning, in the words spoken, and, perhaps, an increased pressure on young people in care to rebel, to express themselves and their ideas regularly, if not safely.

"I'll tell Sadie," Ryan finally said. He then changed the subject. "Look, Wally, here's the deal. Erin needs a roommate and I need a place."

"That's fine," I responded. I looked at Erin and asked, "Where do you live, Erin?"

"A basement suite...near Hamilton Elementary. With my girlfriend," she added. Her response was flat, and I wanted to pursue it further.

"Is there anything I should know?" I asked, wandering in the dark. Ryan had taken more than his usual care to introduce his plan to move in with this new friend.

"There's a hitch, Wally," he said.

"My hitch, I'll tell him," interrupted Erin.

"Shoot."
"I tried to get welfare, but they don't seem too ready to help."
"Why?"
"They say I can live with my mom."
"And what do you say?"
"I say I can't."
"Why?"
"My business."
"Fair enough, but it becomes their business when you ask for money."
"Bullshit!"
"Life's full of it," I replied.

So we had stalemated. My day was drawing to a close, and I needed to speed up my information gathering, not only from Ryan, but from his friend as well. It seemed to me that Erin might more easily discuss her situation if Ryan was not in the room. I'm not the most insightful of men. People always have small secrets clinging to them like barnacles on oysters. On the other hand, she might have shared every blessed little mystery she possessed with Ryan and speaking to her alone would be an utter time waster. Selfishly, I decided to have a private chat with her. The odds were Erin would be a much more pleasant conversationalist than Ryan, and I needed a break from his outbursts.

"You know guys," I pondered aloud, "for me to help the situation, I need just a bit more information. Ryan, I'm going to page Sadie, and if she's free, would you do your duty and report to her? If she isn't available, I'd still like to talk with Erin alone. About her; not about you. Is that copacetic?"

They both shrugged their version of compliance. I dialled Sadie Cohen's office, told her I had a young probationer in my office who desperately wanted to fulfill his obligations to the court and god and country and could she squeeze him in now? Sadie oozed with workplace camaraderie.

In the wink of an eye, she was at my door to harness Ryan and usher him down to her office.

"Okay, handsome, come along," she invited.

Ryan turned a blond-bearded pink, left the office, and led Sadie back to her office.

Sadie Cohen had been involved in the corrections business for over 30 years. She was as tough as they came. She'd survived over 15 years in the federal prison system. Eventually she decided that she wanted to be at the front end load of the equation rather than, as she put it, "the ass end of justice." Her Brillo-pad-textured grey hair sprayed out of her head like the Bride of Frankenstein. She had an in-your-face direct approach and loved not only shocking youth but placing heavy demands on them. Her vibrant, insistent personality won over most of the young toughs, male or female, who found their wings clipped in her aviary. Judges often ordered specific young felons directly to her as a condition of probation or bail. Her peers seemed to accept this special distinction, likely because she was very open and available.

On the other hand, she acknowledged that she didn't feel all that influential with the withdrawn ones, the loners, the ones afraid of their own shadow, the ones who killed cats or abused infant siblings or shoplifted underwear and the like. She went out of her way to offload those types of offenders in favour of the ones with jam, with moxie, with heart. Ryan fit somewhere in the middle, but he stood up for himself. She worked well with his sort of agonizing tussle with life.

The office was calm after Ryan's departure.

"You already have a roommate?"

"Yup. Gina."

"She staying? Leaving?"

"Up to her."

"Of course, it would be. Does Gina want Ryan to move in?"

"There isn't any choice in the matter."

"Okay, I may be the enemy. I hope not. I would appreciate you being just a little straighter with me. Okay?"

She gave me a thoughtful-looking glare. I returned the look with my best "I'm on your side; screw the World Bank in the process, but choose your answers carefully, nonetheless" smile.

"Ryan isn't Gina's favourite person for sure. But he doesn't bug her all that much." She paused and added, "She likes that Rock gets along with him."

"Rock?"

"Big mother of a German shepherd."

"Named after The Rock?"

"Nope. Rock Hudson."

I wanted to ask why but couldn't bring myself to. We'd likely come back to it, and if we didn't, I could accept that.

I changed course. "Who'd you talk to at the welfare office?"

"Some nasty piece of work," she volleyed back.

"Ooo-whee! That's helpful."

"McLeod, Mac-something-or-other. A Scottish name, I think."

"If the bagpipe playing lady said you could live at home, is that because she talked to your mother?" I asked, again in my softest, kindest voice.

She offered up a faint grin at my even fainter joke. "You think you're pretty funny, don't ya?"

"Only with a receptive audience."

"Right." She smiled. "You think I'm receptive?"

"I was hoping," I answered. And I was.

"Okay, maybe she was Irish. Hell, I can't tell."

"Do you have her card?"

Erin mimed a ripping up action.

"Which office?" She told me. I knew the worker. I couldn't recall if she was Scottish but wondered what else she could be.

"So what did Phyllis MacDougal do?"

"She called my mother, who knew what to say, knew what she was supposed to say, agrees with me living away from home…most of the time…and she forgot. She bloody forgot what we'd rehearsed. That screwed it all up."

"You rehearsed?"

Erin looked nervous, like she had been too forthcoming.

"Well, maybe not rehearsed. More like, mom needs help remembering what to say. She gets rattled."

"We all get rattled about some things, Erin."

"Her especially."

"How long have you been away from home?"

"From her home? Forever."

"So there's a big story here. You want to tell me?"

She had told it before, had it down pat, and delivered it with a matter-of-factness that belied the hurt.

Erin's mom was a band groupie at Erin's birth. Erin was raised on the road with no day-to-day routine and no idea who her biological dad was. When she was six, child-welfare authorities apprehended her in a motel in Sudbury. Her mother and some male acquaintance had passed out from a noisy all-night boozathon. Eventually, she was sent to live with her maternal grandmother in

BC. Unfortunately, her granny had a cerebral hemorrhage and died suddenly when Erin was twelve. She again found herself in care.

A couple of foster home placements and two years later, she was placed with her maternal uncle. Her mother had settled down somewhat during this period and she had moved back to BC with Erin's toddler-age stepsister. She slowly re-familiarized herself with her mother and got to know her sister for the first time. Erin's uncle was a little shaky at parenting, possibly because he was only in his mid-twenties. He worked in a warehouse and afforded little supervision for Erin. Last year it was decided by the social worker, her uncle, and her mom that she should leave care and live with her mother and sister. However, that bottomed out pretty fast. Her mother still liked to party, was very ill with some disease Erin didn't want to talk about, and seemed to Erin to be constantly on the verge of losing her second child to the state. Erin had strayed into drugs, "serious crack-cocaine" issues, she said, and had only been clean for five months. To stay straight, she had to limit contact with her mother's addiction. Her uncle had a girlfriend now and was too busy with his own life for her to go back there.

Two months ago, with a little bit of money she'd saved from part-time work, she'd moved into her new suite with a girlfriend. She was trying to maintain a presence in the Keyhole program, which I knew was an alternate school program in the next city over. She spent as much time as she could with her sister, who was now ten, but was really afraid that if she lived at home, she would "disintegrate."

"Disintegrate?"

"Yeah. Like the Columbia. Blown apart into a billion pieces. It's just, you know, time that I do it myself. It was good with Granny. She was great. She had a good job; she knew what she was doing. It'll never be that good again. My uncle, my mom, it's like 'Parenting for Dummies' with them. And even then they don't get it. Takes way too much out of me."

"So, you want to keep your own place, take in another roommate, and what? Continue with school, I suppose?"

"Yup," she said, with a strong whisper of a voice, like she needed to put emphasis on her answer but dug deep to say it.

"And you think you can make it work with Ryan as one of your roommates?" I asked rather dubiously. "Roommates are hard work."

"I've learned some stuff from Gina. Ryan just needs to know the rules. And know his ass will be kicked out if he fucks up."

I looked at her as if to say that his whole life had been an endless ass-kicking.

"He's told me some pretty crappy stuff about his life," she said, answering my silence.

"And what have you told him about your life?"

"Hmmm," she said, smiling. "Enough. Not everything, but enough so he knows we've travelled a bit of the same highway."

"What's between the two of you?" I asked as delicately as I could muster. "Boyfriend-girlfriend?"

She smirked in the kind of way your betters humour you. "Just a guy friend. Jeanette's pretty possessive, even if I was interested, which I'm not. Does it really matter anyway?" she asked.

"Not the morality of it. I'm thinking of a program we have, Youth Agreements. Pays better than welfare, but we do a contract. Your history would suggest to me that you'd be eligible. However, the state requires an offering. You can have lovers; you just can't live with them."

"Why's that?" she asked.

"Because you're a child, and because, well, the state is a prude," I replied. Not a very comprehensive answer, I was thinking.

"You're the state," she accused. "You're the prude!"

"Guilty," I fired back. "Guilty as charged."

Chapter 5

Cathy and Wally
Wednesday, November 14 (evening)

I repeat it to myself often, usually in the car, where I believe it's permissible to talk to your inner speeder, when you are your only companion, when little swirls of venom can be let loose. Safely, mind. But released to free you up from stewing all day. Stewing is part of the job and needs to be expelled on company time.

When I am in my little mobile stew pot, I espouse my strongest creed. I am a punctual man. I am a man who always arrives on or before the appointed time. Well, you say, is that all you are? Is that all you are proud of? In a profession that has incredibly poor PR, is that the sum total of who you are? Balls!

When people think of social workers, I imagine they think of liberal do-gooders, perpetually frazzled and late. A bit trite, but that's what they likely think. I think it. We are nothing more or nothing less than a superficially perceived profession.

A sad truth, however, is that many of the social workers of my acquaintance like to rant. I like to rant. Sometimes that makes us late.

Risking being late for my after-work drink and after-work rant with Cathy, I drove Ryan and Erin to her place. I finally got around to asking her last name. It was Mulaney. The house was a two-story stuccoed affair, and entry to Erin's suite was off the carport. The carport was cluttered with junk, old appliances, sinks, pipe, and assorted used lumber. I saw a lot of off-the-carport entrances in my work.

Erin invited me in for tea, and even though I was late for my drink with Cathy, I accepted. It might prove to be a teachable moment. Or a snoopable moment, anyway.

Erin's suite was a mess. The bathroom, bedroom, and kitchen were separated by hanging silk curtains that looked liked well-worn kimonos. The living room was jam-packed with couches, unpacked boxes, three TVs, a stereo, and an old coffee table. On almost every flat spot in the room, cans and other assorted receptacles were overflowing with cigarette butts. The suite reeked of stale smoke and cigarettes. Self-preservation dictated that I resist the offer of tea, but one of the prices of working with people is that you accept them, their habits, their grunge and all, as you find them. The room was a public health disaster, but a little boiling water in a teapot was a relatively benign proposition. Nevertheless, I would pay close heed to the kettle's whistle.

Erin made the tea and cleared some space on one of the battered couches for me. Once the tea was steeped, we sipped our liquid and listened to Big Brother and the Holding Company. I commented that Joplin had been dead and gone twice as long as Erin and Ryan had been alive.

Erin said, "She could really belt out her music. You don't have to be old to know that."

"I'm an ageist through and through," I confessed. "Try not to be, but I'm stuck with it; older is superior."

"In music, maybe," she agreed. "But nothing beats being young. Nothing. My mother had the best time when she was young." And then she added, "Having me made her old."

Her painful comment gave me a small inkling of the guilt she might be experiencing.

Ryan sat off in a corner of the suite, fuming or meditating, stewing in his own vinegary juices, I assumed. Erin was enjoying her retro-music; I was emotionally flatlining from a tough day that was destined to stretch into the wee hours.

Before I had given them a ride home, we had agreed to pursue the youth agreement strategy for Erin. That involved some paperwork, an assessment by me and a drug counsellor, and approval by my supervisor. It also entailed Erin's submitting to our expectations and allowing an outreach worker to assist her. The biggest hurdle for her would be tolerating the state's involvement in her life again. She had had way too much of that over her few short years and appeared to me to be weary of that domination.

I drank my tea quickly, reiterated my willingness to speak to Ryan's father about the intercepted inheritance, confirmed with Erin that the youth agreement process would begin tomorrow and that the outreach worker would contact her at home, or possibly at the Keyhole program, and left.

Though I was half an hour late for my drink with Cathy at the Out Inn, I still managed to arrive 15 minutes before she did.

We sat in a small booth against the back wall of the bar. I was nursing a glass of red wine. Cathy ordered a glass of white.

"How was Tessa?" I asked.

Cathy leaned back in the plush leather armchair, smiled like I remember I must have once smiled, and said, "Bubbling. Just bubbling. She's really snagged herself a good deal. Her landlady is, how shall I say, one of the good Christians. At least, that's how it appears. A true Samaritan. And renting to a teenager is almost always a Samaritan's act."

"Bloody courageous too," I added.

"Cynic."

"With Tessa, it's likely a slam dunk. I mean, she's a pretty together kid. The damage to her has been kept to a minimum."

"I suppose. Anyway, she's pleased as punch with the place. Mrs. Garnett, the landlady, looks like she could use some youthful help around her house. She has these two yappy dogs that don't get out much. Tessa will walk them every day and get reduced rent."

"It might be better if she pays full rent and gets a rebate in cash," I suggested. "Though, to be honest, it depends on how tax-pure Mrs. Garnett is."

"You have a larcenous turn of mind, Wally."

"Larceny has nothing to do with how my mind turns," I rebutted.

"The rent's the rent. Labour's work. I think it's important to keep the ledger straight."

I nodded, silently acquiescing to her virginal honesty.

Perhaps I was too quick to reject Cathy's proposition that I have a larcenous mind. Time, and the unending nuisance of trying to adjust the bureaucratic beast so that the decisions we make are primarily human decisions, had transformed me from a meek, compliant servant of the government into an aggressive, challenging, manipulative advocate. I came to believe that all of the rules and statutes I was obliged to operate under were imposed so that nothing beneficial could be achieved.

I had had no epiphany, no bolt of lightning striking me, guiding me towards this understanding. In fact, I consciously came to my understanding of the power and the purpose of bureaucracies from the film *The Great Escape*. In the film, great hordes of recaptured Allied prisoners who had shown considerable skill in escape are moved to a new, bigger, better, brighter, escape-proof prison. The prison is for lifers, though I suspect the Nazis had no plans to extend the lives of their war captives beyond victory. All of those prisoners of the war prison bureaucracy must have expected to be swallowed whole, consumed by the prison, especially if Germany had won the war. Similarly, for those of us who are chained to our work, any bureaucracy is a prison, and we must plan our own escape. No matter what they say, we are being held against our will. As a worker, I was truly being held against my will. I was probably one of my own guards, but my willpower was diminished, as is the capacity for self-determination for all prisoners of forced labour. Yet, for all its clumsy, correctional-centre qualities, I embraced my bureaucracy for the bondaged beauty that it was.

I instinctively expected the legume-counting fiscal police to swoop down at a moment's notice on our small field operation, haul our benevolent asses into a torture chamber, micro-examine every file recording, cheque, and voucher we had ever issued, and ensure the penultimate orgasm, an accountant's pièce de résistance, by taking back every benefit, every scrap of systemic largesse we had ever been able to wangle for the youth and families who received our services.

Not that any of the youth in our system who live on their own keep polished records. And different programs have different expectations. Often it's a matter of mindless providence which program a kid lands in. The youth agreement program, relatively new, is a bit of a hybrid. The youth are neither fish nor fowl; because of their issues, they qualify for contracted financial and social work support. The contract is very specific and spells out all of their costs. Youth in care are eligible for a similar program called independent living.

Any written contract they have is more flexible. It's a marvellous thing to participate in the bureaucratic upbringing of a child.

"Wally? Come out, come out, from wherever you are."

I gave my head a shake and caught sight of Cathy looking at me as if my spirit had left my body.

"Boy, did you zone out," she stated with emphasis.

"Sorry, I was lost in thought. Seditious thoughts of corporate skullduggery, no doubt."

"Fine," she said, "don't be so sensitive. I get your point. I'll ask Tessa to pay full rent. Any other arrangement between her and the landlady will stay off the books. Out of the file and in the wind. But you know, this sort of clarification only works for a kid like Tessa."

"We do what we can, when we can, for whomever we can. Let's talk about the Prentice case, shall we?"

"I have to say," began Cathy thoughtfully, "that Carla Prentice seems genuinely concerned about her daughter. Workable…if we can get them into counselling."

"That's always a big *if*," I added somewhat needlessly. "Kids like Skylark aren't really ready to examine their behaviour."

"And O wise worker, you know this great generality because all youth are wired the same, I am assuming," she added with an appropriate dollop of grinning irony.

"I hope I'm not implying that. Am I sounding that jaded?"

"It must be the booze. You are usually quite a bit more open-minded."

Of course all youth weren't the same. It's an occupational hazard to wander off into the swamp of blatant oversimplification. It's always tempting to sound wise, but every time I do, I crash back to earth like with a hackneyed thump.

"Okay, forgive me. And I agree with you. Carla's earlier failure to follow through with her son, Jordan, must be a great motivator for change, I would think."

"When I was at Tessa's I called Dru Janes. She told me there is a long-time street worker on the downtown east side named Manny Cardenas. Great guy, good advocate she says. Have you heard of him?"

"Name's familiar. I don't think I've met him. Could've I suppose. Maybe I've spent too many years in the burbs," I lamented.

"Yeah," she said with that sardonic pitying tone I'd been playing to, "to be so old, to know all the action in social work is on the inner-city mean streets. And here you are, trapped in suburbia picking up litter."

"Okay, okay, I'll give up my hang-dog blues if you'll just show a little more respect to my years of experience."

"Happy to," she said. "This pity jag was getting on my nerves. What's brought it on?"

"I'll maybe tell you tomorrow, when I know myself," I offered with a wink.

"Anyway," she got down to business, "I called Manny Cardenas. He not only remembers Jordan Prentice, but he keeps a sort of unofficial tab on him and other young people who've come his way. He does street rounds as many nights as he can. He'll be working the streets tonight and said if I want he'll call me if he comes across news about Jordan. I said fine, call anytime."

"How late does he work?" I asked.

"Didn't ask. Does it matter?"

"You want me to go with you if he calls?"

"That would be nice. Why, is there a chance you wouldn't go?"

"Not if I was asleep. You get to be my age, you need your sleep. You relish your nocturnal moments."

"My sex life is nobody's business but my own," I clarified.

"All too true, you poor old man. Look, let's can the cheap chitchat. Will you go with me if he calls? He says most nights he calls it quits about midnight, unless the situation demands."

"Okay, as long as Kate approved the overtime, I'm with you. The hell with my beauty sleep."

Of course Kate wouldn't have pre-approved overtime for this or any kind of fishing expedition. Overtime is a very contentious issue in our work. Often, the circumstances of a case are fluid. Whether you do something or don't may not make any difference. The arbitrariness of the next step is hard to communicate to your superior, the one who has a limited overtime budget, the one who wants workers both to do the job well but not overdo it. Efficient moderation is the theme.

We switched to club soda for a time and then decided to catch a revival of *The Battle of Algiers* at a retrospective cinema in the heart of the city. That would take us up to almost the time Manny Cardenas punched out. *The Battle of Algiers* is a startling film that simultaneously captures the oppression of occupation and the intensity and fanaticism of urban guerrilla warfare. I have seen it a number of times over the years, and I am always frighteningly impressed by the images of women as human grenades. Cathy had never heard of the film, so I was hoping to expand her political awareness somewhat.

We had a quick dinner at a small bistro a few blocks from the cinema and made the late showing by nine. Three minutes into the film, Cathy's cell erupted and we scurried outside.

Manny Cardenas told Cathy that he had met an acquaintance of Jordan who thought he might be squatting in an abandoned house around Broadway and Commercial. Manny emphasized that the information was a few days old; squats are plentiful; they are often unsafe. Arriving unannounced could be perilous. However, there really wasn't any other way to check them out. As Manny still had the old picture of Jordan that Carla had sent him a number of years ago, and that all important human connection that was manna in the human services arena, he was amenable to rendezvousing with us to check out the abandoned house. While I would have preferred to go back into the movie, Cathy was game for the adventure so I was snookered. I would have preferred to request a police escort; that would have been the smart thing to do. However, despite providing us some likely needed security, it would undoubtedly threaten the illegal inhabitants and jeopardize any cooperation that might be forthcoming. It would also identify the dwelling as a squat, information the police might not yet have, and thus further antagonize any resident squatters. In any case, given his experience on the street, I was relatively content that it should be Manny's call.

The upside of asking for a police escort would be that the neighbours would be just a little wiser about the decline of their neighbourhood. The odds were they knew the current use the house was being put to and had already complained. I let these competing thoughts reverberate in my cortex while Cathy and I walked to our respective cars.

She had agreed to plunge further into the pulsating inner city and pick up Manny Cardenas outside the City Hope Hotel, a single-room-occupancy rooming house/hotel with a scummy little pub on the main floor that I had encountered in my university underage beer-swilling days. I drove with my thoughts, alone, and met them at a well-lit Safeway parking lot near the address Manny had been given.

Manny Cardenas looked to be about 45, although evening floodlights tend to add to one's age. He was 5'8" or so, stocky in a well-fed, weightlifter sort of way. Dark complexioned, he had a broad smile that added to a rather plain, puffy face. He also leaned to the right, as if there was some imbalance in his skeletal makeup. His black hair was styled enough to hint at better grooming than I practised. Having a reasonable head of hair will do that.

Cathy introduced us; we shook hands and started walking out of the lot.

"We've met before, I think," Manny mentioned as we strolled past the Skytrain station entrance.

"Could be," I said, struggling to remember where and when that might have been. I was notoriously bad with names, but faces were usually my stronger suit.

"It was Angie… Angie Gravelle."

And then I remembered right away.

"Of course. Stupid me. Wow, that was a long time ago. At ASU. The hand-off."

We stopped to wait for the light at the large intersection at Commercial and Broadway. It was almost 10:00 p.m., and the street was alive. Cadres of youth were engaged in every conceivable transaction. Drugs were being marketed; young, already worn-out bodies of girls and boys were being sold for whatever they might bring; turf was being staked out; mayhem was being plotted, midweek in the city's ever-wicked winter fest. Traffic was animated, full of animus and raunchy sounding-off. Horns honked, sirens wailed, the occasional scream flew through the air like a knife-thrower's blade, but without any precision.

It was hard to stay in the moment as I thought back on the ragged life of Angie Gravelle, another of my notable early failures. It had been almost 20 years since I had transferred her to the Adolescent Street Unit, a special team of social workers who worked with those tough-as-asphalt youth who settled in the hard-ass core of the city. My next-to-final meeting with Angie had been in the ASU boardroom, more an enlarged cubbyhole really, rather than a functioning boardroom. It had held various boxes and suitcases at one end, three end-to-end Bingo tables and about 30 different styles of chair design. The meeting had consisted of Angie, who was just about to turn 16,

Faye something or other, the intake ASU social worker, her supervisor, Dan Pebbles, Art Hughes, who ran Thesis House, a specialized treatment home that had been Angie's last placement before she absconded to live the good life on the streets, one or two other street service workers, and Manny. It had been a quick meeting, more a formality than something of meaning, and was over in all of 15 minutes.

Meetings like that, meetings where files were transferred to new workers in other offices, were always hard for me, especially early on in my career. Transferring a youth to ASU was especially sensitive because it signalled that all of our suburban tricks had fizzled, and that we had to abandon the kid to a darker chapter. Don't get me wrong, the workers on the team and all the outreach personnel who supported them were exceptional people. But from my perspective, I was almost like a relinquishing parent no longer able to keep my child safe. That's how it felt anyways. It felt shitty.

"Sorry I forgot you, Manny. Jesus, that was a long time ago. We were both a lot younger."

"I'm still young, amigo," Manny replied, implying perhaps that I might not have stood the test of time as well as he thought he had. Was he reading my heart I wondered?

I hate this maudlin side. It's usually so damned inappropriate. But I still thought of Angie and how difficult it had been to transfer her on. Not that there was any other choice at the time. I had ceased to be of any service to her.

We crossed Commercial, and walked a few blocks beyond the intersection until we reached a cross street.

"We'll drop down a block and go down the alley," Manny indicated. "The squat is at the end of the block."

"Wouldn't the main street be safer?" Cathy asked.

"A bit safer, I guess," whispered Manny. "But a lot more public. If anyone is there, Jordan or some other homeless person, I don't want to screw up their housing. It's likely a corner house, so we can check out the rear and the side and figure out the best way to approach it."

The alley was dark except for a faint sliver of winter moon. The only lights that were on were motion detectors that we activated by walking too close to garages. Manny suggested we keep to the middle of the alley.

The last house on the left still had its old address number on the garage, though we could barely make it out. A streetlamp opposite threw a little light.

The backyard had a bit of a junk-strewn look about it but seemed surprisingly clean, if somewhat weedy.

"Looks empty," I commented.

The windows on the rear and on the non-street side of the two-story house were boarded up. We took a quick jaunt along the sidewalk to the front and saw that the windows along the street side and the front were similarly boarded up. The front door had also received a plywood coating.

"Wait here guys," Manny said as he pulled out a flashlight from his knapsack. He went around to the back and entered the yard. Cathy and I waited by the lamp pole, clearly not hiding.

"I'm thinking of getting a new pet," I whispered into Cathy's ear.

"What sort of a pet, Wally?" she asked in her second-banana voice.

"A wild goose."

She lightly punched my shoulder.

"A goose would do you a world of good," she deadpanned, and left me wondering who might administer such a treatment.

In less than a couple of minutes, Manny beckoned to us with his flashlight.

"There is a basement door with a false front lock and clasp. Do you guys want to wait here or what?"

"Look," I said, "It's probably breaking and entering. God knows who is hibernating here, if anyone. There's no good choice. Cathy, you wait if you want. I'll go with Manny."

Even as I whispered this sage suggestion, it sounded stupid. All my going would do would be to leave Cathy unprotected outside.

"Right, maybe you stay Wally and I'll go with Manny."

"So, it's settled," Manny said, summing up our banter "we're all going."

The ceiling was low in the unfinished basement and the smell of human waste overwhelming. We found the stairs to the next floor, tested them for sturdiness and proceeded up.

As Manny put his hand on the doorknob, he spoke out "Hello in there. Don't be afraid. It's Street Outreach worker Manny Cardenas. Forgive the intrusion, we're looking for Jordan. Is he here?"

There was no answer for a moment. Manny repeated his apology for the encroachment.

"Look, if someone's there, I'm sorry for intruding. I was told Jordan sometimes crashes here."

"He ain't here, man. Why do you want him? Who told you he was here?" the male voice asked.

"We don't want to cause you any grief," Manny answered. "We just want to talk with Jordan."

"You're already causing me grief, just being here. Are you going to tell me who's talking trash about this place?"

"Look," Manny said, continuing to avoid the who-told-you question, "Do you know me…my name? It's Manny C. That's what they call me down on the street. Have you heard of me?"

"I heard of you, man."

"So maybe you've heard that I don't screw people over? Have you heard that about me?"

"Maybe I've heard that," said the voice. The speaker seemed to be speaking a little more loudly or had moved closer to us.

"So, could you tell me when you last saw Jordan? Could you do that?"

"Well," said the voice, "let me check my social calendar."

A humorist.

"Today? Have you seen him today?" Manny asked, sounding just a bit peeved.

"Yeah, he was here last night. Left this morning. Noon maybe," said the voice.

"Alone? Was he travelling alone?" Manny asked.

"Why do you care?"

I could sense Manny debating with himself about what to say next.

"The people with me, they're looking for Jordan's sister. We thought he might know where his little sister is."

"Who are they? Who's this we? Who's there with you, man?" the voice said in an edgy, agitated manner.

In some quarters, the profession of social work can engender a less than unruffled response. Any rapport Manny might have built could be eviscerated if our noble profession was mentioned. Still, not telling the truth might easily lose him credibility as well.

"They're social workers. Jordan's sister is missing and they just want to find her…make sure she's safe. That's cool, isn't it?"

"Yeah, man," the voice said after a brief pause, "that's cool. It's a fucked-up world. Someone has to look after the little sheep."

"So, was she with Jordan?" Manny persisted.

"Not last night man. Night before. That's why he left this morning. To look for her. She was supposed to either go home or come back here last night and she didn't come back. He got all bent out of shape and went out to look for her this morning. Said don't wait up. She didn't go to her mother?"

"No," Manny said. "No, she didn't."

"That's a bitch, man," the increasingly sympathetic voice said.

"Yes it is," said Manny, "it's a bitch."

Manny whispered for Cathy to give him a business card.

"Hey buddy, we'll split now. I'll leave my card and one of the social worker's cards. Her name is Cathy. Have Jordan call us if he would. Or you, if something comes your way. Okay?"

"Sure, man. Will do."

"We're leaving now," Manny said to the voice.

"You'll see yourself out, right?" said the voice, almost with a gurgle of humour.

"You got it, buddy. Thanks for the hospitality."

"The absentee landlord's casa is your casa, man."

With that parting salutation, we descended the stairway into the cellar, exited the house, closed the door and secured the false-front lock, and walked back to our cars.

"Thanks a lot, Manny," Cathy said. "You don't think that was Jordan in there, do you?"

"Nah, that was an older guy, I think. Wearier voice. Still, it doesn't take long to age on the street. Twenty-year-olds become forty in a flash. I tend to believe him. I maybe saw Jordan three or four months ago. I think that was someone else. Anyway, at least you know there is a strong likelihood that the girl was there the night before last."

As we walked along Broadway to the parking lot, the street was still quaking with nightlife. I looked at Manny, and he seemed to be in his element. Though this wasn't his usual beat, he spotted some youth and young adults he knew. He acknowledged them, and they reciprocated. It had been a long day for me, however, and I was exhausted. Cathy looked pretty fresh, not unexpected for a 31-year-old. She was still young enough to manage late hours and stressful expeditions. I could not say the same about myself.

I chivalrously offered to drive Manny downtown, but Cathy took pity on me and said I should go straight home. She obviously could see the worn-out old man in my eyes.

I accepted her offer, was home in 15 minutes, and was soon tossing and turning in a pretty fair impression of sleep by midnight.

Chapter 6

Carla Baynes

If anyone had ever taken the time to ask Carla Baynes what she was up to with her life, she would probably have been struck dumb. Since her early teens, that was the question that most often stuck in her throat, choking her with its inability to be expressed. That hint of curiosity we all hopefully have some glimmer of remained, for Carla, a dark mass of unspoken whispers. Even if someone had broken through and reached Carla with a caring solicitation about what she was doing, she most likely would have shut him or her out.

For Carla, the predominant sense of her preteen years was that they were mostly uneventful and flat. She had no knowledge of her father. No one in her small family ever spoke openly of him. Baynes was her grandmother's name, so sometime around age eight or nine she came to understand that whoever her father was, she was not destined to carry his name. Most of the time it just didn't matter. She was not the only kid being raised in a one-parent universe and carrying her mother's name. That was just the way it was, a common situation, growing more common every day.

When she was six years old, she and her mother had moved out of her grandmother's house into an apartment in Burnaby. The apartment building was chock full of mothers and children. Her mother worked shift work in a paper mill, and Carla was often babysat by an assortment of her mom's friends, other single-parent women for the most part, who either hadn't made the leap to employment, or, as was mostly the case, were fellow shift workers. Depending on her mom's shift, Carla either got to sleep in her own bed or had to be hauled off to a strange bed in another cramped apartment. Even if she had slept in the bed before, it would always feel strange. And usually it wasn't a bed but a couch, or cushions tossed in a corner. Sometimes her mother would leave her at the sitter's all night. She would have to wake up with strangers, plopped into their routines, feeling like some second-rate appendage in someone else's life.

One morning, her mother came to fetch her from a sitter's, and she wasn't alone. This is Brian, her mother said. He is going to come and live with us. I'm tired of living alone, her mother said to her and to the babysitter, all the while looking with moon eyes at the new fellow, Brian. Carla remained silent, uncertain how to express to her mother that she didn't live alone, that she, Carla, lived with her. She knew her mother knew that. So she assumed her mother meant something else when she said she was tired of living alone. The clearest understanding for Carla was that children didn't count really on adult radar. While this didn't sit right with her, she was aware this wasn't the time to clear the air.

They drove to their apartment-home in Brian's car. As soon as they got in the door, she should have torpedoed herself to her bedroom. But she didn't; damn it, she didn't. Instead she tried to hold 8 year old court on the couch, stake out some communal turf, and let this fellow know who was really in charge. But she quickly learned she wasn't in the driver's seat. After a few it's-small-but-we-call-it- home trite-isms, her mother sat down on the couch next to her and started to share unwanted, unrequested, really unnecessary information.

"I work with Brian, Carla," her mother voiced. "We've been seeing each other, dating, darling. Give Brian a hug, Carla. Hug him tight, sweetie."

Carla had not been raised to embrace family, let alone strangers. Carla pulled the blanket up over her and resisted her mother's entreaty to wrap her arms around this man.

"She's a shy one, Janie," he said, "like her mom," as if he knew her. Her mother leaned forward to lift Carla up from underneath the covers.

"Shy my ass. She's downright rude."

"Give the kid a break, Jane. She's still half asleep." Peeking out from under the blanket, Carla saw the man pull her mother back from the edge of the couch and make enough room for him to sit down.

"Go get me a coffee, Janie, and let me get acquainted with cute little Carla." He rested his right hand on top of the covers, on top of her covered legs. He leaned over and whispered, "This is a bit of a shock, eh kid?"

He smelled of summer flowers; his breath thickly wrapped her in a bouquet of knotty stems. It strangled her throat. Her mother was framed in the archway of the flat's tiny kitchen, moving away from her, moving towards the kettle and the stove.

"All I have is instant, Brian. Will that do ya?" she heard her mother ask.

"Anything you've got is jake with me, Janie," he said in the direction of the kitchen. Her mother was now out of her view. He brought his hand up to Carla's face and ran his palm over her left cheek. His smell was ferocious, sweet and slightly sickening, not unlike the perfumed odour that rose from the casket of her great aunt Eloise.

That had been her first and only funeral. It had been a long time ago, when she was four or five. They were still living with her grandmother. She had been woken, first by the phone call and then by her grandmother, moaning in what must have been terrible pain, drinking from the bottle of white alcohol, and speaking loudly and incoherently to her mother. "She had it all," she had heard her grandmother say to her mother. "That bitch had it all. Money. Didn't have to slave at a job. Didn't have to lift a bloody finger in that sashay fancy-pants house. Selfish bitch! No bloody respect for the sanctity of her own bloody life."

Out of the corner of her wary eye, she saw Brian let his hand flutter down to the left side of her thigh. It came to a feathery rest on top of the blanket that shielded her. The image of her great aunt's casket rushed to her mind; that same scent that spilled from the casket into the cloistered air of the funeral home was spilling over her here in her own home.

"Sweetheart," she heard her mother call from the kitchen, "do you want some cocoa?" Brian's hand abruptly lifted, as if propelled by the sudden insertion of her mother's voice. As she watched his hand float away she found herself trying to force her voice to answer her mother. Something. Anything. Her voice box was dry and seemed to tighten, like a string drawn around her finger meant to help her remember some important small detail but doing nothing more than cutting off the blood and hurting. Perhaps sensing her paralysis, Brian said, "I'm sure she'd love some cocoa, Janie. Me too. Mix my coffee with some of the cocoa, will ya? Do you have marshmallows?"

"Coming right up, my loves," her mother replied, not in her real voice but the voice of an old woman trying to sound childlike, a stranger's voice.

As the coffee, cocoa, and wherever-did-that-brat-hide-those-marshmallows were brought into the living room by her mom, Carla took advantage of the action and shifted to the old overstuffed chair they had inherited from Eloise. Well, claimed, she supposed, rather than inherited. It turned out Eloise had frittered all her money away "on young studs." At least that was her grandmother's take on it, and she made sure everyone knew it on every occasion they had gathered together in the years since the funeral. There was some money, apparently, because her mother had used whatever she had been bequeathed to escape Gram's house.

"Pass her the blanket, Brian. Pulleeeeeeasse," squealed her mom.

"Sure thing, kiddo," Brian shot back as he bounded off the couch, blanket clutched in his fist, and quicker than a woolly wink, he was tucking it all around her, stuffing the edges of the blanket in every crevice; almost mummifying her.

"Oh Brian," her mother cooed, "that's so sweet. Isn't that sweet of Brian, baby?" her mother asked as she handed her the cup of cocoa. Carla took the welcome drink and smiled a faint smile in hopes of putting the whole "aren't we going to be just the best second-hand family" fairytale to rest. But she knew she would have to say something, offer some acknowledgement that Brian was just the greatest guy in the whole jumbled universe, and you couldn't get a much sweeter deed from a man than to wrap up a child in a cozy warm blanket just as she was being brought hot chocolate.

"Thank you," she almost whispered.

"Thank you, BRIAN, sweetie," her mother emphasized. "His name is Brian, and you'll have to get used to it because we'll be living together."

"Ease up, Janie," Brian softly admonished her mother. "Hold your horses. She's just met me for pity's sake." Brian reached over and squeezed Carla's knee through the blanket and added, "These things take time. And we've got forever."

With that threat of reassurance, her mother and Brian went into the kitchen, talked a bit, and then adjourned to her mother's bedroom. Carla sat there, wrapped in her blanket, and, warmed by the cocoa, tried to imagine the future, tried to believe that their lives had improved. She was stumped and had no way to describe how she felt about this man's intrusion into their lives. She sipped the cocoa slowly, desperately wanting to journey the few feet to her own bed. With that thought, she fell asleep in her blanketed cocoon on Aunt Eloise's overstuffed chair.

Brian owned a house that he had been renting out. A few months after he entered Carla's life, he evicted his tenants, moved his stuff out of his buddy's apartment (he had moved there, apparently, when he and his first wife parted ways), and she and her mother moved into Brian's house. There was more space, and it was close enough to their old apartment that she didn't have to change schools.

In those first few weeks after they had set up housekeeping in Brian's house, her mother constantly repeated the small advantages of this change in housing. "It's so close to your school, baby girl," and, "I don't know what we are going to do with all this space," and her favourite, and the oddest, "Doncha just feel like the Queen of Sheba, Carlykins?"

Carla wasn't sure who the Queen of Sheba was, but she was sure that if anyone felt like that queen, it was her mother. And that meant that Brian was king.

Still, she did find pleasure in living in a house again. Better still, there was a yard and an old swing set. Aside from the swing and the apple and pear trees, she surprised herself when she started to believe that the best part about living in a house was having a back lane. She decided that this was a truth that she had known before, when they had lived at her grandmother's, but had forgotten. It bewildered her that she could have let go of a such a pleasant bit of knowledge; that back lanes, back alleys, were repositories of small personal mysteries.

One September morning, the first day of school, she awoke at 6:30 a.m., dawdled a bit, eventually crawled out of bed, dressed, and went out the back door. Brian had returned to work on the graveyard shift and would not be home until just before she left for school. She could hear her mother's low, muffled snore rumbling from the upstairs bedroom. She sounded like a giant cat purring up a storm.

There was a bright still summery morning light, and the air was warm and soft on her skin. Brian had cut the lawn the afternoon before, and it smelled like a mountain field must smell, she thought, even though she couldn't remember ever having actually walked in a mountain field.

She walked down the back steps and along the sidewalk to the rear gate that led to the alley. The wooden gate reached just above her height. She stood on her toes and peered out into the alley. As early as it was, a man was walking by. His head was wrapped in cloth, and he wore what seemed to her to be a light summer suit. He had a long grey beard, and his skin was the colour of almonds. He looked at her, and she thought she detected a smile. She smiled back and said, "Hello."

The alley man nodded his head, and said something that she assumed was an acknowledgment of her salutation but was indecipherable to her. He walked on, with a slow, shuffling gait, and as he left the alley and turned south, she saw him look back and wave goodbye.

Carla opened the gate and stepped out into the alley. She knew she had a bit of time to while away, and so decided to follow the alley man. She ran to the corner and saw that he was walking fairly slowly, like an old arthritic dog. He seemed unaware that she was behind him. He walked further down the block to a large stand of trees. Alley man crossed the street, after looking both ways, and disappeared onto a trail that led into the woods. Brian had said that there was a small community park a block away. This must be it, she thought.

Though she was tempted to follow alley man into the small forest, her courage failed her and she returned home.

The next morning, curious about the alley man, she arose as early as she could and parked herself by the gate. With a comforting predictability, alley man made his way down her back lane. With an audacity she rarely displayed, she opened her gate, walked into the alley and sidled up to alley man.

"Hello again," she said.

"Hello, young girl," he replied.

She had assumed that he did not speak English.

"I'm Carla," she said.

"Hello, young Carla," he replied. "My name is Mr. Sharma."

"My last name is Baynes," She wanted to say that Baynes was her mother's last name but chose not to confuse the matter of her parentage, especially to a stranger.

They came to the end of her alley.

"Where are you walking to?" she boldly asked.

"Just around the neighbourhood. I usually only walk a few blocks in the morning. It helps me to get my old blood moving. You might not understand how blood atrophies if you don't move your body." Mr. Sharma paused.

"This is not a problem young people are familiar with. But to answer your question, I live a few blocks over. I walk this way, down the alley and back through the forest."

They in fact had reached the entrance to the little wood.

"Thank you for the company, Carla. It's best that I go into the woods alone," Mr. Sharma said.

"Why?"

"I have to be home soon. I will pick up my pace and be there in ten minutes. I work today."

"Goodbye, Mr. Sharma," she said, and the alley man disappeared into the small neighbourhood woods.

She walked back down the alley, and, as she entered the yard, Brian drove into the carport. He parked, jumped out of the car, rushed up to her, grabbed her arms just firmly enough to cause her to jerk back in pain and whispered emphatically, "Carla, what the hell are you doing wandering about?"

Brian's aggressive demand startled Carla. She sensed that she had better not mention the alley man. As she tried to form a safe answer, to compose a simple tale of getting up early and meeting a stranger to walk with, Brian screeched into her ear, "Hell, what do I care what a little cow like you is doing. Get in the house." He shoved her in the direction of the back stairs and swatted her behind. Her mother, wearing a slip over her bra and panties, poked her head out of the upstairs bedroom window and yelled to Brian.

"Why are you hitting her, Brian? Stop it now."

He yelled back, "Shut up, Janie, and get dressed for Christ's sake. I'm not hitting her

As her mother and Brian squabbled, she noticed that the next-door neighbour, a man in a white shirt and tie, had come out of his house, observed the altercation, and gone back inside.

"Bullshit," her mother said. "I saw you swat her as plain as day."

"Discipline, Janie. That's what I administered."

"What on earth did she do that you had to hit her?" her mother asked, continuing her upper-window, half-naked interrogation of Brian.

"I saw her, Janie. Down the street by the park…talking to some old *raghead*."

"Who?" she asked.

"No idea, Janie. While you're snoozing, she's creeping out of the house and doing whatever she wants."

"Bring her inside, Brian, and we'll get to the bottom of it. And stop hitting her."

Brian took her by the arm and half lifted her into the house. In seconds her mother had dressed, and the three of them gathered in the kitchen. They made coffee and sat her down and asked her who the old man was.

She wished she could find a way not to answer. By this time she was sobbing buckets of salt tears, and was choking back her breath so violently that her chest hurt as if some weighty block was pressing down on her ribs.

She finally told them about seeing Mr. Sharma and talking to him.

"We were just talking."

"About what, sweetie?"

"Hardly anything. I just met him."

And nothing had happened, except that a loud and angry argument between her mother and Brian that had created somewhat of a split between them. Carla was not unhappy with this turn of events, although it would be weeks before she gained any benefit.

At school later that week, she was called into the principal's office. A woman who said she was some kind of worker talked with her about the incident in her backyard. Carla told her about the alley man, Brian being angry, the word *raghead*, because she had never heard it before, and the fact that she was afraid of Brian because he was loud.

That night, the same worker came to her house shortly after she arrived home from school. The woman met with Brian and her mother, while Carla was asked to stay in her room.

Later, after the worker woman left, after supper, she was sent to her room earlier than usual.

As she was getting ready for bed, Brian came in and sat her down on the bed.

"Carla, Carla, Carla. You *are* a troublemaker, aren't you? This is now the law. My law, and if you know what's good for you, you're going to have to give some serious thought before you do ANYTHING (he shouted it like older boys yell GERONIMO! at the pool when they wrap their arms around their bent legs and launch themselves off the diving board). ANYTHING, you sorry little troublemaker! If one of those goddamn meddling social worker bastards so much as whispers to me that you've talked to them, someone is going to DIE. DIE! You stay in the god-damn yard from now on. You don't go off with people. You do what I say. And you don't talk about OUR business to strangers. Not to anybody." And as he reached his lecture's crescendo, he grabbed her arms, shook her with the force of a freight train, smiled, and said through his clenched teeth, "Or there will be hell to pay. And you can't afford my hell. Now get to bed and think about all the trouble you've caused your mother and me."

He left the room, turning out the light as he exited. She crawled under her blankets and sobbed. Later, her mother came in and hugged her and told her to go to sleep. "You have to do what Brian says, little girl. He's in charge now."

True to her mother's words, Brian was clearly in charge from that moment on. They were living in Brian's house, Her mother never failed to call it that, as if actually giving it the name "Brian's House" sanctified it in some way, placing it on a par with all the other famous houses like the White House, Windsor Castle and, the Hermitage, which she had seen a picture of at Gram's once.

After a time she began to sense a fullness to her days. Her needs were provided for, and she languorously fell in with what passed for the rhythm of Brian and her mother's life. Her mother invariably deferred to Brian, who was her caregiver almost more than her mother.

As often as not, Brian and her mother ended up working different shifts at the mill. This had a number of ramifications for Carla. She spent more and more time imagining that she was on her own, which suited her just fine. It wasn't really that she was left unsupervised. It just seemed that way. Usually her mother or Brian was asleep in the house, or waking up to go to work, or coming in from completing a shift. On very rare occasions, she actually was on her own. Even when this occurred, she could almost hear Brian's voice echo "MY LAW" in the air. Though this was clearly an unacceptable form of parental supervision, it was a necessary by-product of how they found themselves living their busy lives. And it went hand in hand with certain maturing expectations. For instance, Carla was taught early to prepare meals. Both Brian and her mother were excellent cooks but often begged off cooking because of their work schedules. They enjoyed eating and in particular enjoyed eating at the same time every day. If Brian was expected home a little after 4:00 p.m. and her mother was too tired to cook dinner or was working the afternoon shift, Carla was expected to hustle home immediately after school and whip up a meal.

Of course, initially she had some culinary failures, but after a time, and not too much yelling from her mother, she was able to assemble a few casseroles, cook spaghetti with her own homemade canned tomato sauce, make rice, and fry up some chops or links. Even if a meal tasted off, Brian was always complimentary. Her mother, on the other hand, berated not only every failure but even many of her cooking successes.

It seemed to her that she could actually visualize the growing chasm between herself and her mother. Worse still, this escalating antagonism was in direct proportion to the diminishing gap she so fervently did not want between herself and Brian. She was losing her mother, and Brian had become her rock, the one who made every decision about her. She feared him as one would fear a junk-yard dog. He controlled their lives, and what most confused her was that she found herself more and more cozying up to him. He scared her so much that she shook when she thought of him. At the same time, he was an excellent provider, and there was nothing she could do about it.

Chapter 7

Millie Hunt/ Kevin Jacobs
Thursday, November 15

I have an old king-size mattress that occasionally seems lumpy. When I am overtired, the mattress, far from being a comfortable older friend, becomes an aggressive enemy. It seems to become a bed of shifting stones that denies me the pleasure of a moment's rest. That was the feeling I had when I woke up Thursday morning. The alarm clattered at 5:45 a.m., my habitual waking-from-the-dead-of-sleep time. Even with the questionable condition of my bed, an ancient holdover from my long-fizzled marriage, I just couldn't eject out of it right away. I turned on the radio and listened to the travails of the rest of the world: Bin Laden was running out of places to hide; eight foreign-aid workers rescued in Afghanistan; a loving couple in Maine arrested trying to rob a convenience store. News of exceptional tragedy serves a purpose, I think. It lets you know that, by some miracle, you are still alive, still able to greet the day, play your part in the great charade. Buoyant from my survival, I jumped out of bed, showered, dressed, had some tea and toast, and was out the door by seven. There was frost on the ground and dark clouds threatening from the western sky. I was not looking forward to this day. Whatever trap Gord Lafferty had planned, I would be the poorer for it by being ill-prepared. And I still had to negotiate through a morning shift. A quick review of my appointment calendar reminded me that a parent, Lazlo Doig, had agreed to come in at 9:00 a.m. to discuss his son Walter. I also needed to get started on paperwork for Erin's youth agreement, arrange for a home visit by the YAG worker, and have an assessment done.

By nine I had reviewed all of my e-mails, attempted a few file updates, started the Youth Agreement process for Erin, and downed three cups of coffee. I had even closed my office door, not a regular practice with me, to seem more efficient.

Lazlo Doig arrived on time and we chatted about his son. The family, which consisted of the father and Walter, had been in the country for only three years. Mr. Doig was a machinist who worked hard and expected his son to do the same. Mrs. Doig had died shortly after their arrival in Canada. I had already met a depressed Walter, who was staying with the parents of a school friend. Mr. Doig also seemed to me to be depressed. I was becoming depressed for this poor family, who seemed to have lost their emotional core with the sudden accidental death of Irina Doig.

Lazlo Doig wanted his son home and seemed willing to engage in grief counselling in order to lessen both his and Walter's pain, as well as Walter's resistance to returning home. I knew it would be a squeeze to get them into counselling, as there weren't that many child welfare concerns, Walter was almost 17, and the whole damn system was stretched just to deal, barely, with major crises.

I was as honest as I could be with Mr. Doig and got his agreement that I would forward a counselling referral. In the meantime, I would complicate his life further by involving a parent-teen mediator to meet with both him and his son, separately at first, to try and sort out a temporary solution. I advised him as well that the likelihood of counselling happening in the foreseeable future was slim, so much would ride on the efficacy of parent/teen mediation. I did not tell him that the state did not place much importance on the struggle he and his son were engaged in. Telling him that would help no one. Especially me, if he chose to complain about my candour.

After he left, I word-processed the results of the meeting, called our contract mediator, and left a voice message with the details.

Cathy peeked in and thanked me for my company and help the previous evening.

"Too much to expect a call from Jordan, I guess?" I commiserated.

"Well," she reflected, "that expedition was a category five long shot, wouldn't you say?"

"I think you're being excessively optimistic," I laughed. "Still, it was a bit of an adventure. Need a few of those from time to time."

"Pretty grungy adventure if you ask me. Pretty damned gloomy too, I might add." She hesitated and then asked, "Angie Gravelle? What's the story there?"

I guess whatever morning light was shining in my wrinkled elder visage dimmed, and she added, "Sorry, Wally. I'm being too snoopy, right?"

"No, we're teammates. We teach each other. You have to feel free to ask whatever. And I have to feel free to delay my response. Still, in brief, Angie, as you probably guessed, was a kid client from my stone age, when my learning curve had barely begun to ascend, when I still had rocks in my social worker shoes; in short, when I was a baby dinosaur."

She tired of my prehistoric metaphor lobbing and switched topics. "We can talk about her another time…say, I was thinking, could I invite you over for dinner tonight? Sevenish? Nothing fancy?"

I was flattered. A friend inviting me over or…god forbid, was this an overture? I had never been to her place. Most times, work was work and relationships stayed there. At least that was the boundary I had erected after an early misstep.

"It's too short a notice, isn't it? Cathy said. "Look, it was just my way of thanking you for last night."

"You don't need to go to any extra trouble, Cath. But I never turn down a meal. Dinner tonight would be fine."

My phone rang. I waved Cathy adieu and said, "Good. We'll talk later."

It was Millie on the line. "Wally, I apologize, can we reschedule? I've got a wildcat to deal with."

"Wildcatting social workers?" I asked. "Impressive."

"If only," she replied. "Hotel staff. At one of our unionized hotels upcountry. The local rep has requested someone with a fresh perspective to sort it out."

"Can I ask what the bone of contention is?"

"You can ask."

"And I have, haven't I?"

"Quick study. Look I don't want to leave you in the lurch. I may be gone at least till Monday. I can try and find someone else to assist today."

"Christ, Millie, I like being left in the lurch," I announced. "This whole thing is a trap of some kind anyway," I emphasized in my most sincerely paranoiac voice. "Truth be told, I don't want to have the meeting. But if I've absolutely got to walk into Gord's web, I want your spidery skills at my side."

"Fine," she said, "I'll call him, emphasize that I simply have to be away till next week at least…set a tentative time…are you good for noon next Tuesday?"

"Yup, whatever I've got, I'll make time," I said, looking at my day planner and seeing that I had a lunch date with Monica Maggins, a ward and teen mom who was struggling to hold it all together. I'd make a point of seeing her sooner. I'd meant to anyway.

"Good. Now he may insist that we meet. He may also take some precipitous action depending on what the issue is. If he seriously threatens a suspension, what do you want me to do?"

"If he's threatening suspension, it probably won't matter whether we meet or not," I offered. "You know the way it works, Millie; if they have an inkling of cause, they suspend. I've been the steward for enough poor souls who've been kicked onto their backsides by the hint of a misstep; the managerial prerogative of this organization is to prejudge, scrap the jury, and rush to execution. I don't know why I would expect any different treatment from them."

"We've talked about this before," she reminded me. "Activist stewards get it coming and going. As protected as you are by taking a stand, by representing members in their darkest employer-initiated moment, you also poke your head up and make yourself a target. How you present sometimes sets the tone." She paused. I could almost see her grinning. "You weren't ready for a sermon, were you?"

"You're suggesting that I haven't always been as diplomatic as I could have been?"

"We all have to work on our diplomacy skills," she conceded. "Anyway, the die is cast. They'll do what they do."

"I think it would be more politic if you called Gord and rescheduled. Do you have time to track him down? I don't think he's here."

"I'll do that. I've got his pager number."

"Let me know what he says."

"Who else would I tell?" she said, and hung up.

I called Monica's school and asked that she be paged. Youth hate to be called over the school sound system, but I wanted to arrange a new lunch date as soon as possible. It turned out not to matter, because she was absent. I could think of no good reason why she was away from school. I called her at home and got her answering machine. I left a brief message saying that we needed to find a new time and suggested today or tomorrow.

I hung up and my phone rang almost immediately. It was Brenda Fisher, Kevin Jacob's probation officer.

"Wally, you'll probably get a call, but I wanted to let you know that Kevin Jacobs is at YDC."

Her news wasn't unexpected. Kevin was very familiar with the Youth Detention Centre, our handy regional kid lock-up. Like a second home. Like his first home, unfortunately.

"When did he get picked up?"

"Surrey RCMP drug squad visited a house last night. A whole rack of young offenders having a really uncool, midweek party. The cops were just driving by. Kevin took a flyer through a rear window. He has a few cuts, but whatever he was on numbed the pain."

"Thanks, Brenda. When's he appearing in court?" I asked, knowing that it likely would be this afternoon if he hadn't appeared this morning.

"Surrey Court is full to overflowing, Wally. He'll be there this afternoon. Look, you know they'll hold him. He's been on the run for three weeks. No need for you to go."

And she was right. Technically right. The juvenile-court zoo breathed its own air and, for a repeat offender like Kevin Jacobs, —a 17-year-old ward in name only because he had pretty much given up on us a long time ago—, the appearance of his guardian was, at best, a fatuous formality. It was, however, a formality that I tried to preserve whenever time permitted. I called the juvenile facility and was told they had transported Kevin earlier. I then called the Surrey Court and was told that yes he was there, yes he would appear this afternoon, and no, I couldn't visit because there were too few sheriffs, and too many felons. I then called Jackson Dewar's law office. Their law firm has the contract to represent ministry youth in conflict with the law in a couple of Lower Mainland jurisdictions. Surrey crime keeps them hopping. Jack Dewar's legal secretary told me he was in court but that she would page him. I said Kevin was in cells there, and I wanted to visit him; and it would help if Jack would smooth the way, given my lowly station. She laughed and said I should make my way to Surrey Court and she would make sure Jack would assist.

Back in the warm fuzzy days of the 1970s, a wonderful change came over some of our court facilities. Family and juvenile matters were given their own court space. This meant that the formal and correctional facility tone of court was tempered, modified in such a way that mercy had a better chance of breaking through. It was an expensive proposition, and only a few communities were able to do it. Specially sensitized judges were installed as judicial consciences, jurists with humanity who could render decisions that coupled law with community wisdom.

But those times are long gone, lost to "efficiencies" and other cost slashing excuses, ever-present political expediency and, strangely, but predictably, memory. For there is no trustworthy entity in the larger, ephemeral overlay of the land that measures the loss of a system and its impact on a society. Everything shifts, adjusts, alters, and, ultimately, accepts.

There was one community where the judge became too immersed in community life, joining a board and becoming part of approving a loan to an employee to buy a car. Government money. A no-no, but also an indication that intimacy breeds conflicts of interest, breeds those small kinds of corruption that come back to bite you on the butt.

Many communities, both small rural and larger urban communities, had lost their courts to the political fever of fiscal rationing and regionalization. In place of smaller, community-friendly courts, large legal edifices arose; unfriendly, multi-purpose concrete structures, intent on humbling and depersonalizing the individual. I loathed entering the Surrey Court, but that's where I needed to be. I left another message for Monica to confirm lunch, not for today, but for tomorrow.

I took one of our office's cell phones and asked front office staff to let Gord know how I could be reached. Just as I was heading out of my door, Millie called back to say that the best she could do was leave a message for Gord about the need to change the meeting time and to call her.

It was turning into a sunny day. I took a little extra time to make what was usually no more than a half-hour trip.

On journeys like this, often via back roads that laced themselves through farmland and the very tips of suburban sprawl, I felt like I ought to remit at least a portion of my pay. The journey was always a hybrid pleasure, part vacation, part plane crash.

I parked three levels below ground and scurried out of that car chamber into the rank-smelling elevator. I spent the next half hour looking for Jack. Eventually he appeared outside one of the large arraigning courtrooms. He filled me in on Kevin's current legal quagmire.

Kevin Jacobs had been apprehended at age two from drug-addicted parents. He was a beautiful baby, but had serious heart health issues initially that required surgical repair. For reasons never fully determined, he was a screamer, not merely colicky, and went through a series of infant foster homes, each one unable to manage his infant pain and means of self-expression. At age four, his extreme wailing had moderated somewhat, and he was adopted by an older couple who lived in the Cariboo. The social worker who facilitated the adoption may have had some doubt about the new family's viability in providing a home for Kevin, and couched her concern by commenting that the adopting family was "chosen because they were cattle farmers and seemed to have a wealth of patience and perseverance," qualities the child would unhesitatingly demand of them.

At age seven he was apprehended because of allegations of physical abuse, and returned to the coast for assessment. After a brief time, the adopting parents consented to relinquish guardianship. Kevin was back in the system.

He was an immensely angry seven-year-old, violent and unmanageable. He was so disturbed that placement in a foster home was deemed unlikely, and another adoption a pipe dream. He spent the next six years in a treatment facility. Eventually, a specialized caregiver was contracted to make a home for him. This was a relatively good, creative, but costly move. However, the prognosis was clear that he would likely begin to act up in the community. True to that prediction, he started to shoplift, assault other youth, and develop a keen interest in stealing cars. By age 15, he was being arrested at least once a month.

I had been Kevin's worker for the past four months, his previous worker having transferred him to our team during a relatively benign month of calm. The rule of thumb on cases being transferred prescribed that they shouldn't be transferred in a time of crisis, or with incomplete business on the books.

I had met him three times in total; the first time at the transfer meeting; the second time two weeks later in the special care home of Grady Gains; the third time at this same court six weeks previously. Grady was paid in the vicinity of $5000.00 a month to provide a home for Kevin. He had one other youth in his home, a 15 year old boy who had been with him for two years. Grady's full-time job was to provide a consistent, nurturing environment for these two youth. Kevin facilitated this by being absent most of the time.

Part of Grady's responsibility was to attend to court matters, be there as a support. Before I had left the office I had called Grady just to let him know that Kevin was in custody and that he would be appearing in court in the afternoon. At least I informed his answering machine. I had no doubt Kevin would already have called him if he'd had the chance.

The system expected contractors like Grady to ease the responsibility of the social worker and occasionally they did. Whatever direct benefit kids received from this enhanced level of care, the gap, the fissure that existed between the youth and the system, was enlarged. The upside was the promotion of a committed caregiver; the downside was the bureaucratic specialization of social work, the watering-down of the profession to the point where we were removed from the grit of our more extreme client's lives.

I followed Jack through a long corridor to a locked metal door under closed circuit scrutiny. He buzzed and we were let in. The walls were a grim institutional yellow, a loud, intense tinge that seemed to demand attention. A Sheriff led us to a door, unlocked it, and ushered us in. The room we entered was the size of a closet. There were two chairs facing a glass barrier separating a mirror image room of the same dimensions as the one we were in. The high yellow walls of the corridor were replaced by a pale green that looked washed out and insipid.

My mindless speculation ended when a ragged looking Kevin Jacobs was escorted into the booth opposite us. He was wearing street clothes, stained blue jeans and a dirty white t-shirt. He was thinner than when I had seen him last. He was a good looking kid when he was able to care for himself. His skin was light brown, a hue that reflected his mixed parentage, a Cuban father and a Caucasian mother. His hair was black and looked like he had recently had it styled. He had a bandage on his forehead and a couple of bandages on his arms as well as some obvious scratches. He nodded to Jack, who had represented him at least twice before, but didn't seem all that pleased to see me.

"I don't want him here," he said to Jack, pointing the middle finger of his left hand at me "Why can't they keep out of my fucking life? Are you going to be able to get me out of this piss-hole, Jack?"

"Not without Wally's help, Kev. And even then, the court likely won't be smiling on your recent antics. You can't continue to disrespect the court and expect you can come and go because you want to."

"Then you're saying you can't help."

"Listen up, Kev. Aside from being found in some drug house, and fleeing the police, you've got outstanding charges and a recent failure to appear. And that was not your first failure to appear. Right?"

Jack was not telling Kevin anything he didn't already know. The likelihood of the court releasing him today was as remote as his being able to unravel the spiral his life had taken from birth.

"I want to see Grady," Kevin shouted. "He'll help. He'll tell the court I can stay with him."

"Lower your voice, Kev. We can hear you. Grady is on his way. He'll be in court this afternoon. If you are going to get out, the court has got to be convinced you'll stay put somewhere. Grady's. Somewhere. How do we convince them, Kev? Any ideas?"

Jack Dewar was giving a pretty fair imitation of a social worker. He was tossing the problem back to the client, engaging him, demanding that he articulate what steps might be necessary for him to take to resolve his dilemma. And while I knew it was a good imitation, I was also aware that Jack had no illusions about Kevin, that he knew that Kevin simply didn't have the insight to answer the call to reflect and take ownership of his problems. That didn't mean that Kevin didn't know what to say, to regurgitate what the court wanted to hear. It simply meant that whatever Kevin churned out, it would be nothing more than his painful version of smoke and mirrors. The court didn't like smoke being blown out its ass nor false fronts, the house of mirrors the cornered conjure up to extricate themselves from the legitimate shackles their actions have led to.

For half a minute , Kevin looked to be absorbing Jack's demand. He furrowed his brow, squirmed to make an escape plan present itself. The effort seemed to exhaust him further and he collapsed into the chair, a fuming dirigible, deflated once again.

"I hate being in jail," he said. "I hate it!"

"Good," said Jack. "Then you need to remember that you hate it, hate it more than anything else. And when you think you hate Wally or the system or somebody on the street looking at you funny, and just asking to be taken down a peg or two, then," he paused to deliver the haymaker, "then that's when you remember you hate prison more then all of that other stuff."

It was a powerful lesson. I wish I'd delivered it.

It was time for Jack and Kevin to have their confidential legal strategy chat. I left the room and waited for Jack, who joined me in about five minutes.

"You don't have to stay for court. He'll be held over."

"I know," I said. I felt like I had met my own minimal expectations of guardianship care for Kevin.

"Call me with the score after the game, will you Jack?" I asked.

"You got it," he replied.

As we parted, I asked him, "Did Kevin say where he was living for the past three weeks?"

"All over the map. Here and there. He did say that he spent the past week, up to last night, at the home of a friend."

"It's good to have friends," I offered.

Out in the foyer I started to call Grady. A passing Deputy Sheriff kindly interrupted his serious business in order to shift me outside, beyond the "don't use the bloody phone in here" barricade. I finished dialing. Grady confirmed that he would be in court, even though I emphasized that Kevin was not going to be released today.

It was just past noon. I called the office and there were three messages. Monica had called and was at home and was up for lunch today. Millie had confirmed the rescheduled meeting was set for next Tuesday. Kate Morris had left a message for me to call in or check my cell. Gord Lafferty had also left some verbal leavings, polite but cryptic. I called Monica back and agreed to pick up her and Samantha, her daughter, in about a half an hour. I then called Kate.

I had no idea whether Lafferty had shared whatever issue he wanted to fling at me with her.

"Kate, hi," I said when she came on the line.

"Wally, what's going on?"

"With?" I asked.

"Give me some credit," she said with just a faint tone of restrained edge.

"If you mean with Gord," I took an informed stab in the organizational dark, "I don't know. He's got something he wants to bring to my attention and has advised me to have union representation. It was scheduled for noon today but had to be reshuffled. Why?"

"You're saying you don't know what it's about?"

"Right. Not a clue. Do you?"

"An old case of yours. Angie Gravelle. The closed file was requested by Gord and it came in this morning. And you can't think why?"

"No clue, Kate. Angie has been out of care for over a decade."

"I don't like not knowing what's going on in my office. Straight up, you can't think why Gord should be perusing the Gravelle file?"

"Believe me, I don't like surprises. Especially management surprises," I lamented.

"When is the new meeting scheduled for?"

"Tuesday. Noon. At the office. But Gord may have something further to say about that. I'm keeping my head down."

"Why?"

"Because he more or less threatened suspension," I said. "I would prefer not to be suspended."

"I need to talk with him." she declared.

"Be my guest. I'm surprised he hasn't taken you into his confidence already. Look Kate, I need to get to Monica's. We have a lunch date and something is going on with her. I'll be back at the office before three. Will you be in?"

"No," she replied, "there's a supervisors' meeting set for 1:30. Gord chairs them. I'm surprised he went with the original time today for your meeting."

"Maybe he knew it would be brief. Are you in tomorrow?"

"Nine," she said.

"We'll talk then."

"Let's structure it a bit, Wally. A mini case review. Maybe just your high profile heartbreakers. Okay?"

"They're all heartbreakers, Kate. Okay, see you in the morning."

I returned to the parking catacombs and headed out to Monica's apartment. During the drive, I first thought about Kate and then, as I came closer to Monica's home, I thought about her. Overlaying those two distinct thought threads, I harkened back to Angie Gravelle.

Supervisors like Kate Morris were organizationally neither fish nor fowl. It was a fusion position really, meant to funnel leadership from the top and placate soldier unrest below. What her position was mostly designed to do was to screen, to filter the sediment that goes up and down the sluice. They had to be a wary lot, foxy and sharp. A percentage at her level would be groomed to rise up the ranks. They would be constantly tested for organizational loyalty, organizational survival skills, and personal loyalty. The personal loyalty test would be in regards to their superiors. When the ink hit the paper, who did they support, the worker or the boss? And how well could they hide their corporate yearnings. To be successful in the position, the supervisor had to engender loyalty from the team, the workers on the line. To climb the ladder, the organization had to be first in their hearts.

I suspected Kate had maxed out her climb. Unless I was mistaken, she was a client-and worker-oriented leader. But it was still early days.

I sometimes regretted the slow pace of my ladder climbing. I also regretted that I saw so many snakes coiled amid the rungs. At every opportunity, I took satirical aim at the snakes, who I knew were simply bureaucratic travelers seeking their place on the ladder. They were not usually poisonous. More frequently, they were venomously dull, tedious and scaly, more liable to smother you in *perhaps* and *maybe* and my favourite, *"there's a better way to come at this Wally."* And if you spent too much time with them, became one of them, they would suffocate you with their pandering, simpering ways.

I could never be one of them. And I really hoped Kate kept her distance.

Chapter 8

Monica Maggin,
Thursday Afternoon, November 15

As I got closer to Monica's, my thoughts drifted to her and her 18-month-old daughter. Over the years, I had been the social worker for a handful of young mothers, children 15, 16, 17 years of age, who tackled what I considered the toughest job going; one I had failed miserably at. Often they came at the duty of parenting with no real experience of having been parented themselves. Many of their parents had lost their traction along the way, and their children had been set aside. Some were outright abandoned, but frequently it was my impression that they had been set down on the corner, so the parent could rest up. If the parental recovery moment proved excessively long, pernicious time would not permit them to resume their parental chore.

I was an apologist for the parents. Harsh assessments of their character failings served no purpose. If the parent was still alive, reunion was always possible. Most of the youth I worked with craved that reunion, although often they would not admit it.

When a pregnant youth came my way, I was scrupulous in not attempting to influence her about the decision to parent or not to parent. For many, the struggle to decide was as intense as any struggle they would ever endure.

Monica had come to my office one Monday morning two years earlier. She was three months pregnant. For the previous six months, she had been living with her mother. Prior to that, she had lived with her dad from the time her parents had split up when she was six. Her bond with her father was a powerful key in her development. His death from cancer six months earlier had been preceded by four years of escalating illness. She had become her father's confidante and nurse. There had been significant acrimony between her father and mother and contact with her mother had been minimal. When her father died, she had no other option but to go live with her mother.

"Oil and water," Monica had said describing her relationship with her mother the first day we met.

Denise Shaw, Monica's mother, had not taken to her estranged daughter. She was a hard working realtor with a long-standing, live-in partner, and Monica had not blended well into their domestic arrangement. The mother-daughter bond was further tested when Monica disclosed not only that she was pregnant but that she was obligated to keep the baby. She felt this obligation because she had suffered the loss of her father, and knew that he would have wanted her to keep any child of hers. From my experience, this wasn't a casual, impulse-driven decision. I admired Monica's resolve. Her mother and stepfather tried to understand her position, but, though they never articulated it clearly, it was fairly obvious that Denise Shaw and Ray Comeau did not want to end up parenting the infant. Even though they insisted that she either terminate or relinquish, she held her ground, and this precipitated her expulsion from the home. I apprehended her, and in a matter of weeks, she became a state ward. She lived in a good foster home until Samantha, her beautiful child, was six months old. Finding a foster home that can care equally for the infant as well as the infant's child-mother is a challenge. Eventually, Monica's foster parents, and the foster mother in particular, found themselves increasingly concerned about Samantha's welfare. Small tiffs over day to day care started to simmer. This predictable conflict was exacerbated by Monica's occasional comment that maybe she should have relinquished. She had tried to involve Samantha's father, a young man she no longer dated, in the baby's life. He was relatively transient, and the foster parents discouraged his half-hearted attempts to play a part.

The placement cracked under the weight of the conflict. Because there had been a marginal, yet legitimate, concern about the care of Samantha, Monica agreed to allow her Samantha to be brought voluntarily into care at age three months. This essentially technical gesture allowed the foster home to receive more funds for her care, but it also served to formalize Monica's desperate and wavering plan to relinquish. Complicating the situation was the appointment of a social worker from another office to be Samantha's social worker. The intent of this was to assure that the baby's interest were protected and kept separate from Monica's interest. Though this was a reasonable approach, it also served to create a wedge between the interests of the mother and the interests of her child. Something had to give. Monica decided that she and Samantha should move out on their own. The voluntary care agreement ended and the complexity of two workers came to a close when I negotiated a rocky ceasefire to any protection concerns. This happened even though I had ignored a directive from our chieftains in Victoria who were uncomfortable with the image of two social workers from two different offices working at apparent cross purposes. This conflict had evolved, plausibly enough, as I assisted Monica in her corner, and Samantha's social worker struggled to ensure her baby's rights and safety were in place.

For the past year, Monica had lived on her own with her baby. I took her out to lunch once every two to three months. She attended school as well as a young parent's support group. I thought she was doing just fine.

Monica's apartment was located in a large, rundown complex, part of a string of four-story apartment buildings that had seen way better days. I parked in the rear and walked through the open-corridor underground parking to the front entrance, buzzed her, and she let me in. I took the frail elevator to the third floor, got out, and walked the hallway to her apartment. The door was ajar. I knocked and she hollered from somewhere inside for me to come in.

I was saddened but not surprised to see that her housekeeping skills had barely improved. She came out of the bathroom holding Sam on her hip, looking thin, waiflike and smiling, and said, in a pitch more craggy with weary age than her more usual chirpy, tone, "Say it Wally. It needs a cleaning."

"Consider it said," I agreed, reaching for Sam. She handed her to me.

"Fresh diaper?"

"Yup."

"I'm honoured."

"The place might be a shambles but she's spic and span. Look Wally, let me dress her and we can go."

I made a face at Sam, got a smile and a gurgle, and gave her back to Monica.

I could barely tie my own shoelaces when I was her age. I had been coddled and exempt from obligation as a teen, both blessed and cursed by inspired adolescent indolence. In hindsight, I wondered what part of my shallow teen know-how allowed me to support youth like Monica. None of my experiences came within a moon shot of her life, or the lives of young people similar to her.

Shortly, Sam was dressed and we lugged car seat, diaper bag, and a couple of other baby trappings that meant little to me, into the elevator, down to the main floor, out the building, and quickly to my car.

"I was thinking Japanese, if that was to your liking, Miss?" I said, knowing Monica's culinary tastes were somewhat more sophisticated than many of the youth I dealt with.

"Where were you thinking…Yoshihara's?"

"Yup." We had eaten there once before, and I had promised we would go there again.

It was a short drive, and we were there quickly.

The hostess showed us into a private room and we settled in to the intimacy it afforded. The restaurant had a small low chair especially meant for securing babes while adults dangled their feet in the well below the table.

We ordered two specials that included miso soup, a tray of delicacies including tempura veggies and prawns, California rolls, and green tea.

"You want to know why I'm not at school?" she asked.

"No mystery there," I offered. "You were destined to go to lunch with me."

My stock answer generated a small smile. I had offered it only to give her time to gather her forces to share what was slowing her down.

"My mother called on the weekend. I haven't spoken to her since I was at the Bensons. And then, it wasn't really speaking…strictly yelling."

Carol and Ted Benson had been the foster family for both her and Sam. Monica still wanted to have a speaking relationship with them but the struggle between the previous social worker for Sam and me had left a lot of emotionally charged fissures. One of those was the slow repairing of the rift between Monica and her mother. Denise Shaw, contrary to what I had expected, took a shining to Carol and Ted Benson. Denise seemed to appreciate the safety and care the foster family directed to both Monica and Samantha. However, once Monica started to assert herself, Denise landed smack dab on the side of the Benson's. It was a logical landing emotionally, adult to adult, but it widened the divide that had been closing between Denise and Monica.

"You must have been glad to hear from her? It's been over six months of cold shouldering," I said optimistically.

"Yeah… glad… for about a minute."

"So what, I have to extract everything you're feeling? Like a dental shrink?"

That got a small smirk.

"Oh Jesus, it was great to hear her voice. She seemed to be happy to hear mine but then she started asking all sorts of questions about Sam, was she getting enough food? Was I missing any school? Wasn't it about time I went back to Carol and Ted's? It turned into a humongous bitch session."

"So, she called just to bitch at you?" I asked.

"Maybe not," she conceded, "but it didn't take her long to work up to it." After a gasp of breath, she added, "Actually, she was calling to tell me she and Ray were getting married and she wanted me there."

"Super," I chirped in.

"She just wears me out, Wally. Mothers and motherhood just suck the life out of me some days. I went to school yesterday but I just couldn't get out of bed this morning."

Confessions of exhaustion from one so young invariably wore me out. Aside from listening to her maternal woes, I had little to offer. I had successfully tied my own hands. Denise had pretty much slammed the door in my face once I had gone for a permanent order for Monica. And taking Monica's side when she moved out of the Benson foster home had sealed my consignment to hell. Keeping the lines of communication open between youth and parents was often the key to their growth and survival. Many times I had been able to provide that intermediary conduit role. In Monica's case, I wasn't able to and there really wasn't anyone else in her life that could.

What might be needed now was a trusted middleman, a go-between, someone who could renew the healing that events had failed to scab properly. I could think of a couple of choices; Kate Morris could intervene, put me modestly in my place by appealing to Denise to help her find a way to patch things up as long as Wally was kept out of it. Another participant in Monica's life was Sheila Reicken, her teacher. Sheila had spent the past decade developing a young parents program within her school, an inclusive program that supported young parents to fully participate in learning, provided skilled daycare, and normalized as much of their lives as possible.

Lunch arrived and we dug in. There wasn't a whole lot Sam could eat but she took a bit of the miso soup.

"So," I asked, "besides marauding mothers, how are you doing otherwise? Dating?"

"Like when would I have time?" she snapped back. "No, I want to and I don't. But I'm not. Between school and my parenting support group, that's about all I can squeeze in. Darren has visited a few times and he takes me out, or sits Sam and frees me up a bit."

Darren was a young man who had known Monica when she lived with her dad and they had a pretty stable, seemingly platonic friendship. I had met him once on a home visit. He had been a neighbour of Monica and her dad's in the last couple of years of his life. Early on in my involvement with Monica, I had requested a CPIC check on Darren just to insure that he was more or less on the up and up. On the surface, he was just what he seemed, a young single guy with a caring heart and no criminal record.

The balance of lunch was quiet. The food was good and we chatted about the past, and more importantly, what the future might hold for her and her baby. I restrained my barrage of focused questions, preferring to kick back and enjoy the moment. Social workers on my team actively used lunch moments to engage our clients, share small social interludes we are invariably nourished by.

Maintaining a balance between the professional and the caregiver was the goal. I had worked with some social workers who actively shunned the sort of intimacy shared lunch and open conversation permitted. Breaking bread with teens had always seemed to me to be a valuable activity, and I built service plans around that kind of relationship. There were youth who would have none of it, youth too damaged to find any value in those sorts of quiet times, or who simply had other things to do with their time. And that was fine. I likely had a limit to my capacity to relax and share simple pleasures with youth. But I wouldn't intentionally be the one to set that limit.

As I was driving Monica and Samantha back home, I raised the notion of finding an intermediary to talk to her mom. She knew Sheila a lot better than she knew Kate but she agreed that Kate should give it a try. If she failed, Sheila, as her teacher, had a better, less threatening chance. I told her that I would ask Kate to touch base with her mother and see if we could get her agreement to participate in mediation, or some process aimed at finding a less painful way for them to communicate.

I dropped them off and got back to the office a little past 2:00 p.m. A big lunch, last evening's late hour carousing in the abandoned house, and too little sleep had worn me down.

I checked my e-mails and phone messages. I am a bit of a throwback as far as phone messages are concerned. Some years earlier, we were compelled to accept electronic phone messaging. As a proud Luddite, I could not bring myself to add one more beeping, ear-slaughtering electronic doodad to my limited wired world. While the rest of my office mates had accepted their new toy, I had simply refused. If someone called the office and wanted to leave a message, one of the front office staff would take it. It was a simple act of defiance, not much understood except perhaps by those people who were paid to take messages and provide related supports to people like me.

It wasn't a stretch to see that in the very near future, professionals would be responsible for all of their record keeping. There might be some ethical benefit to having sole responsibility for the work, the documentation and the outcome, but what it also did was isolate the social worker, and that isolation accelerated the burden of personal responsibility that most workers were shadowed with. In and of itself, this was a reasonable complication, but most, in my experience, buckled with the weight of it. I had crumbled some months earlier with the insurmountable tonnage of it all. All of my layers of culpability had crushed on me, like multiple streams of lava, and eventually, inevitably, predictably, I had hardened into immobility; I had become frozen in the moment, my own petroglyph.

As much as I hated to admit it, I needed to rest my eyes.

I walked to the front of the office and told Roberta that I was going to take a catnap for 20 minutes in the family room, where we had a sofa.

"Wake me in twenty, will ya Rob?" I had asked.

"Are you feeling okay?" she said, in a very concerned voice.

"Absolutely. It was a late night. Did Cathy tell you about our adventure?"

"She did, at coffee."

"Well, maybe I'm just showing my age," I replied.

"It's about time," she smiled.

"I love you too," I said. "By the way, when is Cathy due back?"

"She said three, Wally. But you know she sometimes runs over time with her youth."

Didn't we all sometimes, I asked myself. You could never give the youth we worked with enough time. They would invariably suck the soul out of you. Maybe that was our role; someone for the dispossessed to feed on, to be nourished by our energy and wellness. And there were some very healthy practitioners in the field. On that sheen of professional ice I saw them skate so well. In the taut skin of the professional, all the jiggles of misgiving, the waves of apprehension, and the currents of despondency were held in check by that tensor bandage of expertise.

But I had my own self-doubt, my own limits. The work culture I was immersed in did not really embrace the sort of examination that would encourage serious reflection. If it did, there would follow the compunction to effect change. And change was actively discouraged. I mean, who had the time?

"If you would wake me at three, I'd appreciate it, Rob"

I fell asleep in seconds. It wasn't an appreciably large couch, but I squirreled into it and faded. I never used to nap. When I was younger, I could function on five or six hours of relatively uninterrupted sleep. Those times had slipped away from me, and my body and restless mind needed to adapt to the ways of the older worker. My favourite dream reappeared. I am in the warm sun, the topography is flat; the road I am walking on leads away into some far-flung hills. I am thirsty, and water instantly appears. A cool spring gurgles by the side of the road. I lower myself to the side of the stream, drink, and am quenched. Hunger overtakes me. Food materializes. I sit at a table by the roadside; there is a checkered table cloth, red wine in a clay jug, goat's cheese, an assortment of olives, and warm bread fresh from the oven. I feast and quaff the wine. A breeze blows in from the sea, waves softly lap onto the beach that has replaced the road I was trudging on.

I lie down on the sand and sleep, and dream of the mountains I will climb when I am rested.

Roberta roused me at three and I was refreshed.

I put in a call to Kate's cell so as not to forget that I had tapped her to make a pitch to Denise Shaw, Monica's mom. Kate's mediation skills might strike a chord with Denise. And I had to think that Kate and Denise each shared that ability fancy dancers have to sashay around the social dance floor without stepping on toes. Both were required to schmooze and suck up to a wealth of people. That was the core skill set of both their jobs; networking. Whatever worked to improve Monica's sense of her own worth.

I prided myself that I did the same sort of thing without selling out. There were obviously lots of days when I could delude myself in this way.

I called Cathy and she said I should drop by around seven.

I putzed for the rest of the afternoon. At five, I went for a swim at the local pool and did fifty laps. All right, forty. But I had planned to do fifty.

I got to Cathy's apartment a little past seven. I had had to park two blocks away, having forgotten how little space was available for the itinerant guest visiting west-enders. As much as I felt slightly inconvenienced, the pedestrian in me couldn't help but praise the planning foresight that kept the streets small as the high-rises intruded into this neighbourhood. The sixties were a boom time; a massive population shift delivered tens of thousands of immigrants from the country, the other provinces, and the world, to this jewel by the sea. And everyone wanted to live downtown; the cultural life of the city broke free from staid Anglo-Saxon repression, the tedious flat-lined fifties. At least that was my sense of that decade, the one that had seen me toddle into my teens.

It was an older west end apartment building, four floors of soft-yellow fifties stucco. The entrance had a New York brownstone feel, high broad steps, and a depth of style that led you to believe, if you let your mind wander a lot, that you were back at the turn of the century, and that, behind those grand oak entrance doors, a timeless mystery was about to unfold.

I was having a pleasant time conjuring up the notion of a relationship with Cathy. There is certain liberation to be had in having an affair of the mind. Warmth envelopes you, a secret, musky warmth that adds an oddly satisfying dimension to a friendship.

I had picked up a bottle of domestic white earlier in the day. Sadly, only the November weather had chilled it, but a few minutes in the freezer would put some snap into it. I took the elevator to the top floor of the building. It opened onto an exceptionally wide hallway with a nine-foot-high ceiling. The carpet was somewhat worn but had the remnants of rich deep-blue dye and flowery patterns. The walls were graced with framed family photographs of the half dozen tenants who lived on the floor. Cathy had once told me that the building owner strongly encouraged the notion of a shared hallway as portrait gallery, and it seemed to have struck a nostalgic chord with her and her neighbours. I rang her apartment bell and she let me in. She looked great, dressed in shorts and t-shirt and a hefty, efficient-looking apron.

"Wine," I offered, handing the not-quite-chilled bottle to her.

"Take your coat off, Wally, and hang it in the closet," she said, taking the wine and heading into her small kitchen.

Soft jazz was playing in the living room. It was almost familiar. I have no ear for music but am heartened and rejuvenated by familiar pieces that chance my way. I took off my coat and shoes and wandered into the kitchen after her. She had placed the wine on ice and then turned to check whatever was cooking in the oven.

"It won't help your waistline, I'm afraid," she warned. "Eggplant parmesan. Heavy on the cheese."

"Thanks for the heads-up. I should have brought a burgundy…a red of some kind."

She reached into a cupboard and removed a bottle of Merlot. "Help yourself Wally, and pour me one, will you?"

I found two wine glasses, poured the wine, put hers on the kitchen counter and wandered to the living room. Cathy had a corner suite that was blessed with a wall of windows on two sides. Not ceiling to floor, but clearly designed to let the eye wander out into the street and catch a view of far-flung hills and a glimpse of the sea.

"I like this view, Cath," I said with my back to her. I spoke softly, which I often do when mesmerized by a pleasing view, or when holding a glass of wine.

The West End had a frenzy of trees that, though they had been defoliated by seasonal change and horticultural endeavour, still gave a sense of a forest family visiting town for a few days. What they mostly did, amidst the low-and high-rise obelisks, the sheer volume of congested humanity which claimed the layered urban air, was bring an intense sense of calm to anyone with time enough to stare, time to spare.

"You say something, Wally?" Cathy asked from her kitchen.

Of course I had uttered nothing worth repeating, nothing other than a simple observation on the view. Yet it was more than plain commentary on the vista. It was one of those moments when the brain is stilled, when the heart is composed, when the body at rest.

"Only commenting on the view, Cath."

Cathy came into the living room to pay a tad more attention to her aged guest.

"It's great isn't it? I loved visiting my grandparents here. Growing up in the burbs was stultifying but here, well it was sheer fantasy. I remember spending hours sitting at the window, peeking out and spying on the world. It was great fun. Still is."

Though it was a rental apartment, it had been in Cathy's family for over 50 years. Her mother had been born just after her maternal grandfather, Cameron Cowan, had shipped out overseas with the Princess Patricia regiment. During the war, her grandmother, Sylvia Cowan, and mother, Betty, had bounced around quite a bit. There had been a massive housing crunch, and people doubled and tripled up just to ensure a roof over their heads. When Cameron Cowan was demobilized, they rented this apartment. It had served as the recreational and residential heart of the family since that time. Holidays were cramped and crowded affairs and Cathy had relished every family event.

As the years progressed, Sylvia and Cameron resisted every overture to leave. The death of her husband five years ago had hastened her own death, according to Cathy, but she refused to abandon the apartment. The family had held a series of meeting to discuss how best to continue their half-decade tenancy. Cathy's mom had other obligations as did most everyone else. Though Cathy often described feeling compelled to assume the lease, she couldn't imagine living anywhere else.

"How's your wine?" she asked from the kitchen.

"I'm good. Thanks."

"Dinner will be about another 10 minutes," she said, coming up to me. "Take a load off. I'm wiped from last night. An old guy like you, why, you must need a nap."

"Had one at the office," I replied. "I meant to ask, did you hear from anybody about Skye?"

"That was the strangest thing. I had a message from one of her friends, Sue Gainsborough. She called at noon, and I was away from my desk. The voice message didn't really say anything other than Skye was fine and please stop chasing her. Odd."

"She was probably calling from school. Did you try and reach her there?"

"I called Heather Slocum. Do you know her? Counsellor at Pierce School? She told me Sue was turning into a truant type. There most of the time but away enough without permission that it was concerning. Skye even more so. I called the Gainsborough home but only got the machine. I was hesitant about leaving a message, about it actually being heard by her parents or maybe setting them off. I thought I might swing by there tomorrow."

"All of this begs the question," I ruminated, "how did Sue know you were 'chasing' Skye?"

"I'm not chasing her, Wally."

"I beg to differ. That's what we are doing. It's okay, Cath. Child savers sometimes have to run these sad youth down to ground. Don't be so sensitive."

"Right," she said in a manner that closed off that area of discussion. "Back to your question. How did Sue Gainsborough know I was involved?"

Only a few people were aware that youth services had been drawn in. Carla Prentice may have mentioned our visit to her daughter's friend. That would make some sense; desperate parent heats up the phone lines trying to scare up some news about her missing child. But beyond Mrs. Prentice, only Manny and the man in the abandoned squat were aware of our curiosity.

The bigger question was really why Sue Gainsborough would feel the need to kibosh a search for her friend. I could sense the distraction of a tangent inching its way into an otherwise pleasant evening. As few pleasant evenings as I might have, even those that did chance my way often easily fell prey to worry and speculation. Mastering your own universe is a constant challenge when you work with vulnerable people. Some social workers and similar types, givers, the emotionally starved and needy, those who intentionally or accidentally substitute a real life with the visceral demands of their work life, never enjoy the primacy of their own thoughts, their own inner privacy.

I wavered constantly.

"You should call Mrs. Prentice in the morning," I advised.

"I think I'll do it now," she countered, going to her daybook to get the number.

On another occasion I might have said tomorrow will do, but this sort of impulsive need to know had been one of my irresistible compulsions some years back. A question burrows into your brain, like toasting nuts, heating up your thought processes, getting in the way of your down time. It pisses you off; such a small itch to scratch. You finally convince yourself that there will be little harm in making just one call to answer the damn question.

"Damn," Cathy said. "I don't have her number. She grabbed her phonebook. "A couple of C. Prentices, but no Carla. Must be unlisted. I think I knew that," she muttered.

"After-hours will have it," she finally said, and called them. She identified herself, gave her home number, and asked them to call her with Carla's number from the electronic file. A couple of minutes later, the callback came and she jotted the number down.

"Thanks, George, I appreciate it," she said to the after-hours worker, knowing how much they loved being an answering service.

"I'm going to call her, Wally. Sorry."

I nodded. She needed to know, and for that matter, so did I.

She punched in the 10 digits and waited.

"Could I speak to Carla Prentice?" she asked.

"Mrs. Prentice, I'm sorry for bothering you so late. This is Cathy Baker from the youth team."

She listened for a few seconds.

"No, no, I have no news about Skye. The reason I was calling is that I was wondering if you had mentioned my visit yesterday to anyone."

"No, it wasn't meant to be a secret. It's just, well, I would appreciate it if you could tell me whom you might have mentioned it to. More to the point, do you happen to recall mentioning my name? Or my colleague's name?"

I could vaguely hear Carla Prentice's muffled voice, deep in the receiver.

"So you can't recall mentioning our names to anyone?" Cathy asked, just to be certain.

"Sorry to sound so mysterious, Mrs. Prentice. I appreciate your time. Is there a good time to reach you tomorrow? Before four? Fine, I'll touch base in the afternoon. Thank you. Goodnight."

She hung up, went into the kitchen, asked me if I needed more wine, to which I nodded in the affirmative. Being a responsive host, she brought the bottle to my nearly empty glass and poured.

She set the bottle down on the coffee table and sat next to me.

"So if she is telling the truth…I believe her, Wally. People typically don't name-drop social workers, do they?"

"Only in vain, Cath. Usually, we become part of the dark family secret, whatever it might be. There's little to boast about knowing the likes of us," I said, in a fake pirate intonation.

"So that leaves us Manny, and the hermit," she resumed.

"Unless someone overheard you at some other point. It may mean nothing. The youth cell phone tree has more links than we could ever imagine. And there are no mysteries in social work. Except why we ever signed up, maybe."

"Maybe food will cheer you up," she announced, and we sat down to a filling eggplant parmesan and salad dinner.

Cathy offered me her couch as the wine won its little skirmish with my sobriety. I was unfit to drive, and too cheap to pay for a cab.

Chapter 9

Kate
Friday Morning, November 16

When morning came, when what I took to be the beginning of the following day arrived (which was not as easy an undertaking as one might imagine, given the thick dark cloak of night that surrounded me on Cathy's couch, and the foggy remnants that hung in my brain's closet), I huddled there in the morning, straining to hear Cathy stir in her room. My hearing clearly was less than it once may have been; I heard nothing.

Abruptly, like a dervish, she charged out of her room, decked out in baggy grey sweats, said the place was mine for an hour max but then she needed to reclaim it in total, and was out the door in a bolt for a run. My watch had the temerity to suggest that it was 5:30 a.m.

It had been years since my drinking demons had permitted me to languish overnight in a young woman's apartment. Like some mangy carpetbagger trussed up on a flea-infested burro and led to the edge of town, I gathered my clothes and dressed. In a flash I was out the door.

The early morning air was cold, but there was no rain. I stood on the sidewalk at the bottom of the steps to her apartment building and struggled to remember where I had parked my car. The slight morning breeze carried the fragrance of muffins, likely from a nearby Davie Street eatery. Coffee smells poured into the mix as well. My stomach gurgled. Though it was as dark as danger, the street was alive with morning exercisers, walkers, joggers, dog strollers, street denizens, and java addicts seeking someone else's brew. This neighbourhood had the activity a suburban mall might have a few days (or a few months) before Christmas. The only difference was that here the roof had been rolled back. My neighbourhood would tremble with such a display of ferocious morning movement. It was as if all these high-rise dwellers couldn't wait to taste the crack-of-dawn air and live the urban dream. In my neighbourhood, only the odd shift worker, hotel maid, and the perpetually homeless would be caught dead out this early.

Parking recall kicked in and I sauntered the couple of blocks to where my car had spent a lonely night and drove on home to shower and change. I was at work by 7:30.

No matter when I start working on Friday, the day seems to drag. For others it may scamper by, but for me, it seems interminable. It may be that I add to the stretched-out tediousness of my work Fridays by reserving most of the day for paperwork. Even with my meticulous planning, the day often gets away from me. The unplanned problems of people intrude. Paper is easily dispensed with. However, if you suffer too many out-of-control days, your paperwork stacks up like grain in a silo.

I was also anticipating my nine o'clock meeting with Kate. I liked to be supervised...in moderation. Kate usually gave me my head, as if I was some old racehorse with a few good runs left in him before pasture time.

To prepare for my meeting with her, I printed off my caseload and began to review the list. Currently, I had 33 open cases. Though above professional caseload guidelines, it was relatively manageable. Whatever the size of a worker's caseload, what really mattered were the demands each case made on you. A corollary to case size was that the worker needed to be level-headed, emotionally fit to service each case, each kid, appropriately.

Over the years, I had become the sweeper, the cleanup guy. As other workers moved on, as offices were merged, as new styles of service delivery evolved, I stayed and cherry-picked the interesting cases. These last few years on the specialized youth team had been the most rewarding for me. We mostly serviced youth 16-18 as well as a small group of former youth in care 19-24 who were eligible for post-majority monies. Our attempt to service Skye Prentice and her mother was a bit of an anomaly given Skye's age but we thrived on being able to help when we were of a mind to.

The 16–18-year-olds fell into four categories: youth in the care of the state, youth on agreements, youth receiving some level of support or assessment (and occasionally they were assessed as eligible for an agreement or state care), and families with youth still at home and unlikely to need more than skilled mediation.

Of my 33 cases, five were family-service based, 14 were youth in care, eight were youth on agreements, four were youth in an initial assessment phase, and three were on post-majority.

Whether the boxes the system had created for these young people have any substance, I found them useful. They spoke of a tiered array of responses to the needs of youth. Realistically, this small arsenal of bureaucratic weapons, used equitably and judiciously, served the citizenry well. The fly in the organizational ointment was, as always, politically-dictated policy shifts. And these shifts were always rolling in on us, unexpected tsunamis of reorganization and adjustment.

The next hour and a half dragged on as I assembled updates on my most difficult cases. I always attempt to prioritize them, primarily for my supervisor's sake, but also as a means of understanding how best to respond and assist the youth for whom I have varying degrees of responsibility. Kate consistently needs a clear sense of what her workers are doing and a crisp knowledge of all of the youth and families receiving service on her watch. By nine, I had a fairly serviceable list and walked two offices down the hallway to Kate's office. She hadn't yet arrived, so I went to the coffee room, refreshed my cup, sauntered into the front office, and advised Roberta, who was on switchboard, that I'd be in Kate's office for at least an hour.

By the time I got back, Kate had arrived and was removing her black poncho, her signature winter cloak. Kate Morris had been my supervisor for the past three years. We had similar backgrounds in that neither of us had started out to be social workers. She in fact had been a musician for a number of years, on the road with a punk rock group called the Dead Bohemians. When we were making acquaintance five years earlier, Kate struggled to explain how she had made the transition. I however had no difficulty in seeing that her kindness and personal strength were harmonizing characteristics that led her into a most suitable profession.

For me there was a certain perverse pleasure in being led by a refugee from punk rock.

"Wally, good morning. Look, get comfortable. I want to grab a coffee. Need topping up?" she asked, whizzing by me.

"Naw, Kate, I'm good."

I sat down and stretched in the chair. Kate returned before I had a chance to compose my thoughts.

"Sorry I was a little late. You know I always shoot for nine on the dot," she said. We had had this conversation a hundred times. Kate has an almost six-year-old daughter, and her needs regularly occupied Kate's mornings. "Shooting for nine on the dot" was a standing gag. Kate lived 40 minutes away and had to negotiate the tunnel or the bridge daily, each of which could jam up in an instant. Because she worked evenings once or twice a week with groups in the community, she didn't need to come in at "nine on the dot", and it wasn't expected. She expected it of herself, but that was her demon.

Once she was settled, she opened her case management book, a large ledger used to track all of her workers' cases.

"Okay, I am ready," she stated as an opener.

"Me too, Kate. What do you want first?"

"What I would like," she phrased carefully, "is some information about the Gravelle case. What can you tell me?"

What could I tell her, I wondered? What she really wanted to know is why Gord would even threaten me with suspension or worse. What she also wanted to know was how whatever action crashed down on me would affect her, me, and ultimately the team and my cases. What she wanted to know was simply beyond my knowledge.

"I can give you my take on Angie Gravelle, Kate," I conceded. "I don't have a clue what Gordo has up his sleeve. Did you read the file?"

"I looked at it. Old files aren't quite as well documented as we expect today."

"Actually, I thought I kept pretty good records. She was one of my earliest youth in care."

"Did you have any contact with her after she went to ASU?"

"Direct contact? No," I replied.

"Indirect?"

I thought about it, and I didn't want to lie to her. I also didn't want to tell the truth. Mostly I didn't want to unnecessarily open an embarrassing can of worms.

"No. No I don't think I did."

"Then why does Gord want the file?" she asked in a frustrated tone.

"I sincerely don't know, Kate. I wish I did. I guess I'm going to have to be on tenterhooks until Tuesday. Until then, we both have to let it rest. Can you do that?" I asked, with a sharper edge to my voice then she deserved.

Taken aback, Kate let it go.

"Okay, I'll put that down to frayed nerves, Wally. Maybe I was pushing. For that I'm sorry. But I don't like your temper. Please keep it in check."

I nodded, choosing not to give voice to my embarrassment at speaking harshly to her.

"Caseload then?"

"Right. I do want to save enough time to ask a special favour regarding Monica Maggin but let's cover the rest of the caseload as long as we get back to Monica."

"You keep track of time, Wally. I'm all ears."

"Will do. Let's start with the post majority. I have three in contract. All three, as you'll remember, were signed off last September. Jordan Sloan is turning twenty-four in December, so he's on his last PMS legs."

"He's at Langara, isn't he?" Kate asked.

"Yup. Completing his fourth semester. Fair marks…still unsure what he wants."

Jordan had worked as a construction labourer once he left care. It was hard for him to give up a working wage for the life of a student. Like others I'd known, it had taken him a few years to mature sufficiently to consider the benefits of a poverty-infused student existence. He'd been fairly straight up that he knew he would kick himself if he didn't access the Post-Majority Services dollars. I thought that was as good a reason as any. He now had two years of college under his belt, a taste of a possible future that had eluded him before, and one more substantial option.

I continued with my remaining two post-majority youth.

"Cassie Moran is on her first contract, attending BCIT…studying mechanics. Deserves to be renewed in the spring. One tough young woman."

We both knew Cassie well. Kate had worked with her even more than I had, even though she was nominally on my case load. Cassie hadn't allowed any grass to grow under her once she turned 19. Both Kate and I and her longtime foster mom, Mel Caruthers, had repeated ad nauseam how precarious PMS monies were and that they needed to be used speedily.

Contracts were typically six months long. The program had been a late season innovation by an earlier government. Foster parents and social workers, as well as the youth-in-care movement, had all been vociferous in arguing that, because the state was at best an inconsistent parent, children in her care often struggled once they aged out. One means of redeeming them, fortifying them, was to provide educational support after they turned 19. The first version of the program had been weak and limited. In short order it was expanded with few limiting controls other than regional budgets and worker enthusiasm. Subsequently, fiscal restraint struck like a virus, and the program was shaved down to a two-year maximum. All along, age 24 was the cut-off. Kate was right about our region. We were one of the few that had no waitlists. Our office in particular had vigorously implemented the program, as we did with as many new youth-support initiatives as we could.

"I took her to lunch last week," Kate added.

"Good," I replied, not the least envious. "Students need to be fed regularly."

"What about Stella Walters?" Kate asked, anticipating me.

"Stella, Stella, Stella," I said in my obligatory, albeit puny, Brando voice. "I don't know, Kate…I'd like to talk with her and verify that she's sticking to the plan. That hairstyling program she registered in was iffy from the beginning. Not the program. It always felt like she grabbed it out of a hat though. I know she was getting desperate; next thing to homeless much of the time; bouncing all over the Lower Mainland. I had a hell of a time keeping tabs on her even when she was in care. Now, I have so little time to even pretend to offer her support. Not that she's checking in more than the bare minimum. The whole thing may be a con."

"You need to follow up pretty quickly, Wally. Management has issued machetes and is looking closely at this budget line. Amongst others. Nothing is safe from the grim fiscal reaper, I'm afraid. Even small-potatoes programs."

Kate was a farm girl, even more than she was an ex-punk-rocker, and mostly favoured wholesome vegetable and barnyard metaphors.

"It's such a cost-effective program, Kate," I whimpered in a half pathetic, half-muted-anger voice.

"As I was saying," she resumed, "they are getting slash-happy. Most regions have to keep waiting lists for the PMS program. We've never done that. Never. We may have to pretty soon, and that would be plain bad news."

She caught her breath.

"We have got to be a lot more rigorous with how we do our PMS contracts Wally. They already think we've been lax. Hell, we have been lax. Not anymore. Otherwise we won't have any program. We will need to cut any wastage to avoid that."

Point taken. I nodded. Rigour was one of my talents. Well, bureaucratic rigor mortis, that is.

I made a note to visit Stella as soon as possible.

Having dealt with the PMS cases, I next gave Kate a thumbnail sketch of open intakes. We had reviewed all of them at our team meeting on Wednesday except for Erin Mulaney. I briefly filled her in on Erin's inaugural appearance at the office on Wednesday afternoon, our discussion, and my home visit.

"The paperwork's coming," I promised, and she smiled.

We both embraced the youth agreement program, and she didn't need to tell me it was vulnerable as well. We also agreed that they (they being the brains trust who developed programs that just couldn't be kept simple, manageable and locally driven) had screwed it up on a number of fronts, not the least of which was the long stack of paperwork required.

I then went through my youth agreement caseload. The only one that seriously worried me was Jimmy Hollinger. Jimmy had come to us a few months earlier. Dru Janes had heard about a young man hunkering down on a strip of sand by the river and later discovered his camp on one of her regular scans of isolated out-of-the-way spots. He had been bivouacked there since summer, and by late September, when she encountered him, the weather was turning, and he was somewhat amenable to offers of shelter.

One morning earlier last month, Dru had brought Jimmy in to meet with me. I had been expecting a beaten-down, pungent, smashed-up kid, but that's not what I got. His clothes needed upgrading for sure; but they seemed clean, and he had a lovely scent not unlike jasmine bath oil.

He was also a good-looking kid, with soft, smooth facial features, straight nose, eyes as blue as the prairie sky (his description of his eyes), light-brown hair nicely trimmed, and a smile as broad as the Mississippi River. And ten thousand tales of woe.

"Yeah, my mom and I didn't get along pretty much from the get-go," he said in a faint maritime brogue.

"How come?" I asked disingenuously.

"My sister, being 15 years older than I, attended at my birth. When I was six or so, and after being a little bastard to her, messing her room and causing her all sorts of grief, she told me."

"Told you what, Jimmy?" I asked, falling into a well-worn snare. "Well sir, she told me that when I was coming out of my mom, a slippery, sloppy newborn squawker, well sir I was ten pounds if I was a gram, and mom was a wee thing, and my sister says she screamed out, "I'm gonna hate this heathen creature. Not even breathing on his own and he's torturing me."

I smiled and asked, "Did you both survive your birth?"

He smiled back and said, "Things improved some after that. But I was the last kid of three. Each of her pups was born bigger than the last. She couldn't imagine giving birth to one larger than me."

Things may have improved after his birth, but his mother was 33 when she had him, with two teenagers, 15 and 16, and few prospects. After his birth, to get away from Jimmy's father, whom his mother considered a bully, they left Newfoundland and settled, after a time, in the North End of Winnipeg. In a few years, it was just him and his mother. His brother joined the armed forces, and his sister married her boyfriend and moved down east.

As folksy and entertaining as Jimmy presented, his story became a lot more painful. His mother just sort of got lost in Winnipeg, and drifted into drugs and increasingly abusive relationships. Eventually Jimmy came into care on a revolving door basis.

Every time his mom got it together, he went home, wherever that might be at the time. The chaos of her intermittent bouts of recovery didn't help Jimmy develop any structure, but he loved his mom and flew to her any time he could.

"One of my workers, JayCee, she understood my mom. She just told me what I guess I knew, that my mom was broken and that's the way it was."

"A good way to say it," I conceded. "Some people are broken, like a bone. Like a bone that never heals properly."

"Christmas last year was gonna be our first real Christmas in years. My brother couldn't make it. He was posted overseas… in Germany. My sister Gay, her hubby Matt and their two kids were driving down. It was looking good. I'd been back with her a month. Crowded little one bedroom apartment."

"What happened?"

"Nothin' new. One of her buddies hooked her up. She got into a scrap with some woman. Cops arrested her. They finally released her after New Years.

The rest of us made do but it was a downer. I made up my mind to get away. Westward Fuckin' Ho!"

Jimmy needed a boost and the youth agreement program seemed fitting. I never spoke directly with his mom, a modest prerequisite to gain access to the program, but the financial worker in Winnipeg confirmed that she consented. We could have arranged some telephone contact and the file documented that we would try. One of those little tasks that needed to be done, might get done, didn't really matter if they got done until the accountants wanted to check it off. Until that day, Jimmy got the support we had to offer.

Kate and I continued for the next hour. I presented little sunshine and sorrow sketches of the youth on my watch, and she accepted most of my observations, but consistently pushed me to identify work tasks in relation to each kid, tasks that would hopefully benefit them but also address bureaucratic chores that needed to be done to ease the inevitable wrath of the auditors.

After two hours, we had reached overload. Kate likely still had some gas but I was plainly looking for short cuts, little diversions to show my mental exhaustion. Supervision is considered to be a valuable process for social workers to engage in. How you do your job, how you are at it, how you reach decision points, how they mesh with the rules of the game; all of these intricate steps need to be policed to ensure purity of action.

Even though I had become weary with the length of this meeting, we had done some good work.

"Let's do Monica," I said and Kate nodded.

There was no need for me to summarize the steps we had taken with Monica. Kate was painfully aware that I had exercised excessive advocacy with her. The worse part for her when the mandarins were squeezing my professional oranges was that she essentially agreed with my position of support for Monica.

"I think it's maybe time to try and inject a mediation process in the Maggin/Shaw family."

"Monica would be up for that?" Kate asked.

"I think so. She just had her first contact with Denise in six months," and, I added, "a phone call from Denise inviting her to her and Ray's wedding."

"Good."

I looked troubled

"Not good?" she asked.

"Denise is a tough-minded woman. She offers an olive branch: the invitation to the nuptials; and she smites Monica down with a barrage of questions, questions that are hostile opinions about how Monica is doing. More of the same, but with the invite."

"You have a plan?"

"I'm about as welcome as Dick Cheney at a gay-pride parade," I said.

"It would be a big step to have Dick attend, don't you think?"

"Forget the metaphor. I've been unable to come up with a half-decent one all week. Point is, Denise hates my guts, as do the Bensons. Monica trusts you and is open to having you contact Denise. If you can initiate a sit-down, come up with some ground rules for Monica to attend the wedding, everyone wins a little respect. There's no guarantee that Denise wants any outside interference. But Monica wants an escort. She needs our help or they'll torpedo her sure as…shooting."

"Isn't there some one else?"

"Monica and I talked about Sheila Reicken. I think Denise has some respect for her. But we figured you could, if necessary, promise to keep me in check. I'm the bad guy and if it takes me having my character assassinated to improve Monica's relationship with her mom, so be it."

"What are you saying? You want me to sacrifice you on the altar of family reunification?"

As Kate asked me to clarify my request, I couldn't recall ever having this sort of conversation before. What was I asking her for? To do whatever it took, within some practical ethical bounds, to make life better for one of our youth clients. Even if that meant offering me up as a scapegoat. It would be a painless ritual for me. For Kate, it would have a different outcome. She might have to say, or imply, negative things about one of her staff; suggest, ever so delicately, that I may have stepped over the line. She would have to be careful not to give Denise Shaw ammunition to file a complaint either with the ministry or with the Board of Registration. We were sailing into shallow waters ethically. The only justification was the best interests of our client and our assessment of her welfare. Kate would do well to talk out what it was I was expecting her to do.

"I won't undermine you, Wally. There's no percentage for you or me or Monica. But I will call Denise and see if she will meet with me."

"Fair enough," I said. "Good. I know you'll do what you're comfortable with."

"Will you call her today?" I added.

"I'll call her when I call her. Give me a break."

I'd stepped over the sheepherder line again. Always pushing, that was my style, always doing other people's jobs.

I shut up and we left it at that.

It was just past eleven in the morning. The supervision session had been unexpectedly draining. On any given day, I try not to get wrapped up in more than five or six of my cases. Other cases may demand nothing more than small bureaucratic massaging; they are done almost by rote. Emotion doesn't often enter into this sort of routine. If the day is going tickety-boo, the lives of all my youth cases, both current and past, don't pop-up into my everyday thoughts. I seem to mostly have the capacity to file them away in the waiting room and select them as time becomes available. Or so I tell myself.

I was at loose ends. Though it was still an hour away from my lunch time, I couldn't bring myself to settle down and tackle paperwork. Just as I decided to run out and get a burger, I heard Cathy's voice down the hall. She came closer, and in seconds, she was sitting down opposite me looking a wee bit flustered.

"Thanks for the loan of your couch."

"Anytime," she said somewhat sourly.

"How's your day unfolding?" Cathy had something to tell me, or so her body language seemed to say.

"Crappy! Sometimes you just can't see the freight train coming."

I gave her my "stay off the tracks but even that won't save you" look. It was an obscure look of mine and I doubted she could read it well.

"What happened?"

"I just saw Tessa Wednesday. Well, you know that. The whole point is to be there for them. Listen. Be someone they can trust."

"Tessa okay?"

"She's fine, if you call being pregnant fine."

I nodded and held my tongue. Cathy would add to her words.

"She called me this morning. I think she was surprised I answered. I think she was hoping to get my voice mail."

"I do that sometimes; call people when I'm betting they're out."

"She seem startled when I answered, apologized for not telling me when I visited. Oh, I was cool. Listened attentively. Empathized. She doesn't have a clue what she wants to do."

I offered a smidgen of sage advice. "You know it's a process. She's told you. She'll want your help."

"Oh, I know that. I know! I know! I know! I just wish it hadn't have happened to her."

But Cathy knew pregnancy happened to all sorts of kids. Some you expect to get pregnant. Some, well you have this little silent bet going with yourself. You bet this is one kid whose gonna be smart; gonna be lucky; gonna beat the odds. Sometimes you're right. Cathy had invested a lot of her professional hope into Tessa. We would talk about it later, have a fuller heart-to-heart about the way we measure the work we do. One way is to try and protect the higher functioning ones from some of the bad stuff that trips other kids up. How we do that is a bit of a mystery. We try to draw them in under our wing; we put as much extra support as we can into their placement; we probably occasionally treat them as equals, certainly the older ones. We give more to these kids; often they have taken less from us.

Of course there is no way to quantify the emotional investment we have in the lives of any of the kids we work for. Yet, whether we admit it to ourselves or not, we are constantly weighing input and output. Our bodies keep track. When we burn out, all that turns out to be is our bodies acknowledging that too much is going out and too little is coming in.

"Any more on Skye?"

"Nothing. I thought I might try and track Sue Gainsborough down this afternoon. Maybe she actually goes to school."

"It's Friday afternoon, you know. If she's a weekend street kid, she's revving up."

"Do you want to come with me?"

"Check with me later. I've got my own laundry list."

It was still Friday morning and all I had to look forward to was an oppressive Friday afternoon, loose-end tying. I could hardly wait.

Chapter 10

Danielle De Sousa
Friday Afternoon, November 16

I ran out at noon to pick up a veggie burger. Smothered in onions, mushrooms and dripping with plastic cheese, it tasted almost real.

In the early afternoon Cathy checked with me again.

"I'm off to Pierce Middle School. Heather Slocum says Sue Gainsborough's there. Says she'll try to hang on to her but I'd better hurry. I'd like some company."

"Best offer I've had today. You drive." I said.

It took fifteen minutes to get to the school. Pierce was a monster of a modern instructional facility. It was built in partnership with the Department of Parks and Recreation, a means not only of unifying education and recreation but of spreading out the cost. The added dimension attracted lots of adults. There were many more doors to enter and exit. It may have been good fiscal sense and some form of beneficial social policy was getting done, but it was just too damn big to my way of thinking.

It was quicker, or so I thought, to park in a recreation centre parking space and rocket in through the mall-like entrance to the other side. As we entered the foyer of the school, we were bowled over by a fast moving young girl. She was past us and out the entrance in a burst. Cathy lost her balance and landed in a large potted plant. As I was offering her a hand, I caught a glimpse of Tom Chaney, the principal of Pierce, pull up. He was vibrating.

"Lost her," he said, short of breath.

"Tall girl, pretty, good runner?" I asked.

"Sue Gainsborough. Yeah. She punched Heather and took off."

"Violent kid?"

"Not usually. Been harder to manage of late."

We went back to the counselling area and spoke to Heather. She had been shoved but seemed all right. I had had dealings with Heather on a number of occasions. She would go to the wall for most kids, particularly the ones who had been hobbled by a regrettable family life.

"She's just not a violent kid. Some are. Some have reason. Not Sue. And besides, it was more of an accident than a shove."

"As far as you know," I chimed in.

"An accident," she stated with authority. "I wasn't straight up with her. I should have told her Cathy wanted to talk to her right off the bat. Instead I gave her some song and dance about her marks…not untrue. Anyway, I switched gears and told her the truth and she booted it out of here. I made the mistake of getting in her way."

"You don't think you're making excuses, Heather?"

She looked at me coolly and nodded. "Of course I am."

I couldn't believe how casual Heather Slocum was presenting. Being brushed aside like so much litter by a careless kid couldn't have happened to her all that often. Counsellors like Heather were unremittingly considerate advocates. They saw their mission in life as making sure the school hung on to the child against all of the damaging forces that conspired to unplug young people. At the same time, they had to maintain credibility with an increasingly zero tolerant administration. Aggression meant suspension. Violence on the school premises meant expulsion. Assaulting a teacher got you the electric chair. Or the equivalent: a mental health committal order.

"Look Heather," Cathy asked, "just so this hasn't been a total loss for us, is Deidre Chang here?"

"No. In fact, while Sue was waiting, I asked her if she'd seen Deidre. She said she was grounded."

"Grounded? Has she been at school this week?"

"No. I called her home. No answer."

"What do her folks do?"

"I'm not sure. I've only met her mother. Quiet woman. They haven't been here in Canada all that long. A few years. Struck me as very traditional."

"Deidre?"

"Hardly. She's hungry to assimilate."

"Would Sue go to Deidre's?"

"I suppose. But her mom would be there. The dad is away a lot. Business. Hong Kong, I think."

"Anyone else at home?"

"A granny, possibly. And her older brother, Wilson. He may live there at least some of the time. Attends UBC."

Cathy and I had already had one wild goose chase this week. Monday was a much more suitable time, I believed, to chase undomesticated geese a second time. Less pressure. Less chance of failure.

We left Heather and the principal discussing whether the police should be called. I couldn't see the point, but zero tolerance for any physical attack on a teacher seemed to demand a call to the gendarmes. That was the problem with absolute decrees and the like. The American third strike rule was a starker version. It removed the option of choice from the court's response. And the poor sap committing that final crime would know with some certainty that he'd better not leave witnesses. Some saw this as a fringe benefit to the sanctity of law and order. You didn't have to waiver, to equivocate. The rules of the three strike rule (or, in case of schools, zero tolerance) were to blame for any blunders in the commission of crime, in sentencing, any remorse any participant might conjure up.

No one wanted violence perpetrated against teachers, or anyone else within schools for that matter. If the police were called, and they actually attended, Sue Gainsborough might be suspended for rushing away in panic from school and, intentionally or not, bowling over her counsellor. The facts wouldn't matter; opinion wouldn't matter. Her intention, or her uncontrollable impulsiveness, would require that she be smote down, administratively speaking.

Cathy drove the few short blocks to the Chang home. I called into the office on her cell to check on messages and scope out any other emerging issues.

One of my investigations was simmering to the surface. Some weeks earlier a young woman, 15 or so, had come to the office. Her father had hit her, and she wanted to know what could be done. I explained that if she reported it, we would investigate, likely with the participation of the police. She seemed hesitant about giving me any details, her name for instance. I pressed gently, and she bolted. A few days later she called. She said her name was Danielle. She explained that her family was Portuguese and her parents were very traditional. She had started to date a Sikh boy and her father had found out. He had hit her and grounded her. He had never hit her before. She had always been an obedient daughter. The day she had come to see me, she had skipped school to do so. The school had notified her family of the truancy, and she was grounded again. Dad hadn't hit her again but he was drinking and she feared he might. I asked her for her address and she hung up. I star-69'd the phone but the home number was blocked.

I had dutifully notified the police about the earlier visit, the report of the hitting, and the subsequent call and had promptly forgotten about it, filing it under things to do if I get a name.

Danielle had just called again asked that I come to her house. Quickly.

I filled Cathy in and we opted to swing by Danielle's home. I debated calling the RCMP to explain that backup would be useful and perhaps essential. Given the earlier hitting report and the potential for violence, I decided to notify the police and was advised that a patrol car would attend as soon as possible. No promises; after all, it was Friday. I said we would start the visit and hope the police wouldn't be needed. It was Friday afternoon, and I was being somewhat careless.

Danielle's home was in the southern part of the city. We parked across from the address she gave. There was no sign of the police. We waited ten minutes. Nothing happened. Then Cathy noticed a girl walking along the side of the house, along the path leading from the backyard. Right behind her was an adult male, speaking loudly. We rolled down the window. The girl was crying.

"No, I won't," we heard Danielle say.

"Get in the house."

"No Poppa, I won't."

The man I presumed to be Danielle's father reached out and grabbed her by the arm. She tried to shake him loose. He used both hands and pulled her back into the yard, out of sight.

"I don't know," I offered. "He didn't really hit her. Just your everyday, two-fisted, fatherly grab."

"We should check on her," Cathy said.

"I'll do it. You just keep an eye on the situation."

I exited Cathy's car and hurried across the street. Father and daughter were going through the gated entrance to their backyard. I increased my speed, and as I approached the garden gate, caught sight of them struggling near a rear door of the house.

"Is there a problem?"

The struggle stopped, and Danielle shook her father loose.

He looked at me with a glare of rage. "Who are you? Get off my property!"

I wasn't sure Danielle recognized me. She stepped further away from her father.

"It looked to me like there was a problem, sir," I stated in my friendly, formal, just-happened-to-be- passing-by voice.

"The only problem buddy, is you butting in to my business. Beat it!" His manner was neither friendly nor formal. It was direct and to the point.

I wasn't sure that addressing Danielle would serve to de-escalate the situation. Danielle seemed uncertain as to what to do. She took another step away from her father. He didn't wait for me to decide my next overture.

"Danielle," he shouted, "Come here."

"Can I…?" I started to ask if he might be interested in what I might have to offer, some help or wisdom. Clearly I was advising that there was a problem.

There were some tools resting at the base of a partially completed shed. Danielle's father reached down for a hammer lying on a chair.

"Get off my property, buddy. Now!"

He surprised me. He may have surprised himself.

He flung the hammer in my direction. Not directly at me, perhaps not meaning to hit me. Still, it whizzed by fairly closely. Cathy had just rounded the corner of the gate. "Wally!" she screamed as the hammer hit the gate and ricocheted on to her arm.

"Oh Jesus!" Danielle's father recoiled.

Right behind Cathy, a police officer appeared.

The officer's sudden presence immediately chilled the situation; that and the presumably inadvertent assault on Cathy.

The feverish father-daughter air got frostier.

After I gave the cop a quick recap, Cathy and I took Danielle aside. The officer and her partner (who followed right on her heels) zeroed in on the hammer-hurling father.

The intervention took about 15 minutes. Danielle was still pretty jittery, and not a little wary of her father. She thought it might be best if she stayed elsewhere for at least a few days. Her mother, Carmen De Sousa, had recently left for a month's visit to family in Portugal and her absence had escalated the father-daughter conflict. She was expected home in two weeks. Danielle was sure things would quieten down after she returned.

Danielle got on her cell and called a friend. She spoke to the friend's mom, as did I. She would be more than welcome.

I advised the police officers and Rick De Sousa of the plan.

Mr. De Sousa was not happy.

The police officers explained to the father that it appeared that he and his daughter needed a timeout.

"You can see that, right?" he was asked.

He struggled to admit it. "I like to…to fix my own stuff."

"We appreciate that, Mr. De Sousa. Honestly," the lead officer commiserated. "But things got out of hand here. You may not have meant them to, but they did."

De Sousa nodded. He seemed to be the kind of guy who just didn't want to put his shortcomings into words.

The officer asked again. "You gotta tell me, Mr. De Sousa. I need to hear it. You need to hear it."

De Sousa squirmed and contorted his face. It was such a struggle for him. Finally he said, "Damn it, I know. I let her push me over the edge." Blame was still easier for him then responsibility.

Afterwards, the officer and her partner determined that, because Danielle and her father, Rick De Sousa, were willing to discuss the situation, charges would be a needless diversion for the time being. Cathy and I spent an hour completing our assessment and felt moderately comfortable that a dosage of counselling might actually benefit the family. The hammer-chucking episode concerned us, but De Sousa was eventually excessively apologetic. He knew he was lucky not to be charged. As upset as he was to find out his daughter had spoken to me earlier and had gone even further and called me, he reluctantly acknowledged that they needed something, some way to straighten her out. He was willing to help. Danielle was used to believing she was the problem, had been conditioned to accept it. Her mother, she mentioned to us as we drove her to her friends, had always been blamed by her dad for any problem they faced, anything wrong with their child. Counselling, she figured, couldn't make it any worse. I wasn't so sure.

After we left Danielle De Sousa at her neighbourhood sanctuary, Cathy drove me back to the office. The plan now was that I would pick up my car, and we'd both drive to the Chang home and perhaps to Sue Gainsborough's. It was after four p.m. I had a ream of messages. I scanned them and decided they would all keep. I gave after-hours an electronic alert on the De Sousa family situation. I then followed Cathy to the Chang residence.

It was getting dark, that oily-wet November darkness that slips in by 4:30 or so. A light rain had started to fall. The evening rush hour was well underway. As I tried to keep up to Cathy, I roamed all through the events of the week. The De Sousa family, being the most recent, kept pushing its way into my thoughts. Friday is an awful time for a child protection worker, at least those of us who want to have a restful weekend. I couldn't shake the image of Rick De Sousa beating his daughter to death. We had weighed our worst-scenario fears when we made the decision that there was something workable about the family. The odds were that Danielle would spend a week or two with her friend. She and her dad might actually talk during that time. A counsellor would be on board sometime in the near future. With help, they might rise above the flare-up.

Or he'd kill his daughter to save her from her hormones. If that happened, our careers would be toast. Mine was winding down; the risk was less. I expected I'd end up some wretched old bastard living in a single room, munching on crackers and bananas, pissing my pants at least once a day, gradually remembering less and less of my life. Cathy was the more courageous one: she still had a life to flesh out.

Yeah, Fridays. It was only at the end of the week that you were more cognizant of everything you still had to do, if only there was more time. There was never enough time to do the best job.

I caught a glimpse of Cathy's car up ahead, saw that she was turning into a new subdivision, and followed.

She pulled up at the Chang residence. I got out and walked up to her car. She hadn't moved, but was clutching the steering wheel and looked to be crying. I tapped her window, lightly. It startled her.

"You okay?"

She waved me off, opened the door and started to get out. I touched her arm to be gallant. She winced.

"The arm? Sorry. We should have checked it out."

"It'll likely bruise, but the hammer barely touched me. Is this what social work is all about? Crazy people throwing perfectly good hammers at you?"

"I confess it's never happened to me. Though, once, I was doing a brief follow-up on a runaway kid. I went to this house where she was supposed to occasionally stay. The only one there was a downstairs tenant doing some repairs. He was, to put it mildly, uncooperative. A problem guy, I suppose, with authority issues. I turned to leave after an unproductive exchange and, I don't know, heard this swish of air. The jerk had actually swung a ball peen hammer in my direction. Not to hit me. Just to emphasize how unwelcome I was. A dismissal with attitude."

It wasn't a remotely funny story but it got a smile out of her.

"I'll be fine. Let's get this home visit over with," she stated emphatically, and led me to the door.

It was a mega-house, the sort being built at the time, the sort in demand by many new Canadians who may have lived cramped lives in their home country and wanted as much space as they could get. The subdivision we were in had been constructed a couple of years earlier on what was once a large, gentle field, vacant, serving no purpose other than allowing the passing eye to appreciate a small vastness. Richmond once had many such spaces, green fields that went on for miles. Now, only a few solitary pastures remain, surrounded by a proliferation of increasingly massive homes. Not too far from our office, in the southern reaches, two horses run free in a couple of acres that adjoin a fading farm. The whole property is surrounded by a chain link fenced subdivision, now, quietly strangling the open space.

Cathy knocked on the Chang family front door, waited a few seconds, and then pushed the buzzer. I like to do both as well-knock and buzz. When you are usually unwelcome, you go the extra distance to gain entry.

I whispered that I was running out of steam and hoped no one was in.

The door opened. A tall woman, likely of Asian descent, dressed in a white silk suit answered.

"Yes?"

"Is this the home of Deidre Chang?" Cathy asked.

"How can I help you?"

"Mrs. Chang?"

"And you are?"

Cathy handed the woman her card as she said, "My name is Cathy Baker. We were hoping to talk with Deidre."

"My daughter is in her room. She's unavailable."

"Mrs. Chang, we wanted to ask her if she has seen a friend of hers."

"Which friend would that be?"

"Could we just see her for a minute, please? We'll be quick."

Mrs. Chang looked at the business card. "Child Protective Services? My daughter is very well protected."

There was a hint of accent but the tone was pristine, upper-crust English, exuding a clipped dismissiveness, though I might have been excessively sensitive.

I smiled. Cathy decided to be more candid. "Mrs. Chang. This is not about your daughter. We hoped she might know where her friend Sue Gainsborough is."

"They are no longer in contact, Deidre and Sue."

"What harm would there be if we spoke to your daughter?"

"I prefer not to take that risk. Please leave."

It wasn't exactly a fast shuffle but the intent was clear. We were the risk, the contaminating factor

"Mrs. Chang?"

"I'm sorry if I appear impolite," she said closing the door.

"Me too," I muttered to the fine dark mahogany door as it closed abruptly.

We walked back to where our cars were parked.

"Friendly sort of person," Cathy opined.

"Just protecting her daughter."

"From us?"

"From the immediate, the immediately unknown. In some cultures, once you've closed the door, you're safe."

"Which cultures would that be?"

"The ostrich ones."

She punched me lightly on the shoulder with her good arm. As she did, I wondered if Mrs. Chang actually knew where her daughter was. If Deidre was at home, it was feasible for a protection worker to enter the home if there was an indication that a child was at risk. I had never resorted to swat tactics but wondered if someday I might. There was no legal justification for that type of response now. Rarely would just wanting to *talk* with a teen necessitate home invasion.

As it was, we'd run out of energy. I had anyway.

"I'll tell you Wally, I'm thinking two courses of action right now-home and the bar. Three really. Whistler awaits! I'd better run."

"Have a great weekend, Cath. If you get a moment, get that arm checked out."

She drove off for her weekend.

The De Sousa family was still potentially so volatile that I thought I'd better scamper back to the office, write up my mental jottings, make sure after-hours had actually got my alert, and send in a faxed rush referral for family counselling.

It was after five by the time I punched in the code to gain office entry. Everyone had left for the weekend. All the lights were out except the exit signs over the front and rear entrances. The small entry portal at the front of the building was also lit, somewhat like an AMT cash machine entry common to any bank in the land. No free money here, though. The small light that guided me in even had a nourish quality to it. Night in the suburbs!

Sometimes I wished I still smoked. I am a cowardly, regretful ex-smoker. I sometimes want to resume my smoking ways; I accept that my life may have been extended by quitting. And, like any quitter, I harbour the faint notion that I am in control and that one puff or two is manageable. I like to watch old movies, made in the days when smoking was sexy, when it had a sophisticated, albeit senseless, cachet, a fog of world weariness. I would have given anything to light up a smoke, pull out a bottle of scotch from my desk drawer, put my feet up on the desk, knock back a gulp of fiery booze, and just seem for a moment as tough, as gnarly, as thoughtful, as Bogey.

I had met only one social worker who actually acknowledged keeping a bottle of liquor in his desk. He dressed to the nines, looked more like a Wall Street broker than Bogey. He specialized in family reconstruction and, I suspected, his own slow, alcoholic dissipation. He kept the bottle, he said, "at the ready," anticipating those moments when the dark descended, when the demons squirreled out from under the desk and laid claim to him.

I would never get that morose, I told myself. Never.

As I was still on the company dime, I entered my notes on the file, called after-hours to make sure I hadn't fumbled the electronic alert earlier, called April Wininger, the woman who had agreed to care for Danielle, assembled the referral for crisis counselling, and faxed it off.

I saw the lights of a car pull up in the rear parking lot. A moment later the back door opened. It was Kate.

"Problems?" she asked when she saw me.

"Naw, just playing catch-up. Us old guys, we have to start earlier and work later just to stay even."

"Right," she smiled, walked towards me, and then entered her office which was on the way.

"What about you? Supervisors are supposed to manage their time in an exemplary fashion."

"I have a meeting at Glenbrook Co-op. Just went out for a bite."

I remembered then. A preteen girl had been accused of molesting younger children in her co-op. Once the investigation had been completed, the anger somewhat subsided, and the offending girl and her family moved elsewhere, the remaining co-op families, and particularly the co-op board of directors, had asked for some help with educating themselves and in managing the residual fallout. Kate had once filled an anomalous position of community development worker, a job the ministry had created years back when social planning fever had run rampant. It wasn't a bad idea, especially for the adventurous macro-thinking social workers who filled the positions. I had interviewed twice, but no cigar. I suspected that my gritty demeanour was anathema to the bosses, a position that amused me. Kate had won one of the c.d. jobs I had tried to get. I couldn't argue with her being selected.

"Going in alone?" I asked.

"No. Jill Larch is going to be there." Cpl. Larch worked at the RCMP Sexual Assault squad.

"Piece of cake then," I suggested.

Kate grimaced. "They may serve cake but that's as easy as it`s going to get. A lot of raw nerves still there. Two of the victims still live there with their families. From day one confidentiality was pretty much out the window."

"Good luck. I think I'll head out."

"Have a fun weekend Wally. I'm taking Monday in lieu. See you Tuesday?"

I muttered something equivalent, packed up my gear, and left. The night air was below freezing. I was alone. As I stood there, I realized I had better discuss the De Sousa hammer-throwing fiasco with Kate.

I went back in, cleared my throat and walked to her office.

"Hard place to leave, right?" she asked.

"Oh yeah, I forgot to mention something." I gave her a quick synopsis of the De Sousa incident.

"It is a critical incident. Cathy can do the paper work. You sure she's okay?"

"She needed a drink. Or two. Yeah, the arm was a bit sore but it careened off her. Not a direct hit."

"Okay. Now beat it."

This time I was truly out of there.

Chapter 11

Lindy Lavallee, 1975
Weekends

Friday had been another long, complex day, topped off with an unexpected adrenaline rush. I returned home sometime after seven o'clock, exhausted and just a little brain-dozy. I own a small house on the east side of the city. It's over fifty years old, a 1200 square foot product of the post-war building boom. My father built the house not only to put a roof over the heads of his family but also for its spec value, the first of many he had planned to build for security and a better life; all the values he and thousands of others were forced to set aside because of the war.

Growing up in southern Alberta, he had gained a lot of practical skills. Any kid raised on a prairie farm who paid the slightest attention to how their lives worked learned a wide array of practical tricks and useful tidbits. My father had that country jack-of-all-trades way about him. He could fix a gas motor, frame a house, wire and plumb it, landscape the yard, grow a garden. He could do the whole Megillah.

Though that first house absorbed him and he built it well, there was one thing he couldn't do; one obstacle derailed his empire building, at least for a time. He couldn't budge my mother from that home. Once it was built and we had moved in, she grew suction cups on her feet and refused to leave it. My memory as a five year old can occasionally dredge up their arguments about what to do with the house. Over the years, usually in the early evening when they both were sitting around the living room planning the next stages of their lives, having their ritual night-time shot or two or three of rye and seven, filling the air of our home with the hum of love and laughter and marital blitzkrieging, the saga of whether or not to sell the house and use the profits to lever funds to build another spec house, and then another, was a constant theme.

I envied them their lovingly wrought, rye-leavened living room wars. They would not have called them rituals. It was just something they did because life needed to be directed, planned, prepared. That was their way.

Sometimes, when I veer into an introspective mood, get caught on some interloping lock of nostalgia, I am compelled to think back on my lesser moments, my failures; back steps that I could identify in my life; lapses that had overtaken me along the way. Partly, I do this to keep myself honest. Who better to appraise my life than me? Who better to take note of the gnarls? I have had no one to plan alongside me through the course of my life, except a dispatched wife and the occasional companion who chanced along for a bit of the journey.

Somewhere in my ebbing past, my mid-twenties perhaps, when I was half awake to life, a quarter asleep at the wheel and a quart empty, I sleepwalked into the helping profession. A stint as an on-call longshoreman and an especially glacial shift on a freezer ship encouraged me to seek warmer, less physically demanding labour. Later, after a few years of working in a youth group home, I developed enough interpersonal skills to the point where so-called troubled teens trusted and respected me. Eventually, I was hired to provide one-to-one support 10 hours a week to a 13-year old boy with a dying dad and an alcoholic mom. This involved spending time with him playing street hockey, walking, talking, and generally lending an ear. Through that boy's family social worker, I met Prudence Tait, a resourceful social worker with 35 years on the job. She wanted a decent guy with sufficient stamina to devote 40 hours a week to only one client, a 13-year-old "dynamo" named Lindy Lavallee."

"Lindy gets the final say on your hiring," Pru cautioned

I was still young, somewhat prickly, and countered with, "So, what you're saying is that I have to be interviewed by a child?"

"She's thirteen," replied Pru, "And that certainly classifies her as a child. But she has an acute view of herself as a solo agent. She listens to no one. Nobody has yet made a dent in her armour. It's taken months just to get her to agree to have a youth worker. A gopher-chauffeur, as you so accurately imply."

"So, if I get hired, that's what you want me to be? A kiddy chauffeur?"

"To start with," answered Pru, "that's precisely what I want. And what she needs. She does a lot of traveling around the region. As far as we know, she hitchhikes everywhere. Short of locking her up, which we may yet have to do, the best way to keep her safe is to provide transportation and a driver. I shudder to think of the precarious situations she places herself in."

Though this was a few years before the horrific exploits of serial killer Clifford Olson were brought to light, no-nonsense people like Pru were aware of the risks.

On that sorry note, I was always amazed that there were so few Clifford Olsons. It seemed to me that our mobile society was ripe for a plague of predators who slithered about the land stealing and raping an inexhaustible supply of innocent waifs. They were everywhere, these waifs, in singles and pairs and triads, untethered to much of a home base, unobserved by absent or otherwise engaged parents, wandering into the iffiest of futures, of little value, really, except as economic cogs for some of their vacant parents; disposable victims of evil and violent sexual marauders.

Pru Tait initially suggested that I become familiar with Lindy's story by reading the family's file. This was the first government file I'd ever read and a token but necessary breach of confidentiality, but I didn't know that then and doubt if I would have cared. And I learned something from Pru's openness with the information of others; if you want people to help you do the work of caring for kids, you have to trust them with information. That people who received services from the state had a right to privacy was an unfamiliar concept to me and I suspect to many of those engaged by the state to provide those services. I identified myself as a helper and that seemed sufficient justification for the work I was being paid to do.

The Lavallee family file was three volumes and over six inches thick. Pru had advised me to skim through the forms sections, of which there seemed to be a morbidly sizeable number, and focus more on assessment reports and "running records", a sort of stream-of-consciousness process used by social workers to document every direct, microscopic contact or, in some cases, nothing more than gossip about the family.

I countered the offer to read the massive files with the self-serving request that Pru give me her verbal summary. I admit it, I was lazy and the sight of the files bored me to tears. We compromised with the agreement that she would give me the down-and-dirty Coles notes version provided I tackled the files afterward.

"Trust me Wally," she pleaded, "these files aren't works of art. They're a tough grind, but I want you to be prepared for her. We've documented this family for over 15 years." "That's bloody scary," I responded.

"Scary but essential," she countered. "Make up your own mind but suspend judgment until you have all the facts."

"Fair enough," I said, withholding a long held belief that you never get all the facts until you're dead and, by then, it doesn't really matter. Does it?

"Let's get some coffee and you can tell me the tale of the Lavallee family."

We got our coffee from her staff room and hunkered down in her storeroom-sized office.

"So," I quizzed, "give me the skinny on the Lavallee clan."

"Okay, here goes. And jump in any time if you need to," began Pru. "Corinne Lavallee, Lindy's mom, arrived in BC sometime in the mid-seventies. We don't know exactly when. Doesn't matter in the grand scheme. The Quebec authorities had posted a cross-Canada alert that she was fleeing her husband—domestic abuse—but he had a custody order on their 2 children. They wanted us to return her and the kids if they came to our attention."

"Sorry," I interjected, "she was an abuse victim, but he had a custody order?"

"Yes. Quite unfair, but not unheard of. Anyway, our first contact came from a public health nurse. She encountered Corinne when she paid a home visit to a single dad…oh drat, what was his name?" Pru opened the file. "Richard Garrett. He lived out on the flats in a ramshackle house that he used as a small-engine repair shop. Or was it a small-engine repair shop that doubled as a house? One of those. His ex-wife, girlfriend, whatever she was, had left him with their three-month-old baby daughter. Of course we didn't know this until the nurse reported to us. Richard had hooked up with Mrs Lavallee and her kids, they moved in, and when the nurse came for a visit, she had some serious concerns. The house was littered with kitchen appliances in various states of disrepair; there were mattresses on the floors, only one useable bedroom in this tiny house, a baby and two smallish children, a harried woman with limited English, and an apparently ill-equipped, somewhat distracted father of an infant."

"Naturally we investigated," Pru continued. "The long and the short of it was, we offered homemaker help for the father and baby, liberated a second, junk-ladened bedroom, sorted the Quebec warrant, got Corinne's younger child into daycare, and the other, a boy, into the local school."

"I'm assuming Lindy was one of them?"

"Uh huh. Lindy was about three and Theodore, Teddy, was eight."

"How did the Quebec angle get resolved?"

"The father had fairly entrenched criminal tendencies and had been arrested on a new charge even before we alerted the Quebec child welfare workers that we'd located the family. We weren't inclined to ship little kids back to that can of worms. The Quebec authorities weren't optimistic that Mr. Lavallee, or whatever his name was, was going be able to parent in the foreseeable future. His interim custody order was substantially weakened."

"The whole situation, here and there, sounds like it was high risk?"

"Very. And to add to the risk, the community Corinne and Richard lived in was very needy. Social workers tended to rotate out as fast as a driedel. Still, the file reads like some good, stabilizing, supportive work was done."

"Until?" I asked.

"Well, it seems like Mr. Garrett, though the social worker liked him, was a minor pot dealer, in addition to being a home-based business man. He had diversified interests. Toasters, lawnmowers and BC Bud to name but a few. Corinne had had her fill of criminally inclined partners. After about a year, she parted ways with him and moved one city closer to Vancouver. I've been the family social worker since then. Nine years."

"So, what has made the family eligible for ongoing service?"

"Once Corinne had moved into my bailiwick, she discovered she was pregnant. It took her two, maybe three years to really get settled. As you may know, we had, at the time, a fair amount of affordable housing. She moved often."

"Cheap digs? Yeah, and some rough neighbourhoods," I added for good measure.

Without missing much of a beat, Pru continued. "Corinne moved about quite a lot in our early years. It seems every apartment she found had a drug or prostitution aura about it. Eventually, she found a pretty clean place for herself and her three kids; it was within her means, close to schools. Unfortunately, once she got more settled, she was forced to pay attention to her kids' behavioural problems. They became progressively more serious. Teddy, for all the usual reasons, became involved with crime. He has a year to serve at a youth camp on a three-year robbery-with-violence conviction. He has become an immoral and especially violent young man."

"And Lindy?"

"That's what we want you for. Corinne hasn't been able to control her for years. She has abused her baby sister, Sara, not unlike the way she was abused by Teddy."

"Physical? Sexual?"

"Certainly physical. Teddy likely beat her on at least a couple of occasions that we've documented. Sara had unexplained injuries almost from the get-go."

"Not the mom?"

"No, I'm pretty sure not. Even with the incredible demands her children have placed on her, Corinne has always been co-operative and caring. She's got herself off welfare and works as a receptionist for a non-profit. A success story of sorts."

"Is Lindy with her still?"

"No. Single parents pay a huge price as they pick themselves up and re-enter the workforce. Not always, but painfully often, they lose whatever control they have at home. Lindy went way off the rails and Corinne pleaded that we take her into care. We've placed her in a group home in the valley. That's where she can be found, when she wants to be."

"What do you mean by that?" I asked querulously.

"Where we have placed her, the Shellford Receiving home, they simply can't hang on to her. If they take their eyes off of her for a moment, she's out and away. I don't blame them, really. They've got eight young hellions at a time and usually two or three staff. And all of those kids are high risk, needy, and a handful."

"So," I interjected, "you want me to gain her trust, be at her beck and call, become her confidant and...?"

"Keep her alive, Wally! Keep her alive."

After that succinct introduction to Lindy and her family, I spent a couple of hours digesting the file. Pru then confirmed that Lindy was still at Shellford and got as good as possible a guarantee from staff and Lindy that she would be there when we drove out. We caught the late-afternoon traffic marathon and that, coupled with an inconvenient fog, made a half-hour trip last a good hour and a half. The extra time taken was caused mostly because Pru drove very conservatively. The sluggish commute, and my inadvertent but necessary tailgating in the pea-soup fog, made for a harrowing trip.

Shellford House was a huge, green-and-brown residence located in a heavily wooded, semi-rural setting. The surrounding trees afforded the repository some privacy. The nearest neighbour was at least 400 yards away. There was a small parking lot with four cars. Pru knocked, and a young woman, barely out of her teens, answered the door.

"Hi Mrs. Tait," the young woman said, "come in. We were just sitting down to dinner." With that invitation, her right hand swept our attention to a large dining room with an almost medieval air about it. A number of young people, along with two or three adults, were seated around a large, dark brown wooden table. It had to be 15 feet long. From a distance I could tell it had the carved-in memories of countless idle and transitory young travelers scratched into its well-used top. It had a heft. If anything, it was like a table prop from that old Kirk Douglas film, *The Vikings*. I imagined that the meals served at this table must have often been exuberant affairs, not exactly Viking raucous perhaps, but lively. The table and chairs needed durability to survive the intensity of these youthful diners. Good decor planning was at work here, I thought to myself.

Bowls of food were being circulated, hands were reaching and grabbing, and voices were chattering feverishly. Despite the apparent chaos, there was a sense of control, of modest but effective order. One fellow, dressed in a very loud Hawaiian shirt, who turned out to be the house manager, bellowed out "Ladies and gentlemen, down to a dull roar please! We have guests."

"Who are you calling a lady, Danny boy? 'Cause me, I certainly ain't no gentleman." queried a tall, lanky youth with long, purplish hair and more than his share of zits. He seemed to have a half smile on his face, so his question, presumably, was simple banter.

"Right you are Mr. Barone. My error. Ladies, Gentlemen, and Others."

With that, enough space was created for Pru, me, and the young door-opener, who introduced herself as the assistant director, Hailey Soames, to sit down.

It became quickly apparent that Lindy wasn't at the table. It didn't seem to be a big issue and I focused on my dinner companions and a generous helping of pasta.

The youth were an eclectic mix of wise asses, street-smart urchins, urban throwaways and a couple of indeterminately androgynous-looking others, one who turned out to be the cook and the other a boy in care.

The meal had been winding down by the time we arrived and in short order Jim Helliwell, Hailey Soames, Pru, and I had the table to ourselves. Though youth and staff had dispersed out of earshot, we adjourned to a cramped little office off the main entrance.

"Good dinner Jim," Pru offered.

"Thank Schism," he answered.

I must have looked puzzled.

"Our magnificent chef," he clarified. "Born Mary Smith. Street name Schism. Her *nom de guerre*. I've always believed that life experience is a good predictor of subsequent behaviour. The best kind of cook for a group home is someone who was allowed, for whatever reason, to be hungry as a kid, preferably, but not necessarily, a former kid in care."

With that cogent observation we moved on to Lindy's whereabouts.

"She split about an hour before supper."

"Not a pasta lover?" I asked.

"She eats constantly. Always hungry! In fact she successfully scammed dinner before she left.. Pasta's best reheated, as you know. Well, maybe you don't, but it's like soup in that regard, and because we usually do an activity shortly after the evening meal, supper is often lunch reheated most days. Today, at any rate. Look, I think she'll be back in a bit. She seemed interested in meeting you, Wally. You might want to hang around. Most of the youth and I are headed for a movie. A night of culture! A revival showing of *Jules and Jim* at the university. Couldn't seem to interest her, but the other inmates are game."

"Have staff here formed any specific impressions about Lindy?" I asked as Jim and Hailey started to rise to attend to the evening program.

"I wish I could say yes, that we know this girl," Helliwell replied. "Hailey has probably had the most contact with her. Hailey, anything to add?"

"She's gone most days. Eats well, doesn't really spend any time with any of the other kids. Not anti-social, just a bit of a loner. Sorry."

I waited for Lindy Lavallee to return to her Group home until just past 11:00 p.m. I was a keener in those early days. The *Jules and Jim* contingent had gone, returned and settled in for the evening. Leaving my home number with the night staff person, I departed. Just as I was driving out of the driveway, I spotted a lone figure ambling down the dark street. As the apparition drew closer, I could tell that it was a young woman, a girl really, bundled in a scarf and old mackinaw. She seemed no taller than five feet, with wisps of pale hair sneaking out of a toque.

I decided to let the engine idle and rolled down the window. As I did, bold as brass, the young woman came up to the car and bluntly enquired, "Who are you? You a cop?"

"No, I'm a youth worker. Who are you?"

"Like I'm gonna tell some old fart in a car who I am."

"You're right," I replied. "Don't tell me who you are. Somebody has probably told you before not to talk to strangers. Especially male strangers, at night."

"No, I ain't never heard that before."

"Really. Well, I woulda thought otherwise."

"I talk to strangers all the time," she beamed. "Mostly men, but women too. I like talking to people. Especially strange people."

"I bet you do."

"Yeah, I do."

"So why do you like talking to strangers?" I asked in a slightly bored voice.

"'Cause most strangers don't ask stupid questions," she countered.

"There you go. Just your luck to run into a male stranger, late at night, who just loves to ask stupid questions. Look, it's late. Been nice chatting with you who ever you are. Take care of yourself."

I started to roll up the car window when she put her fingers on the lip of the rising glass and asked, "Say, are you the guy Pru wanted me to meet?"

"I didn't get your name," I said.

"I'm Lindy."

"Ah, you're Lindy. Yeah, I'm the guy. Name's Wally," I said and offered my hand for a high five. She countered with an offer of a handshake. I accepted.

"How come you were leaving?" she asked, with an obvious snicker in her throat.

"Well," I said, "us old farts need our beauty sleep. It was getting late, and our appointment was, like, five hours ago."

"So you don't want to hook up now?" she asked.

It was late, and the heavily exaggerated old fart retort was seeming more truth than banter. I mean I was zeroing in on turning thirty. Nevertheless, there was some fun communication going on between this lippy young girl and me, and I knew sleep had to be postponed.

"No, now's a good time," I said.

"Good. Can we go for coffee?".

"I don't see why not. Can we get some coffee at Shellford?"

"Naw. If I go in there, I'll have to go lights out."

"Really. Okay," I said, "let's go elsewhere for a coffee, but I need to tell them you're with me."

"You're a real tightass, aren't you?" she asked, again with more of a twinkle in her voice then anger.

"We've just met Lindy," I said, "and you know me sooooo well. Hop in."

"You're a funny guy," she said, and got in the passenger side of my car.

I notified the night staff that Lindy was with me and drove to an all-night café. The night staff was a little doubtful of the propriety of my request but she had a houseful of youth to protect and I was clear that I'd bring Lindy back in just a short while.

The café was on the old highway and was jam-packed with a truckers and other late-night denizens, including migrants from a local movie house, and, likely as not, a few random drug dealers holding suburban court.

We grabbed a booth and stared at each other.

The waitress came and Lindy asked if she could order pie and coffee. That sounded good to me, and we ordered two coffees and two slices of lemon meringue pie.

The waitress was back in a jiffy, and we dug into our respective pies. I didn't care that the pie had likely been out in its plastic display housing all day. It was good and tangy.

"God, I love lemon pie," I said.

"HMMMMM" she replied, her mouth as full as a survivalist's larder.

"I'll take that as a sign that you are a member of the lemon meringue brother and sisterhood."

She looked up, a little curious about this odd old fart she was eating with.

"You ever had lime pie?" I asked, somewhat out of the blue.

"No, I don't think so," she answered. "Lemon? Lime? What's the difference?"

"Not a whole lot I suppose. I just wanted to tell a pie story."

"Go for it."

"A few years ago, I went to Mexico. Puerto Vallarta. Ever hear of it?"

"Naw."

"Well, one day I went on a little sightseeing sail to a village a couple of hours south of P.V. The sun was beating down on all us tourists, drinking watered-down Margueritas and trying not to hurl our cookies. We finally arrive at the bay where the village was. No dock. We have to be off-loaded onto motorized launches and driven ashore. Beautiful sandy beach ringing the entire bay. Palm trees, other tourists soaking up the sun, parasailing. And these women, dressed in long multi-coloured dresses, straw hats, selling these warm lime pies on a straw platter. No telling how long the pies had been out in the heat. But I bought a slice. Tart, just sweet and tart from lots of sugar and strong lime. Delicious."

She had the attention span of a drunk. Halfway in to my little lime pie fable, her eyes were wandering all over the café, desperately seeking stimulation.

I've learned a lot since my Lindy days. However, I still like to tell travel tales. They have less impact the higher up the economic food chain you go but stories of faraway places still have status, the allure of the magical, the forbidden. There was also an instructional component to my travel tales. Any of the youth who came my way were ripe for all sorts of exploitation. The most insidious, the most treacherous type of abuse involved being recruited as some manner of drug courier. Twenty years ago, stories were emerging about young travelers knowingly or unknowingly transporting drugs in Asia, sometimes being raped and/or killed in drug rip-offs or, more agonizingly perhaps, arrested as drug mules and spending years, potentially the rest of their lives, in hellholes like the Bangkok Hilton.

All their lives, all these youth had ever been told was that drugs were dangerous. Say no! Stay clean! Smoke marijuana, and the devil will scoop you up in his twisted arms and suck the life out of you, chew up your soul, and leave your mangy carcass in a some back-alley dumpster with all the other trash. Well, a few tokes quickly put the lie to that barrage of gobbledygook. So, if experience and experimentation showed them that fear-mongering fabrications aren't necessarily grounded in truth, they can often easily reject admonitions about drug-related dangers, even the ones with a modicum of truth. Hence my little travel monologues. Aside from the sheer pleasure of telling these harmless yarns, my intent, always, was to first amuse and then do a bit of cross-cultural reconnaissance, some international safe-proofing.

It didn't appear that Lindy was all that amused or intrigued about Mexico and my lime pies.

She had wolfed down the lemon meringue in record time and was on her second cup of coffee. In those days I still drank coffee in the evening, but given that it was almost midnight, I had finished about one-half of my first cup. The sweet tangy pie would likely keep me vibrating for a few hours anyway.

"I should take you back," I suggested, half yawning.

"I ain't tired," she fired back.

"It's after midnight. And I AM. When do you usually sleep?" I asked. "When I want."

"Me too," I said. "And my bed is calling me. Let me take you back, and maybe, if you'd like, we could get together tomorrow."

"To do what?"

"What would you like to do?"

"Oh, I don't know. Maybe visit my friends."

"We could do that. Where do they live?"

"All over the place."

"Do you know their addresses?"

"Are you calling me a liar?"

"No, I hardly know you, Lindy. I'm asking if you know their addresses. Maybe you simply don't know specific addresses."

"Well I don't," she emphasized, "But I know where they live."

"Just like a bird," I suggested cryptically.

"What are you talking about? Birds? Who's talking about birds?"

"Well, birds likely don't know geography all that well, but they have a homing instinct that guides them back from long journeys."

I was venturing into an ornithological landmine of my own making and my own ignorance.

"Look, it's late and I always take my date home. Let me be the gentleman I aspire to be."

She neither agreed nor resisted, and I returned her to the group home.

We arranged that I would pick her up at 10:00 a.m. and go exploring.

I got a few solid hours of sleep that night. Not as many as I would have liked. A few of the less solid ones were composed of draft Lindy scripts, various ways of making a coherent impression on her. I found myself excited by the challenge of getting her to trust me, not to benefit me or my evolving ego particularly, though that was a factor, but for the possibility that I might have something to offer her. That's how I saw the role of helper then. And I confess it's still a prime ingredient in my thinking.

The next day, bright as a button, I arrived at the Shellford group home's door. I hadn't missed her by much. She'd gotten up at seven, showered, had breakfast, played a couple of board games with Schism, and given the impression she was anxiously awaiting for me to show up to go for a ride.

By 9:30 she had split. I was a shade miffed but tried not to take it personally. Our appointment had been my arrangement. She had agreed to it because her sense was that "now was now" and tomorrow was not a fit thing to plan. Her impressively flexible agenda, I eventually discovered, wouldn't allow her to respond to anything but the gratification of her immediate need. That sort of bedlam thinking would be hard to modify. I had my work cut out for me.

I wasted most of the day driving through a number of municipalities hoping to stumble across Lindy. It was a foolish, gas-gobbling exercise. Late that afternoon, I returned to the group home to await my elusive charge.

In time, I made some minor inroads with her. The process was drawn out, dragged out over months. She came to appreciate a ride to wherever she was going. I refrained from criticizing her choices. It turned out that all her friends were dogs, every last one a canine acolyte. She had fashioned some form of feral bond with a host of mutts all over the Lower Mainland. Her seemingly haphazard travels took her to myriad remote outposts, back alleys, cul-de-sacs, dead-end streets, worn-down developments, fishing shanties along the Fraser—innumerable spots where she knew all the dogs, and had, over some implausible span of time in her short life, put out a lot of energy to become an intimate of this street wise, unaffiliated rover brigade. She spoke to them, talked to them with meaning, clarity and friendship, played with them, hugged and cuddled them, rolled in the dirt and the mud with them. It was a sight to behold, one I saw many times over those months I trailed after her, chauffeuring her, chasing after her, trying to have some smidgen of impact, trying for all the world to secure the same sense of trust and understanding she seemed to have with her multitude of mongrels.

I often asked myself what there was in it for her. The answer seemed simple, I decided. Even though any one of these dogs could turn out to be a rogue, none seemed to. That we knew of. They responded to her obvious warmth and welcoming overtures with a reciprocal love and affection.

As peculiarly romantic as I've made it sound, and though my basic task was to protect Lindy from danger, there was a limit to how long she could just wander the back roads of the Lower Mainland schmoozing with the spirited, but undemanding canine population. Larger responsible forces were at play. Educators, senior bureaucrats, animal-control officers, dog owners; all had some say in her Huckleberry wanderings. Any attempt to discuss the larger ways and expectations of the world with Lindy generally proved futile. One warm May afternoon, having cajoled her to help me wash my rust bucket, having almost reached a point of mutual affection, I broached the subject of school in the fall. At that moment she had possession of the hose and cut loose with a spiral of water.

"Enough already! You got me." She put down the hose and stood there looking angry. I found a sunny spot on the curb and sat down to dry out. She came close and sat down next to me. She then hauled off and slugged me on the right shoulder with her left fist. Lindy was a puncher. I rationalized this painful behaviour as a means she had of showing affection, of letting her reach out and touch someone. Her punches were not light-weight taps. They often hurt. I had come to endure her abuse of me; I could abide the pain. There was some residual value in creating a zone of safety for her, of permitting her to express herself in this most unconventional way.

I massaged my pummelled shoulder. "No more, Lindy. See the bruise?", I stopped rubbing so she could see.

"It's perfect now," she said. "I don't need school." Oblivious to my abused body parts.

I gave her a long appraising look. Her scarcely five foot frame, hunkered down next to me, her husky-as-a-wrestler physique, her dirty-blonde hair drag-down damp, dripping from hose misfires, pretty, slightly square, slightly off-centre facial design, her 13-going-on-90 grasp of the captivity of youth, and her wild-child, undomesticated, chaotic rebellion that was poised to collapse. Did she know it was about to end?

"You think you don't. Truth is, you don't really know. There is so much more you could learn."

"I know what I need to."

"I'm still learning. Every day."

"Then *you* go to school."

Back and forth we went, jousting on the sidewalk curb, each with a shadowy vision of what was coming.

An integral part of the planning package that Pru had devised for Lindy was an imminent relocation to a specialized treatment facility in Victoria. That had been gently broached by Pru, Corinne, and me already. Lindy and I had recently gone on a day trip to the home. Just exploratory. She was not hugely resistant. The resource had an in-house teacher provided by the school district. That softened the expectation that she attend school. There were places she could have been placed in on the mainland, however the prevailing view was that a smaller therapeutic home in a new community might offer the chance of changed behaviour. All of us feared that there was some dark canker running through Lindy. In some of the neighbourhoods she ran in, a few dogs had been mutilated. There was a lot of wickedness in the world. We had no evidence that Lindy was responsible. We could barely frame the question.

A month later, at the end of June, Pru, Lindy, and I made the final journey to Victoria. Her mother just couldn't bring herself to accompany us. They said their goodbyes in the family's cramped, warmly oppressive apartment.

The trip was perfunctory, a handoff. I recall it mostly because it was the beginning of my friendship with Dave Waters. And, not to diminish Lindy's transfer, it was on that simple day trip to the island to say farewell to a sad, washed-up child, a child who was almost fully aware that her life had flat-lined in utero, that I gained some sense of the depth of the heartache the young and unattached experience. Nothing specifically happened. On the contrary, it was as if she was a day-old newspaper we had left on the porch of a subscriber, fulfilling our contract, but not really.

Some years later, I saw Lindy on the streets of her mother's home community. She was pushing a buggy up a steep hill. She must have been in her early twenties by then. I had heard that she had become pregnant. Dave had offhandedly recounted her journey back from Victoria, into late adolescence and young adulthood.

I didn't stop as I passed her that day. It would have been so simple to pull over, say hello, and check in on her life; perhaps share a bit of mine, should she ask. It had been a decade since our brief dance together. But I had left her, more than left her; had reconstructed her entire universe; I had been just another paid escort on her dance card. A sheen of professional distance was shining a bit on me that day. I mentally configured the assets and deficits of pulling over. I was still getting use to the sheen. Over time, I found ways to tone down its dazzle. Alas, even now it still has a glare; and sometimes it blinds.

But, as it was, I drove on by as she kept pushing that large buggy up that steep hill, aided by the giant shepherd at her side.

A further period of years later, and I don't remember when exactly, nor who told me, I heard that Lindy had died. Twenty-eight or thereabouts. Way too young to die. Truly too young.

The baby? Or babies? Were there more than one by then? The faithful shepherd accompanying her up the mean hills with her baby and buggy? The lovers she may have had beyond my time as her escort? Her small dishevelled family? The cause of her death, likely before she was 30? All unanswered for me to this day. Even Dave, who, as noted, followed her meandering journey for some years, didn't know. It wouldn't have taken much to find out. But how would the finding out have served me, or benefited me or her? As always, I was perplexed about how much I needed to or should know.

Years later, when the technology made it easier, I fell into the trap of seeking more information than I needed, or wanted, or should have had. Knowledge might be helpful, but it is also addictive.

Chapter 12

Carla Baynes

The morning she turned 16, Carla Baynes had more questions than answers about the meaning of life and her place in the world. Though it was a school day, she was giving serious thought to skipping and spending the entire morning languishing in bed. She had just encountered the soft, rich sounds of the word languishing, and for a brief time, as she lay in her bed staring at the ceiling, letting errant thoughts wander in her relaxed mind, she allowed the long, sumptuous word to roll around her tongue and drip from her lips. She ran the tip of her tongue around the outside of her damp lips and repeated langgggggggguisshhhhiinngggg until it began to seem just a bit ridiculous to her.

Most mornings before this special day, the thought that she might be considered ridiculous would have been mortifying. But this morning, this day that she transcended out of her childhood, this extra-splendid day when she was 16 and not a child, by her own fanciful standards, any longer, brought an understanding to her that released her from her childish concerns. She could feel it spark along her skin from her curled toes to the cushion of her soft red hair. It had to be a spell she thought; some moment of magic that was hers alone; a fleeting trick of time that might only remain as long as she was able to stay in bed.

"Come on Carla. Up and at em!" she heard her mother call from the kitchen.

God, she was bellowing a lot these days, Carla thought. And if she didn't answer her mother's echoing holler, she knew she would come and beckon her from the door. And if she still didn't answer, she knew that she would pour a glass of water on her. It was a ritual they had played for years and the thought of cold water tumbling from a cup onto her bedclothes, just the thought of being wet in bed, had been enough to compel her to get out of bed all of her life. Except that one time, she was four years old, and had decided to test her mother's joking threat. The discovery that there was more to her mother than empty threats was a piece of information well worth knowing, well worth remembering.

It had kept her in check. She had been an obedient daughter most of her life. Well, obedient on the surface. No one was perfect. Carla never wanted to be perfect. But imperfection wasn't an acceptable feminine trait, she had discovered. Even when she understood a little bit more about *her* lack of perfection, she hadn't gone out and boasted that she understood that people were flawed, that sometimes "perfect" was unattainable. It was just something that one day she knew. It was reinforced by being born into a family that was obviously, undeniably, irretrievably not perfect. Brian Scragg's colonization, his invasion into their midst, had elevated them to the pinnacle of imperfection.

"You better be getting up, Carly," she heard her mother's insistent threat. "I'm at the tap; the cup is filling," she added.

Carla could visualize her mother in the bathroom as if she was right next to her.

"Brian," her mother shrieked over the running water, "come and help me. Lazy girl thinks being sixteen comes with sleeping-in privileges."

"Leave her be, Janey. For Christ sake, it's her birthday. Leave her alone," Brian barked his defence of her from their bedroom. Carla had heard him come in after two in the morning. She knew his afternoon shift had ended at midnight, so he must have gone out drinking. Brian could be counted on to hit the bars at least two or three times a week. Her mother hated his drinking and was only mollified when he took her with him. He seemed to know when he had little choice but to extend that peace offering to his wife. The gaps between treaties were enlarging, Carla had noticed.

"Birthday or not, it's a school day. She can't afford to miss many more." Her mother rebutted Brian's argument with the fact that she was teetering on the edge of being booted out of school for skipping too much and just being disinterested. The school didn't really care if she showed interest in their boring product; they mostly had conniptions when she opted to not show up.

"You'll be late for work, Janey," Brian advised. "I'll make sure she gets to school on time."

"Oh yeah, I'll believe that when I see it," her mother sputtered.

"How will you see it, Janey? You'll be at work."

She could hear Brian get out of bed. He grunted when he got up, like a corpse pushing through the lid of its coffin, reaching up into the moonlight, expelling the pent-up groans of the long-dead, shoving the splintered wood and the compacted earth away, reaching into the vampire night.

He clomped into the bathroom. "Trust me, Janey, trust me. I'm up. You get ready and go. I'll take care of Miss Muffet"

"Thanks Daddy. Oooooh!!!" she heard her mother respond to his guarantee and what she knew from experience was Brian's hug from behind, his reach around, his mottled hands grabbing her mother's breasts, two-fingered nipple-rubbing, circling, imploring, softening her up like butter being microwaved, immobilizing her reason, weakening her with foreplay running out of time. Teasing her.

The game was not new. The three of them had played it over and over. Surely her mother knew the rules. She must have twigged by now, Carla thought. Over the years, Carla had sent messages, stares, ESP, time-stamped emissions from her brain across whatever room she and her mother were in; none of the dispatches got through; all of the emissaries died en route. The walls were overrun by Brian's extreme infidelity.

Why was she perspiring, she wondered? Why did her sweat seem to turn to glue? Why did she just lie there, like a sack of rotting potatoes? The back door of the kitchen slammed. She heard her mother negotiate the back steps. She sensed that her mother's footsteps were getting heavier, going down the wooden risers with more force than they use to, than was called for. Oddly, she seemed to be walking faster; her steps heavier, yet more fluid?

The house became silent. Her mother's car fired up. Carla could hear its reverse gear clang into position and the car pull out. Away.

She stared at the baby-blue-painted ceiling of her room. They had lived in this house for eight years. The room had never been painted. She liked the colour, a pretend, dream-blue, sky-like shade. A water mark from some wayward, ancient leak hovered above the foot of the bed. It had been there a while, but she had never mentioned it to her mother or Brian. Neither of them had ever noticed it. Other parts of the house had similar stains, small dark blemishes that might or might not need repair. She didn't know or care all that much; she did sometimes worry that some massive wall of sour-swamp water might be massing behind the mark, poised to burst. She might not like that, she thought. Likely it would miss the bed and she would remain dry. Most times, she didn't lose any sleep over it. It was just there, just being what it was. She had thought she could pinprick the mark; test the water, as it were. Soon, she thought. Soon, she might do just that.

Chapter 13

Jordan Prentice

Jordan left the squat Wednesday morning. Well, closer to noon, he had to admit to himself, to go look for Skye. She had said that she intended to meet up with a girlfriend on Granville Street early Monday evening. The friend, Sue, had to be home by midnight as her parents were cracking down on her, and Skye needed to catch-up on "stuff." Skye hadn't returned Monday night or all day Tuesday. He'd thought he might go look for her Tuesday night, but Bo had scored and they'd partied early and hard, and Tuesday night just vanished.

Wednesday morning, he'd woken up cold, and with the sniffles, that drooling nasal thing that his life had been plagued with. There was not much about his current life that he was happy about. Each day seemed endless to him. When he tried to remember how the day just ended had been, what had happened, what was memorable or exciting about it, he usually came up empty-handed. Sometimes, this lack of memorable moments, highpoints of any kind, frightened him. He knew he had low points, dullened pieces of pain that he remembered all too well.

Those cheap drug highs had been part of his life since he was 13. Gawd! That was the best time he could remember, smoking weed and sipping stolen beer on the banks of the river one warm summer afternoon with Harry and Rachel Hughes. The three of them had spent the day swimming and drinking the few cans of beer Harry had been able to steal from his old man's fifth wheeler.

Harry was his age, but bigger and fatter and meaner. Rachel was 15, older than both of them but slower, mentally slow, but fun and sexy and not stuck up like other 15-year old girls he knew. He didn't know many but hoped to in September when he went to junior high. He didn't understand why Harry and Rachel liked to spend time together. He knew Rachel had a lot of friends but she was always there when he and Harry hooked up. It didn't bother him, because he liked Rachel, liked looking at her, liked to see her form words and speak her wild talk. Harry seemed to slough off his sister's swearing and smarty-pants ways. If she was his own sister, Jordan knew he would be embarrassed, an embarrassment that would likely turn to anger, by her language and her slutty-sexy ways. But she wasn't his sister; Skye would never be as forbidden and foul as Rachel; still, he excused her behaviour, and his pleasure at looking at her caused him to be drawn to her.

They'd come to the river in late morning. His mother was at work and his grandmother was sitting Skye. His mom always asked him to sit her. This time he threw a tantrum and punched a hole in the wall of his room. That pretty much freed him for the day.

As his mom left to drive Skye to his grandparent's house, she had yelled, "Your granddad will be here at four to show you how to fix that hole, sonny-boy. Don't be late."

He remained silent. He had won the day and it was pointless to fire back. But the threat of his grandfather coming at four was an unexpected volley.

"Shit," he said to his feet as he slammed the front door and headed off to meet Harry. "Shit and double shit!" Halfway down the block, he muttered, "Bitch," with a ferocity that frightened him. Every time he cursed his mother out, he felt a sharp blow to his head, imaginary, throbbing, a sudden whack of pain, self-inflicted by his own guilt, and hers.

His grandfather was the boss of all of them. While he sensed that his mother was extremely reluctant to invoke his grandfather into their lives, she had done it before, all too often.

Jordan had seen other grandfathers operate and knew that his grandfather, Brian Scraggs, was an oddity. He didn't patiently teach; he didn't take the time to mentor. He boasted and berated and left no door open for love. A darkness drowned him on the evenings when he was left at his grandparent's home. At 13, he could gaze down the hall of his memory and see only the obscurity, a black wall he could not get beyond.

He rendezvoused with Harry and Rachel a few minutes later. The trail that ran the length of the town beside the train track, though well-known, was little used. There were long strips of shadows that frightened women joggers. Male joggers used it cautiously, aware that there had been two high-profile assaults of runners within the past year; assaults allegedly committed by a pack of teens. Jordan didn't know if the tales were true. He bragged that he often walked the trail late at night, into the dark of the morning hours, alone, prowling, exploring. But that wasn't the truth. Not much true at any rate. One night, running late for his mother's most recently imposed curfew, he ran the trail full-bore, his heart racing like an eggbeater. He later confessed to Harry how scared he'd been, making Harry swear on his own future grave that he wouldn't tell anyone, ever, especially his sister Rachel.

"What do you care what she knows, Jordan?" Harry had asked.

"Just keep it to yourself, motor-mouth," he had replied, using a name Harry's mom and dad often called him.

"Like I can keep a secret," Harry smiled.

"Like you'll be dead if you can't, Harry," he had replied, smiling at the inane threat.

Of course Harry had told the secret of Jordan's fearful run to his sister, just as Jordan knew he would. He wanted Rachel to be thinking of him as someone who had dared to make the late-evening run. She would know that Harry would never have done it. Harry was good at stealing beer and harassing younger kids in the mall, but that was the extent of his bravado.

As the three of them walked towards the river, Jordan cast a glance towards Rachel, who was between him and Harry. She was just a bit taller than her brother, with the darkest black hair, shiny and short; she had a thin pale face that reminded him of Dracula's women, blood-drained, pasty-white skin, lanky and arm swinging. Rachel was wearing her favourite swimming attire, baggy shorts that were snug tight on her middle but whose legs floated up in the water, sometimes revealing her buttock line. She also wore a loose T-shirt that left her whole body free and fluid.

They reached the river. It was a working river, its water brown and warm. The beer, the sun, Rachel, they made the afternoon float on by. None of the three of them had a watch, and Jordan almost forgot his mother's directive to be home at four. After a long, dreamlike time, an afternoon spent snoozing on the sandy bank of the river, Rachel snuggling up close to him and Harry off somewhere exploring, looking for something salvageable, he squinted his left eye and saw the sun was lowering itself. Rachel stirred and rolled away from him.

He had had two beers and a joint; Rachel the same. The smoke had given him a thick head. A small chainsaw of pain ripped at the temple, and his mouth was grainy, like he had swallowed a fistful of sand. He felt Rachel touch his left hand and place it on her belly; her T-shirt had lifted during her siesta, and her soft, supple stomach was glistening from sweat and the invading sun.

"You can rub me here, if you want," she half commanded and moved his hand over her warm midriff. He did as he was told, afraid to do anything that was not permitted. Where was Harry? He didn't want Harry to know about this. For a moment he thought Harry might be peeping from the bushes, jerking off to the sight of his buddy and his sister. That would be just like Harry.

His palm rubbed her belly in slow circles. He could feel himself stir, his penis straining against his trunks. He glanced at Rachel, not wanting to spoil the moment, not wanting to ruin the richness, the magic of it. But he didn't know what to do next. Part of him didn't want the moment to end; this feeling was just right, as perfect as anything could ever be. If he looked at her the wrong way, cross-eyed his mom would say, or if he said something stupid or moved his hand too soon, to the wrong place, it would all come crashing down. He wanted Rachel to take the lead, as she had in moving his hand to her soft tummy. Or did she want him to step up, to make the next move? How was a guy supposed to know?

"So," Grandfather Brian's voice attacked the air, "this is where you meet your skinny little whores?"

His grandfather pulled him erect by his hair. "You have work to do, you little fucker."

Rachel ran off into the bushes as his grandfather dragged him back to the trail.

Jordan tried to break free but Brian's grip was solid. He wanted to scream, to be released from the older man's grasp, but choked back any words. He knew his grandfather wouldn't hesitate to hit him. He knew this because he had an instinct about Brian Scraggs. He had known from birth that this man would use whatever means he deemed appropriate to get what he wanted. Having been raised until he was four by his grandparents, he had memories of how they were together. He knew the tyranny of the man. And now, even though he knew his own mother was leery of Brian, tentative in his presence, quiet and without opinion at the family table, even though he knew she kept her distance from him, she unhesitatingly invoked his authority to reel in her son. Jordan felt trapped by her failure to protect him from his grandfather. His mother was a coward.

Jordan got to his feet and began walking slowly home. His grandfather stayed behind him a dozen feet or so. Jordan continued to walk slowly, his eyes staring down at the path, watching every step he took. He could hear his own feet crunching the rocky trail. He could hear his grandfather's measured steps. He choked on his tears and saliva.

"Be a man, you little whelp. I don't want to see any crying."

Jordan sped up, driven to walk faster, further ahead of his grandfather, out of earshot. Away from his taunts. In truth, his grandfather had only hurled a few nasty barbs his way, but it seemed like they hung there in the air, poking at him, punishing him relentlessly. He felt contrite about the morning's tantrum. Yes, he'd achieved some small liberation. Yes, his fingers had come to tentative rest on Rachel's smooth, wet belly. Yes, it had been worth it, sort of, but now he had to pay, as his mother had threatened he would have to this morning.

They arrived home. He knew his grandfather had already been in the house. A can of spackle was there, as well as all the other hole-repairing materials. He had managed to stifle his sniffling by the time they came into the house.

As a bullish, brooding Brian sat and watched, Jordan repaired the hole in the wall, repaired it as he had numerous times before.

Jordan let go of that earlier time. He wasn't getting anything out of the recall. He shook that past moment loose and tried to focus on his search for Skye.

He went out into the fresh noon air and immediately felt hungry. He scurried down the alley and worked his way over to the Skytrain. He parked himself near the streetlight and started to hit people up for some money. The corner was crowded with panhandlers, and it took him a few minutes to sort out the best spot.

He used the red ball cap that he intentionally kept clean to allow people some comfort in giving him change. Maybe he imagined it, but it seemed to work for him.

"I got a job lined up, sir; spare some change so I can put on the feedbag?"

"Spare change. Invest in me, sir. I'm a good bet."

He knew the use of the word "feedbag" sometimes worked wonders. He didn't know why but knew it was an older word, one his grandfather used from time to time when they had chowed down for dinner.

It was a slow day, but after an hour of non-stop panhandling, he was 10 bucks ahead.

He hurried up the stairs to the platform and caught the next car. In ten minutes, he got off at the Granville Street station, hustled up to ground level, and hot-footed it to the Clearing House for a free lunch. It was a good place, the House; one of a number of places in the city's core that fed, clothed, and housed the flotilla of wandering youth that hung out on the streets. He sometimes went to school, when he was able to be somewhat punctual, when the mood struck. They let him come when he felt the need, although the staff attempted to regularize his visits. Often he went just for the hot lunches, which filled him up and kept him alive. Most of all, he went for the street news. It was the way any brother or sister who cared about street life could keep current, keep track of good and bad drugs, good and bad places and people. He loved the human contact. It swarmed all over him, demanded nothing from him, and accepted him simply because he was there, because he had shown up. Jordan desperately wanted back into the world. He knew places like the Clearing House were only way-stations, transit points to an old life or, with some amazing luck, a new one.

The knock on the Clearing House and programs like it was that they served as magnets; all the tiny lead-bitten human particles flew to the light.

Another knock, the same one really, was that predators paid attention to the human movement at such places. As safe as youth felt, they were also visible to the carrion who wanted youth for trade. Jordan knew that some of these youth were commodities. He was once, briefly.

Now Skye was buzzing around the streets and he was frightened for her, knew she was ripe for plunder.

She'd found him easily enough when she had taken off. He must have been stupid to expose her to Bo. That had been Sunday afternoon. He had never actually lashed out at Bo, but Jordan instinctively knew that he might be cornered into a confrontation if Bo tried to move in on Skye. He'd very reluctantly taken her to the squat, and she stayed overnight. They'd cuddled like they had when she was younger. When he was younger and had more time for her.

She rambled on about life with their mom, how dull it was, even more so since he had taken off. He didn't tell her that her words were almost carbon copies of his lament, his excuse for lighting out. Boredom, and that bastard Brian.

When he had mentioned Brian, she had clammed up. He guessed that Brian was a big part of why she had taken off. Had to be. He should tell her about Brian, had yet to tell anyone, swore he would never mention it. Every day away from that son of a bitch lessened the impact. At least he hoped it did. Every day was different. Some days, when he was active and scamming and bustling about, he easily forgot Brian. Other days, and he wished he knew why this was, the smell of his fake grandfather was all over him, like a scratchy, flea-infested horse blanket.

The squat really belonged to Bo. His full street name was "Bohemian Grove." He did little, except to make the space available to young men and women who needed sanctuary. Bo had a good reputation for finding safe havens and minimizing violence. But Jordan knew there was a price to pay for Bo's services. Bo had small businesses on the side, lining up people to buy ripped off stuff, moving small amounts of drugs between places, and once in a while, getting creepily closer to young runaways, male and female; you just couldn't tell when Bo was going to find a way to suck you in.

Jordan knew Skye was safe from Bo's antics as long as he was between them. Now that Skye knew about the squat, Jordan didn't like being away for great gaps of time, just in case Bo stuck his anemic fangs into his sister. If that happened, he'd have to take Bo out. That would screw up everything.

Chapter 14

Millie-Preparation
Tuesday, November 20

Union rep and snarly advocate Millie Hunt grew up in a militant household. Her grandfather had been an IWW organizer back in the early twenties. He'd wandered the mining towns of western Canada and many of the northwestern American states on perpetual assignment for his ragged and disruptive union. Matthew Wolfsen Hunt had been a free-flowing, unstoppable activist-vagrant.

He was born in Perdue, Saskatchewan in 1884. By 1900, 16-year- old Mattie Hunt had packed his bag and was on the road. He had hopped a train to Vancouver, spent a winter working in the great CP Hotel Vancouver, and then shipped out on a freighter that fortunately avoided sinking until just after he disembarked in San Francisco. From there he travelled America for the next twenty years, mostly organizing for the IWW, returning to Moose Jaw in the early 1920's and buying into a half interest in a hardware store, acquiring a new wife and, in time, three kids. Years of rough living, mine work, and maybe a half-dozen beatings had softened the starch in Mattie Hunt's fabric.

Millie was the eldest daughter of Pepperdine Hunt, the oldest of Mattie's children. Pepper Hunt was born in 1925; a year after Mattie wed Elizabeth Tennant. Three other children followed. Mattie kept his radical union past to himself, but in the late forties, grandpa Mattie began to tell of dark mines, evil mine owners, vicious scabs, brave miners, and the glorious union that wanted equality across the board.

These unexpurgated tales had a significant impact on Millie and led her down the path of union activism. She was well-grounded and skilled.

I had spoken to Millie on the weekend, and we agreed that she would drive out to my office Tuesday morning and we'd grab an early lunch around 11. That would give us time to fuss and fume about Gord Lafferty's agenda.

Tuesday morning passed with the speed of a snail. I tried to lighten up, boost my sagging spirits. Every one-liner fell short of the mark. I avoided settling into my amassing paper overload. My few, albeit necessary, phone calls were stilted; I was clearly distracted. By nine, I closed my office door, something I rarely did, and settled in to thinking about Angie Gravelle.

Over the many years since I'd ultimately transferred her file to ASU, after the end of my obligation to her, I had kept track of her, within my minimal, slightly unethical, vaguely obsessive limits. I'm not sure if I am proud of my actions and I doubt I can explain them; I had, as every worker did then, some capacity to access welfare files. After Angie had aged out of care, she spent a considerable amount of time on welfare. I guess I wished better for her and thought that by monitoring her life from my distant bureaucratic perch, there might come a time when I could intervene, assist her in some way.

I whiled away the balance of the morning giving my memories of Angie some of my patented, introspective attention, going around in istorical circles, reaching no plausible conclusion. Eventually, the morning wrapped up. Millie arrived right smack dab at our prearranged time, and we walked over to a little café on the wharf.

As we strolled in the morning haze, fog still hovering, I confessed that I had an inkling as to why I might be in trouble. I told her about my electronic forays into Angie's welfare file, my compulsion to keep tabs on her, to know about her, her life.

Millie listened to my confession, my acknowledgement that I had stolen Angie Gravelle's privacy, burgled into her electronic life, and pilfered what I wanted.

"There's no excuse, Wally. If that's what they've got, and you admit it, they can terminate you. With cause."

We arrived at the bodega and were shown a table. We ordered salads and sandwiches, and Millie extracted more of my confession.

"Explain it to me. Not only why you snooped but why you think they know or care?"

"There can't be any other reason for calling up the old file. They must have been checking unauthorized accesses to welfare files and up I popped."

"When was the last time you breeched that protocol?"

"I don't know," I carelessly offered. "A couple of years, I imagine."

"It might help our strategizing if you tried just a bit harder to remember your indiscretions."

"There's not enough time to remember all of them," I smiled.

"Humour. That always helps."

"Okay, sorry, it's such bullshit anyways."

"You sound like one of your juvenile delinquents making excuses."

"I wanted to return her property. I was becoming manic about it." I went on to explain about having a box of Angie's memorabilia, how for years I had had this box of stuff she had left in a group home when she disappeared, how I had secreted it under my desk, kicking it every morning during moments of stretching, how it was just in the way and I wanted it gone and how I couldn't bring myself to just throw it out.

"Disappeared? When was that?"

So I told the shabby little tale of how I had lost her, how she had evaporated at age 17, and was only reluctantly returned after being arrested for prostitution in Montreal almost two years later.

"She was gone for TWO YEARS? Christ!"

"Yeah, just about two."

"So what happens when they evaporate like she did, like Angie did?"

"What you'd expect, I imagine. Kids in care take off all the time. It's a rite of passage with them. No different than other kids, except the state is paying nominal attention. And we...we almost expect it."

"Expect it?"

" Well, not the two-year exodus. But most kids worth their salt takes off. Hell, we keep them prisoner. Really, that's what it amounts to sometimes. What *they* think it feels like."

I explained that, after a couple of days, you report it to the police, you circulate her picture to street workers. "I was really pretty new then, Millie, and she was the first kid who...vanished on me. There was no policy to go by, other than involving the police and asking around; her friends if there were any, other adults. By the time she took off, her mother and sister had moved away, to the Duncan area, I think. She was pretty estranged from them. Always on the run. Although, technically, Angie was still a client of the Exiles program."

"What's that?"

"One of our more intensive programs, sprung up in the early eighties. The intention was to wrap a cocoon of support, as one of the therapists described it, around identified, high-risk kids. They tried to do family work, but Angie fought program and family all the way."

As I attempted to distill ancient details of a program long terminated, long watered down into some other funded pool, I tried to reawaken a picture of Angie as she was at 14 when I met her. Muscular kid, hourglass physique, smooth dark skin, anger so intense that she seemed to seethe all the time.

I tried to find the right words so Millie would know.

"If ever there was a kid, Millie, a kid who gave nothing away, left no opening, no passage into her personal world, it was Angie Gravelle. At least that was the way she was with me from the get-go. I may have been new, but I don't think my being more experienced would have made a tinker's damn of a difference."

"So you couldn't charm her?"

"It wasn't like I was oozing with charm back then. Not like now."

"We can be thankful for that."

"Right," I abruptly offered, not as much in the mood for trivial repartee as I usually am.

"So, sketch in your time with Angie for me."

So I did. I gave her the 10-minute version, how I spent much of my "Angie time" moving her from placement to placement, smoothing out a storm of placement issues like coming in late, coming in hammered or stoned, punching out walls, not coming in at all, coming in and then splitting again, dressing provocatively, hygiene issues, noise issues, being a bad influence, and the most typical one, violence.

"That was...is the biggy. She started to accumulate assault and theft charges. We ran out of places for her to stay. It came down to renting a hotel room and rotating shifts of child-care workers to protect her, not to mention the hotel. Because of the accumulated charges, in different jurisdictions, my going-to-court time for her just went through the roof."

"Jesus! What a fucked-up kid!"

"Yeah. Anyway, after about two years, I was reaching the end of my Angie rope. It happens to all workers, I suppose. Other workers would wonder what screwed-up thing Angie had just done. I had thirty or other cases but the thing that was burning me out was her. My co-workers knew what was eating me up; that one case was draped over me like a sack cloth. By then we'd placed her in the Exiles program and she was spending long stretches of time AWOL, on the streets, possibly selling herself. My supervisor at the time, Danny Selkirk, good guy, process oriented, a team builder, he said I needed to transfer her out to the street unit. I put up a fuss but I knew he was right. So we started the negotiations. But before we could fully pass the responsibility on, she disappeared."

"And?"

"Two years passed before we heard from her."

"So, did you look for her during those two years?"

Some might call it looking. I don't suppose I would be one of those. Initially, when she vaporized, I was like everyone else who worked with her. She'll show up we all thought. After, I don't know, maybe three months or so, we began to suspect the worst. She was a tough nut but someone could have taken her. I was so feeble. I wanted to get her picture up on milk cartons. That was the then- current innovation, before the Web. I made little pussy-foot overtures to the child welfare bosses locally. They said they'd checked with Victoria and we just couldn't *do* it. Half-heartedly, I then explained the milk carton idea to Millie and the sluggish delays surrounding that and other meek attempts.

"Why? Sounds like it was a plan."

"Confidentiality. She was a youth in care. They felt that: one, we would be breeching her right to privacy, and secondly, identifying her as a ward might place her at further risk."

"Balanced against the risk of not finding her? Pretty lame."

"I thought so. I pushed it as far as my rebellious streak would allow. Not very far then. Ultimately, I let it slide."

"So you had to suck it up. What happened then?"

"We had reported her missing to the police, of course. She had court cases pending, so the justice system felt shortchanged by her absence. And then, she materialized. About two years after she left, I got a call from the Montreal police; some interprovincial liaison person had spoken to one of ours, who referred him to me. She'd been busted for soliciting. Did we want her? I was so fucking surprised, and not a little relieved. At the same time, I thought, *God knows how tough she is now*, I wondered what we'd be getting back. Big time prostitution! That's what I imagined. In any event, we had no choice. So we flew her back."

"Someone went and got her?"

"Nope, no escort. She wasn't a child anymore. Direct flight from Montreal to Vancouver International. Flight arrived in the early evening. I made the mistake of going to get her."

"Mistake?"

"She'd become a woman, 18, as free as she had always felt she was. And here she was, a woman being forcibly repatriated to a system, to a worker she hated.

I was finding it uncomfortable relating this sordid little tableau to Millie.

"I was at the airport in plenty of time. Like I always am. As a precaution, I had advised the Airport RCMP about the arrival of Angie and the circumstances surrounding her exit from Quebec. The plane landed on time. After the expected delay in off-loading, I actually heard her before I saw her. In the waving strand of disembarking passengers a loud drunken laugh was painfully present, her voice bouncing off the corridor walls. Then she rounded a corner, wobbling, drunk and dishevelled, hanging all over some older guy who could barely walk himself. I should have backed away. But I couldn't think of anything to do but wait till she came closer of me."

And then she was there, in full, uncontrollable bloom.

"Wally! Wally! Wally! Hoowshafuckyadoing?" she bellowed harshly.

With too much makeup, a puffy but somehow less full-face then I remembered, she looked angry and ill. She turned to the guy who seemed to be supporting her efforts at remaining erect and said, "Hey—hey —washyourname?

"Cliff, doll," her friend said.

"Righto…Clifffeeeeee. Thish…thish is the fucker I tol' you about."

Her traveling companion looked to be somewhere between 30 and 50, one of those bantamweight guys, with sharp facial features, hollowed-out cheeks, cunning eyes, a guy who'd knocked around some and hated tall people. My height had always been a problem and I could see it was going to be a source of unpleasantness here.

"Let's check outta here, honey," he said to her.

I needed to get control of the situation. And quickly

"Maybe later, friend. Angie and I need to go somewhere first."

"She's with me, asshole."

With the tenor of discussion, any chance of reasonable dialogue swiftly collapsing to street-level nonsense, any peaceful thoughts I had likely wouldn't carry the day. I signalled to my RCMP escorts, who'd been directed to stand by and maintain order, if necessary. They were good at it. Calm cops, they were used to gently keeping the airport below boiling point.

"Trouble?" one of them asked the bantam rooster.

He had been so intent on winning his drunken little encounter with me that he hadn't seen the police.

He looked at the officer who spoke. I could see him struggle to find a little bit of sobriety.

He had been tamed.

"Nope. None. No trouble. Have a good life, sugar." And he drifted into the airport melee.

Angie was still feisty. "Where-you-goin'-ashhole?"

"He's gone, Angie," I said. "Let's go."

"Where we goin', Wally?"

She was moderately compliant now that her irritating companion had skedaddled. I was ill at ease about driving anywhere with her. I explained my reservations to the cops. It was a slow night. They said they would drive her. A half hour later, we rendezvoused at the same hotel she had hit the road from two years prior. One of the child care workers who had worked with her then was still around, and we had requested her.

After a few informational exchanges, I left Angie in her keeper's hands, thanked the cops for above-and-beyond work, and went home. I was primed for the formal transfer meeting, delayed over two years by her AWOL. It had been scheduled, somewhat hastily I admit, for the next day. In the normal course of events, there was no way her situation could be described as stable. However, the adolescent street unit had recently re-affirmed their willingness to take her on. I had spent two years dreading some awful, final news about her. Now she was safe, alive and about to become someone else's challenge.

Cpl. Ray Baker called me at home the next morning. I still had grapefruit in my mouth when I picked up the receiver. Low marks for home telephone etiquette.

"Wally, it's Ray Baker."

"What's up, Ray?" Ray was a professional colleague. Though we weren't tight, we had conducted countless sexual abuse investigations in concert. He was a fierce cop who hated abusers. Police officers generally seem to have a matter-of-fact approach to interviewing. They detail every step, note it meticulously, like a complete recipe. I always deferred to them. They led, I followed. I knew my place.

He had never called me at home before.

"You at the airport last night, Wally?"

"Uh huh. Picking up a returning ward. Why?"

"The airport detachment got an anonymous call. The caller said he had met a girl on the plane and that she was being forced back west by her pervert social worker."

"Pervert? That would be me, I guess."

"He said she claimed he had molested her years before, Wally. Would that be you, too?"

"You serious, Ray?"

"We got the call. It sounded hinky. If the caller was on the plane, we can probably find out who he is."

"I think I might have met him, Ray. We had words. He was all over the girl. Resented my snatching his golden opportunity away."

"That's what Stark and Wallender said."

Ray had already talked to the two officers who'd helped me out. He was thorough.

"They also said she was a nasty piece of work who seemed a little pissed off at you and the situation, drunk enough to be mildly unmanageable, but, clearly, not afraid of you... in the least."

"That sounds about right, Ray. So, what happens next?"

"I interview her. And you."

"When, Ray?"

"Now, Wally. You ever molest this little girl?"

"Never, Ray. She's hated me from day one."

"That's what I thought. Why does she hate you, Wally?"

"Oh, maybe because I called her on her stuff. Sort of an uncivilized young lady at the best of times. At least before she AWOLed two years ago."

"Good enough reason. I'll chat with Ms. Gravelle today. This should be the end of it, Wally. Unless she gives you up. Has details or something more than drunk talk. Then it's got some legs."

"Thanks for the call, Ray."

"S'long, Wally."

Once before, a kid had come at me. Years earlier, in a youth centre I was working in. One rabbity little guy from a hard luck family got vicious with a floor- hockey stick. I disarmed him. Roughly. Maybe rougher then I needed to. Most kids would have chalked it up to experience. That little whelp reported me for assault. The local cops knew him. They knew his whole family. They told them to keep their wild dog on a leash. That did the trick. That and his older, wiser, tougher brother who didn't appreciate the extra police scrutiny, and who probably saw me as innocuous and not worth the trouble.

After Ray hung up, I sat down. I could only hope that Angie wouldn't make up any lies about me. Wishful thinking! I'd find out soon enough. She had never been an easy kid for me to like. There didn't seem to be much of the world that she smiled upon. Or that smiled back at her. And she had been gone for two years, living a dark grungy life, or so I imagined. I couldn't see her as a high-end whore; more a strung-out, angry street hooker with a habit and a keeper.

Millie thanked me for the honesty. It was the first time I'd told the whole story. My preference was that it be the last. I'd have to keep my fingers crossed when the inquisition arrived.

Chapter 15

Ernie

1977

It wasn't all that long ago that two sets of grey prison walls held court in the Lower Mainland. Both had squatted in the heart of the greater region for over a hundred years. Both had housed generations of sinners, the lost, the corrupted, the irretrievable and no doubt a few who were innocent, or at least less guilty. Both prisons served as constant reminders of unending criminal behaviour and the failure of social order.

Prisons now are out in the country, somewhat to the east, not exactly hidden but camouflaged by green rolling farmland. They are reached, when one is of a mind and has permission, by edging off the freeway and following country roads that weave their way through the rural landscape. These prisons are low-rise affairs that look like large storage complexes, which is pretty much what they are.

The first old-style joint to fall by the wayside was the BC Pen. A serious-time federal lockup, it stood at a bend in the Fraser River, where the river took a hard left to the sea, or an equally hard right inland, depending on which way you might be heading. The pen had stood for over one hundred years. In 1975, its fate was sealed after the death of classification officer Mary Steinhauser, shot by guards trying to rescue her from three inmates.

In 1980, I joined thousands who were allowed to tour the about-to-be- demolished prison. I took a kid named Jesse Bradford, at that moment doing kiddy time in kiddy jail for robbing a fried-chicken joint. Jesse had drifted west from Quebec two years earlier but hadn't lasted more than a few weeks before sticking up a Colonel Sanders competitor. I was part of an effort to prepare him for release. He was a charming, good-looking kid with a smooth patter and a comfortable way. My effort at scaring him straight ultimately didn't work. It didn't help that he claimed to be the youngest bank robber ever from Quebec and maybe Canada. He was proud of his past achievements and had a young Turk's inclination to continue doing what he believed he was good at. He admitted the fried-chicken robbery had been beneath him, and he regretted it; not the robbery but the embarrassment of his venue choice.

Oakalla lasted a dozen years longer than the pen. The pace of development in the Lower Mainland should have crumbled its custodial walls at the same pace as the pen. I never had the pleasure of visiting the pen, except for my brief tour with Jesse. However, I had my first of numerous sorties into Oakalla in the fall of 1977. I went there to visit Ernie.

The summer before, I had been called to meet with Shirley Graham. She was a glossy-looking social worker in her mid-forties, dressed to the nines, moderately aloof from the grime she was employed to sort out. She was new to me. I worked for a small agency on contract. Social workers would request a certain type of one-to-one worker, and the agency tried to accommodate. Along with other specifics, Shirley was seeking a "positive male role model." I apparently fit the bill.

"He's living in a hovel, Wally. We're responsible for him legally, and I want you to relocate him." She had pounced into power mode.

"What's been the problem up to now?" I innocently asked.

"He won't cooperate. That's the problem."

"Do you know why he won't cooperate? Is he content living with rats?"

"I didn't say there are rats."

"I extrapolated. Sorry."

"It wouldn't surprise me if there were rats," she allowed.

"Perhaps I should read the file?" I asked.

"For some history? That would be good. It's not quite current," she acknowledged. She then opened her desk drawer, drew out a bundle and handed it to me.

"Why don't you read this across the hall, and then I'll give you the latest information?"

I was plopped into an empty office and began threading my way through Ernie Thompson's family file. In those days, there was a disjointedness to government welfare files, as if they were constructed without much regard for the past or any expectation for the future. The Thompson file was over 15 years old; at least seven social workers had had charge of it over that time (which was surprising because the myth is that staff were less transient then.)

The file was constructed like a Saturday afternoon serial; major entries documented domestic violence, deaths, expected and unexpected, sudden absences, financial crises. Connecting the highlights were mundane filler pieces, records of phone calls from school staff, neighbours, strangers; calls jotted down, some typed, most hand written, all recording some level of concern about Ernie's behaviours, or his mother's slow-wittedness, or his father's abusive posturing, or his three sisters' slovenliness, as well as the level of care of the 15 or so cats and innumerable mutts. Callers were also not reticent about itemizing their opinions about abandoned vehicles and appliances in the yard, and pretty much every other social and littering issue you could name.

From time to time nearly all of the children of Grace and Arnold Thompson had spent time in one of a dozen foster homes. Workers observed that, on most of these respite occasions, the child placed in care became more agitated and harder to control, but, as if by some mathematical construct, the family appeared to fare marginally better with one or two fewer child-management responsibilities. As the family got a shade more together, the absent child was returned home, either in a planned way when the kids were younger or spontaneously when one or another of the children temporarily in care ran away from their pretend home. Eventually this cycle just wore the family and the system out, and they sought a permanent sacrifice: Ernie, the second youngest, became a permanent ward of the state at age 12. It was akin to popping an infected boil; quite unsightly, but something had to be done.

Not surprisingly, this definitive action by the state did little to really benefit any of the players.

I moved on to a separate opus; Ernie's child-in-care file.

From age 12, Ernie's aggressiveness and criminal disposition intensified. That first year as a permanent ward, he stole three cars, crashing one into a house and injuring an elderly tenant of the home.

The juvenile justice system eventually provided Ernie with the bulk of his housing for the next six years. Brief intervals in between found him nominally placed in short-term group receiving homes, although Ernie was often out and about, accountable to no one save the poor schlep social worker or probation officer not being paid enough, or not psychic enough, to know where he was.

Shirley's last typed recording was over a year old, though there was a collection of more recent case notes paper-clipped together. By glancing at the change-of-placement document section, I could see that Ernie had been discharged from the youth detention centre three weeks earlier and that his stay this time had amounted to five months. He was ostensibly living at Bennett House, a place I didn't know.

I knocked on Shirley's door and returned her jumble of files.

"Bennett House?"

"Rick Bennett is a one-to-one worker we use for the hard to place. Bare bones housing. He's keeping a mattress open for Ernie. I doubt Ernie will go back there. He wants his own place."

"Where is he? Do you know?"

She wrote something on a scrap of paper and handed it to me."Seven-two-three-one Juniper. It's a derelict house. Scheduled to be demolished, I gather. He tells me he's staying there some of the time."

"You haven't been there?"

"No. The fact is, he's threatened me."

"Charge him."

"If I charged every little bastard who threatened me, I'd be forever in court."

"You're afraid of him?"

She looked away. Fear of this young man might be a reasonable response but it also incapacitated her. Once the mask of control, of being in control, was shattered, it was hard to regain it. I didn't know that then, didn't have Shirley Graham's smarts, the wisdom to be afraid of a hurricane like Ernie.

"He's expecting you. Well, not you, but someone like you." She handed me a grainy Polaroid. "This is Ernie. It'll give you an idea of what he looks like, just think bigger, hairier. If he's not at the abandoned house, he mostly can be found at his mother's." She motioned me to give her back the scrap of paper she'd just issued and wrote another address on it.

"Not his dad's address?"

"Grace says he left. I don't know. Sometimes I think she might have buried him in her backyard. He's been out of the home for over a year."

She put on a serious look.

"If Ernie absolutely refuses to go back to Rick's, well, we can't have him living in an abandoned house for too long. Make contact, try and gain his trust, and see if he and I can meet—with you. I won't meet with him alone."

I wanted to tell her that she was giving him a lot of power to control their relationship. But I didn't have to. She knew it, and she was past caring. All she seemed to want was an honourable cessation of hostilities, and if that meant capitulation, likely it was no skin off her professional nose.

I peeked at the Polaroid snap. It was dated three years previously. He was 14 then, slouched in an office chair, this office perhaps, I couldn't tell. He was offering his middle finger to the photographer. He was wearing worn-out jeans, a ball cap with the brim pulled down over his eyes, so the finger gesture was muted somewhat. He appeared lanky, wiry; but a slouch will give that appearance. He had on big black boots, Dayton's or a reasonable facsimile, and a jean jacket. His mouth should have been pinched and ugly, based on her assessment of him, but he was smiling, as if to confuse anyone who thought his body language told the whole story. Maybe he didn't know what he was feeling and wanted to cover all the bases.

I drove to the block where Ernie's appropriated fortress stood. Tall weeds in the front yard and boarded up windows all around made it stick out like a sore thumb. The neighbours would glare at this corpse of a home and feel threatened. It was early afternoon. I should have stopped for something to eat before going on this fool's errand to find this invisible kid who answered to no one. I had reasoned, however, that if I found him, he might well be famished and we could bond over lunch. I was simple back then, my bag of tricks limited. Worst of all, I thought I knew it all. Truth was I didn't know dick. Still don't, some say.

I parked my car across the street from the vacant house. I had a 15-year-old Hillman in those days, a sorry-assed British car with no brakes and no flash. It was also running on fumes. I was half-scared I'd find Ernie, try to drive him to some greasy spoon, and crack up on the way. Not a good way to build trust.

The gate to the yard had been removed. The cement sidewalk was cracked and lush with weeds. At least one tree root had staked out sizable acreage. The lawn on either side of the walk hadn't been cut in quite a few seasons. There were flower boxes, once painted a pale yellow, but now worn and chipped, partially dangling below the windows on either side of the front door. They went well enough with the cream stucco. Glass chunks in the stucco glinted in the daylight sun. What *was* stucco, I wondered for a moment. I didn't care one iota about the composition of stucco, but I still wondered. A bit. I was still married to Jeanne then, trying to get her pregnant so we could pull our marriage out of the fire. She hated my lack of scientific curiosity, accusing me of intellectual laziness. I was happy enough to be considered an intellectual of any sort, even a lazy one.

I walked up the faded, concrete steps and gave the door a knock. Even as I was doing it, it seemed somewhat stupid. The house was abandoned. Anyone using it for free rent more than likely wouldn't be answering a knock at the door

I tried again but all I got for my effort was silence. I took a look around the back. There was a detached, heavily fortified garage at the rear of the property. And more weeds. The patch of earth at the back opposite the fortress garage looked like it had once been a garden. String attached to some sticks might have once held up runner beans. If it had once been a garden, it had long ago been left to go fallow.

Steps at the rear led up to the back door. I walked up and peeked in. No stove or fridge in the kitchen. No doors on the cupboards. Stained, yellowing linoleum on the floor. It was heartbreakingly ugly.

A small concrete stairwell led to the basement. I knocked on both the back and basement doors, just for the record. More silence.

I returned to my car and decided to visit Ernie's mother.

The address I had been given for Grace Thompson was only a few blocks over. I found that slightly odd but understandable. Whether Ernie was a real threat to his family, or primarily a homeless child ever searching for a place to be belong, family would always be his refuge-and perhaps his undoing. The Thompson home itself looked to be one step removed from abandonment, not a whole lot different from the empty shell Ernie supposedly burrowed into after dark. It had the same rough glass-salted stucco and could have come from the same cookie-cutter construction back in the early fifties. Water stains darkened patches of the exterior. The picket fence was missing some slats. A plastic cover was draped over part of the roof—a temporary repair.

An old fridge with the door removed was resting against what looked like a dying cherry tree. Contrary to the family file, there were no more car carcasses in the yard. Chalk up one point for social work intervention.

I knocked on the front door and noticed a smell coming from somewhere. It was impossible to tell whether it emanated from inside the house or somewhere outside. It was a mix of smells, cats, urine and rotting food. I found it almost overpowering. I suppose it was a smell you could adjust to if you had to, but I found it repulsive. I heard footsteps come to the door. It was still a warm summer afternoon. All the windows were open on the front. The door opened. A chubby, pimply teenage girl, chomping on a sandwich, opened the door. A TV somewhere inside the house blared.

"Whadda you want?"

"I'm looking for Ernie."

"This ain't his place no more."

"I know," I said. "Is Grace Thompson here?"

"Mom, there's a guy here," she yelled back towards the inside of the house. A hunk of sandwich shot out of her mouth. "Fuck," she swore, losing another piece of her snack.

"I'm busy, Lo. What's he want?"

"Ernie. He's a cop I think."

"Jesus, that little bastard is always causing me grief. All right, tell him to come in."

I would have been more than content to linger on the porch, somewhat protected from the putrid odours that clung to the house like sandwich wrap. There are some places you don't want to enter.

"I'm not a cop," I mentioned for clarity's sake to the chunky chewer.

"Mom," she yelled, "he's not a cop."

"Then don't let him in. Who the hell is he, as if I really give a fuck?"

"Who are you?"

"I work for Ernie's social worker. She wants me to help him."

"Help him do what?"

"Find a safe place."

"Hmmm," she murmured.

"He's a social-work snooper, Mom."

"Tell him to piss off then. Think for yourself, Lois."

"Piss—"

"I got the message," I interrupted. "Tell your mom thanks for her help."

"Mom," she yelled as she closed the door on me, "he says—"

I was out of earshot, gagging a bit and feeling kindly towards Ernie. No matter what he had become, he was better off away from that home. I was sure of that.

Having no other leads, I opted to stakeout Ernie's borrowed shelter for a while later on in the evening. I arrived back about 8:30. It was still light out but the summer sun was dimming, and the evening had taken on the soft hue of summer nights on the west coast.

I assumed that Ernie would wait until dark before sneaking into his stolen habitat. That's what I would do. Of course, I was beginning to learn back then that people don't necessarily act the way *you* might. That's probably a healthy thing, but it plays havoc when you try to predict behaviour.

As the sun was taking a final shine to the night, I saw, in the near shadows, a tall, husky young guy sauntering down the street. There were a few people sitting on their porches and they seemed to be actively not looking at him. He approached the abandoned house and turned right in as if he owned it. His clothes appeared dirty, or maybe it was the dusky air. He had on a jean jacket that had a giant peace symbol on the back and was covered in small glittering studs. A living, breathing stucco-like jacket, I thought.

I eased myself out of my car and hotfooted it his way. "Ernie, could you hold it up a minute?"

He was just about to duck along the side of the house. He reined himself in and turned towards me. He had a big fearless smile.

"Do I know you?" he asked.

"Shirley Graham says she told you to expect someone."

"So, you're it?"

"Yup, I'm the guy."

"Let's go eat. I'm hungry."

In hindsight, it was clear he had had helpers before, people to ferry him around and feed him fast food. I was the latest of many. He didn't care who it was so long as he got fed.

He also didn't care where he ate. We went to the nearest McDonalds and he consumed three Big Macs and assorted embellishments. I watched in admiring amazement. He ate like a wood chipper, chewing most of his food up, but seeming to swallow chunks whole. He munched and I watched the munching.

Close up, I could see that Ernie had a soft stubbly face, suggesting he was a novice shaver who hadn't used a blade in a few days. It was broad mug, with a strong jaw that reminded me of hockey star, Mark Messier. The rest of him looked stocky as well, if somewhat undernourished.

Afterwards, we each had a coffee, and I explained a bit more about me and what Shirley Graham wanted me to do.

"I ain't goin" back to Ricks. Had enough of Rick. Good guy, Rick, but the place is a dump. I gotta be in control. I want my own place. And it had better not be a dump"

Okay," I said, "It's a bit late to prowl the housing market." How about tomorrow?"

"You good at this sort of thing? House hunting?"

He had zeroed in on one of my lesser skills. Finding places for young people is bloody tough. In any housing market. From what little I knew about Ernie, his life, his style, his ways, there weren't going to be a whole lot of presentable options.

"No," I answered as truthfully as I could, "finding places for young people is tough. And I haven't had much experience.

"You're gonna be a big help, aren't you?"

"Time will tell. So, what's not a dump in your estimation?" He looked as if he didn't understand what I was driving at. "What I mean is, there's only so much money for rent. You've got a limited budget being a kid in care."

"Sometimes I make a few bucks."

"Doing what?"

He smiled a wickedly knowing smile and said, "Odd jobs. Yeah, odd jobs."

He didn't want to say. Why should he tell a stranger? There was probably more going on with this young man than I wanted to know.

I drove him back to the abandoned house and said I would be by at nine in the morning.

"Pretty damn early ain't it?"

"The early bird gets the nest," I improvised.

"I eat birds," he finished the meandering metaphor off. "Raw. I like 'em raw." He licked his lips and scurried off into the darkness.

I fed him next morning at McDonalds, which quickly became *our* place. We became buddies. Over the following week, we devoted every waking hour to finding him safe housing. There were only a few agencies that specialized in coordinating accommodation for the poor. A couple didn't charge. We went to them. They would beat the bushes for landlords willing to rent and match them with home-hungry tenants. These agencies operated on a shoestring, especially when the market was sparse. Landlords willing to rent to teens were as rare as summer snow. Compounding this fool's quest was the knowledge that a poorly integrated teen might easily blow any accommodation the helper could arrange for any one of a thousand sins—having a party, breaking a long list of rules, or burning the place down, either out of stupid carelessness or sinister intent.

We looked at any number of crappy little rooms in basements, rundown apartment blocks and shabby tenements. Ernie hadn't yet grasped how undesirable a tenant he presented. He remained particular. Choosy. Eventually though, with the amount of time on and off the clock that I was devoting to the search, we found a place. Ernie's new residence was one large, sparsely furnished room in a former Victorian mansion, now a relic. Likely, it was a former dining room; the bathroom was squeezed into what was probably a hallway. There were eight other tenants in the building. Ernie was number nine. The place was clean so I had to assume the landlord was finicky and the other renters pretty much on the up and up. Ernie had spruced up some, with a shower at the community centre and some new clothes. He spun the owner a story about school, getting his electricians ticket in the next couple of years, and how he would be happy to help upgrade the wiring. He had a pretty slick spiel. I kept quiet, not wanting to kibosh the deal but still feeling like a grifter.

In quick succession, we had two meetings with Shirley and sorted out the financial and behavioural expectations. Ernie was singularly compliant.

After Ernie moved in, we had a third meeting with Shirley at his new digs. She seemed pleased, especially because the move-in costs were almost within budget. I suspect she was mildly surprised that we had succeeded in taming Ernie's rough and ready hibernation inclinations. We reconfirmed that I would see Ernie twice a week for the balance of my three month contract and get him into some kind of program, or a job, if that came along. Ernie didn't mention his electrical ambitions to Shirley. Maybe it had come up before. I decided to keep that spontaneous, vocational aspiration to myself.

For the next couple of weeks, Ernie was fairly reliable, being ready, by his autonomous standards, within half an hour of my arrival when I came to pick him up. Having spent considerable time on cushions and a hard floor, his transition to a more legitimate sleeping chamber engendered high resistance to getting out of bed in a timely fashion. Nonetheless he was a good sport about my punctuality. We made, and kept, a variety of appointments with training programs, alternate schools and the like. Ernie smiled and schmoozed his way through all of them. I was feeling pretty proud of my emerging child care skills. I had essentially rescued this poor abandoned recluse from his pauper existence, housed him and was well on the way to transforming him into a successful, 9-5 cipher.

One early October morning, not one of my Ernie days, Shirley called.

"He's in jail, Wally."

I wasn't really surprised. I could easily imagine him committing an act of impulsive shoplifting or a B and E.

"What for? When?"

"Last night. He was in a car crash up-country. The policeman who called said he was; there were two women passengers. The car lost control on some desolate stretch of the Trans-Canada."

"Stolen car?" I asked stupidly, though it could have belonged to one of his crash companions.

"Yes," she emphasized, with force.

"Are they okay? Is he—?"

"I was told barely a scratch. But, above all that, the local police attempted to let the car owner know what had happened. They found him dead. Murdered."

Ernie was charged with murder. The two young girls he was arrested with were both juveniles. They were charged with lesser offences. They both said Ernie had killed the old man. The victim was a 47 year old man who evidently thought he had struck gold, picking up two little sex kittens. Once the girls were in his apartment, they let Ernie in. The victim should have been more concerned, more cautious. He was beaten to a pulp.

I moved on. My Ernie job was done. Shirley arranged legal representation for him. She had never before had one of her wards charged with murder. When I later interviewed for a social-work position in Shirley's office, I used her as a reference although, given the allegations about Ernie's murderous rage, I would have questioned my competence, at least a little bit.

Ernie asked her to have me come and visit him at Oakalla. That seemed the least I could do, to say our goodbyes. I had been advised that I might be called as a witness down the line. A witness in his murder trial. It was made clear that I was not to talk with Ernie about the murder or any role he may have played.

One dreary November morning, I drove to that sombre prison. Ernie's lawyer had spoken to the prison officials and cleared the way. I presented my ID at the main gate, and they pointed to a walkway, the path to Ernie's part of the complex. The set of buildings was ancient, Dickensian. It looked out over a fertile valley interspersed with a scattering of older homes.

I had always hated prisons, had studiously avoided prison-movies with their depictions of rancid claustrophobia. If I ever had to relinquish my freedom for an impulsive or deliberate act, it would shatter me. I cherished the ability to choose my own movement, my own journey. Prison is the antithesis of choice. I suspected Ernie would blend in well in jail. He had spent considerable chunks of his youth locked up.

I walked up the stone steps and pressed a buzzer. The front doors opened and I entered a small, locked hallway. A disembodied voice asked my business. I stated who I was and who I had come to see. A loud buzzer groaned and the sliding metal doors opened and I entered to a small foyer. Corridors to the left and right led to to offices. In front of me was, for want of any other description, a visitor's cell. Prisoners were brought to bare cubicles. Visitors entered through a specific door and sat in assigned seats. Glass separated guests and the confined.

A guard approached me and escorted me through the visiting area. Beyond it was another locked door. The guard rang another buzzer, and we passed through to what turned out to be a set of vacant cubicles.

"First time?" he asked.

"It shows?"

"Like a wart on your nose," he replied. "What are you, a law clerk?"

"Child-care worker."

"Right. We don't get many of your type. It's usually lawyers or god's chosen who use these little suites. No bars. Feel safe?"

Before I could reply, he left, telling me to get comfortable and that he'd bring the prisoner when he could.

As I waited, I attempted to isolate the host of odd sounds that echoed their way from other parts of the prison. Wails, clanging, yells. A hellish jangle of sounds, harsh, close, unyielding.

I did not feel safe. How could anyone feel safe in this ugly pit?

The room I was deposited in was painted pale green. It was furnished with a heavy table, with the grim ghosts of many idle gouges faintly visible through a lumpy coat of varnish. There were two wooden chairs, similarly gouged. This Spartan furniture was secured firmly to the floor by metal clamps. Nobody was going to steal these fixtures. Or use them as weapons.

I waited for about fifteen minutes. Doors constantly clashed and clanged.

The guard returned with Ernie. He directed him to the empty chair, the one I wasn't using. It seemed a meaningless gesture, but likely he wanted Ernie to know he needed to sit, needed not to hover. I was glad of that. I didn't want Ernie hovering.

If anything, Ernie seemed bigger, fuller, bulkier. His hair had been shaved to a depth of half a toothbrush. He looked bristly. He wore a white T-shirt and ugly brown pants. He had on socks but no shoes, like he's been called in from his den to the living room.

"Yo, Wally!"

"Hi Ernie. How you doing?"

"Not doing much. Doing time." He smiled at his word play. "Thanks for the visit."

"Least I could do." I didn't know where to go next with the conversation.

"My first time in prison," I confessed.

"Me too."

"But you've been— "

"I've done a lot of stretches in Juvie."

"How does this compare?"

"There ain't any comparison, Wally. None."

I felt obligated to ask him what he meant, what the differences were. But I could sense where that line of chatter might lead and I didn't want to talk about prisons, captivity, and the array of abuses I imagined must be part and parcel of everyday existence behind prison walls. Still, we had a history of seeking housing for him.

"Do you have to share a cell?" I asked.

"I don't. Some do."

"What determines whether you share?"

He looked at me with a frustrated scowl.

"I don't know how this hell hole operates. The guards don't say a whole lot to me. They stay out of my way mostly. Most of the cons are all right. At least the ones I've gotten to know."

"Half of them are drunks and hypes." He stared beyond me. "Way more than half. But that's okay with me—It's a place full of sick fuckers, Wally."

He leaned forward and said, "Take this, Wally." His hand slid across the table and met mine. He seemed to be surreptitiously handing me some small sheets of paper. "Put it in your pocket, Wally. Be careful. They watch all the time." I was so taken aback that I balled up my fist around the sheets of paper and pocketed the material.

"What did you give me, Ernie? What is this stuff?"

"Four hundred bucks, Wally. I want you to keep it for me. Bank it."

"I don't understand Ernie. How do you get money in jail?"

"You don't need to know that Wally. Just be a good guy. Bank it."

I didn't want to know how cash, any cash, got into prison. Ernie was dead right about that. Drugs, sex, bribery. I did not want to know. I had a pretty good idea though that smuggling money or any contraband out of a prison was probably frowned on. Probably chargeable too.

Ernie talked for a few minutes more about the food, his mother's pending visit (her first), and the weather. He made it pretty clear that the only real reason he had wanted me to visit was to be his cash mule. I felt special. Nervous and special.

Finally he suggested I hail the guard.

I waved. The guard came a couple of minutes later. Quick response was not in vogue then.

Ernie extended his right hand. I took his, and we shook. I could swear he squeezed just a bit more tightly then was necessary. The guard told me to hold my horses. He would escort Ernie back to his cell and return for me.

This gave me an additional fifteen minutes to think about Ernie's cash resting in my pocket. I did not use this extended time of reflection productively.

Half an hour later, after the wait and the walk out of the prison, Ernie's cash and I were driving home.

Jeanne had a cousin who was a lawyer. We had met at a few family gatherings. A couple of days after my visit with Ernie, after stewing about how stupid I was to take the money, to walk out of that prison knowing I'd screwed up, blaming Ernie for buffaloing me, I decided to get some legal help, preferably at no cost. I called her cousin Blake. I explained my dilemma, my hypothetical dilemma, or so he insisted.

"Dumb," he replied too darn quickly for comfort.

"Granted," I had to agree. "What do you suggest?"

"Give it back."

"You mean hand it back to Ernie?"

"No, I can't advise you to smuggle money into prison. That's probably a greater crime. I suppose you could give it to his lawyer, but that might not afford you much protection. Just complicate the issue. No, what I mean is, give it to the warden."

"Won't they charge me?"

"Maybe. If they find you took the money out and didn't give it back, didn't tell them, then for sure they are going to drop the hammer on you."

"How would they find out?"

"Your prison buddy is devoted to you? Trustworthy fellow, is he?"

I had to smile. "But why would Ernie say anything. It's his money."

"That's debatable. It's contraband. If it belongs to anybody, it belongs to the state. Either that or it belongs to nobody. Maybe the same thing. It doesn't matter whose it is. What matters is he's not supposed to have it. Besides, there may be some advantage for him in ratting you out at some point. Don't try to anticipate convict logic."

"You're probably right. Still, maybe I should just open a bank account in his name and drop the matter."

"You wanted legal advice. Hypothetical advice. I'm suggesting that you not enhance your culpability. Do what you should have done first thing. Even with the risk of sanction. You're a child-care worker, for Christ's sake. They don't expect you to be very smart."

"And they'd be right, eh?"

"Look, maybe the prison is testing its internal-external security? Maybe Ernie is getting points suckering you in?"

"That's pretty scary."

"Prison is pretty scary. End it quickly, is my advice. See you at the next family reunion."

The problem with lawyers and legal advice is that you still have a serious dilemma no matter what advice you're given. I was tempted to just let the matter drop, to pocket the money and pay with a thimble full of guilt. I would be Ernie's personal bank account until or if he was released. Or I could simply do as he asked and put the money in a real bank. Then I thought of a story W.C. Fields told, of opening bank accounts all around the country. Of course, sometimes he never made it back to close the account, lost track of how many banks he had money in. I might be starting Ernie on just such a fiscally fatal course.

I returned to the prison the following week. It was still November, still dreary.

If anything it took longer for the guard to bring Ernie to me this time. I expressed my distress to Ernie over his cash-flow activities giving him the impression I'd already turned in the money.

"I was advised to turn the money over to the prison, Ernie. You didn't leave me much choice."

His broad face broke out in a large smile. "I figured that's what you'd do. No skin."

"I'm sorry."

"No big deal."

"It's not the only money you've got, surely?"

"Yeah, I still get my allowance."

"I'd better go."

"See ya, Wally."

Not if I see you first, I thought.

I met with the warden after my visit with Ernie. I handed him the 400 clams. I intimated that I had always intended to turn it in. He gave me a receipt. He asked me to write out a statement on how the money came into my possession. I said I would, later. I said I had an appointment I couldn't miss. He said fine, later would do.

I opted not to do the statement. That was the last I heard of the matter. I don't think anybody really cared.

I considered myself lucky. Dumb and lucky. Two months later, I started my employment as a social worker. My office, oddly enough, was right next to Shirley Graham's.

I still think about Ernie. His trial was fascinating. I gave about five minutes worth of meaningless testimony. Ernie smiled at me the whole time, apparently pleased with my kind words. In the end, he wasn't convicted of murder. They gave him two years plus for car theft but no time for whatever his participation was in the death of the car owner. His teen companions admitted that they were so stoned they hadn't a clue what was really going on the night the old man died.

The owner was thought by some to have died by his own tacky misadventure, a suitable end for someone seeking out teenage girls for sex. The sense I got was that some believed his death was justified in some way. I never thought that, but that was the courtroom buzz and the tone of the few letters to the editor that I read.

A few years later, Ernie made the papers again. He had kicked a fellow to death with his boots. Outside of some god-forsaken prairie strip club. He was given a long sentence.

I wasn't even tempted to visit.

Chapter 16

Inquisition
Tuesday, November 20

It would have been smart to put on a suit and tie, dress to the nines, emphasize my professionalism. Gord and his management team would have appreciated the trouble I would have gone to, the high esteem I held them in. It would have been a sign of respect to gussy myself up for their inquisition.

The problem was I didn't have a suit. And if I had one, it would have been at best a shabby old tweed thing, fraying at the sleeves, ballooning in the seat, and stained here and there from drippy foods and drinks from one too many weddings or funerals. For the suit's sake, it was good I didn't have one to misuse.

The upside was that the room, unexpectedly, was not awash in high end three-piece suits. Gord Lafferty had his usual friend-of-the-people style. Assistant Deputy Minister Dylan Kirk and personnel manager Marcia Duncan had also, from their point of view, dressed down for the occasion. The youngish Ms. Duncan was decked out in a grey slacks, a sports coat, and a little bolo tie, set against a light-grey blouse. Her jet-black hair was short and efficient looking. Dylan. He was wearing brown cords and a blue shirt. His overcoat was draped over a far chair. He had loosened his dark-blue silk tie.

"Dylan," I said, "it's been a long time."

"I wish it could be under better circumstances, Wally."

"We wish we knew the circumstances, Dylan," Millie fired back.

Dylan and I had some history. Not much, but some. While worker bees the likes of me had stayed behind to toil and drudge in the trenches, Dylan had filled the leadership vacuum. I appreciated his sacrifice. Someone had to advise the Queen.

"Let's all sit down," Gord suggested. Once we had chosen seats in the boardroom, Marcia Duncan asked if we would object to their tape recording the proceedings. Millie had planned to suggest the same, so we were okay with it. As long as they paid for the transcript and we got a verbatim copy.

Marcia Duncan pulled out a tape recorder from her briefcase and positioned it.

MD: It's Tuesday, November 20, 12:10 p.m. Present are Assistant Deputy Director Dylan Kirk, Area Manager Gordon Lafferty, Union Rep Millie Hunt, Social Worker Wallace Rose, and Regional Personnel Technician Marcia Duncan.

GL: To begin then, and let's be crystal clear, this is a preliminary, fact-finding meeting to explore a serious historical complaint recently come to light about employee Wallace Rose. With everyone's goodwill, we hope to begin this process by asking a series of questions of Wallace Rose to establish context. Mr. Rose has not been advised of the specifics, and with his and his union representative's agreement, we will withhold those allegations until we're comfortable with contextualizing. We recognize that due process requires Mr. Rose be fully apprised of the allegations. However, our hope is that you will consent to not hearing them if only because they are incendiary in nature and might deflect from a cool, dispassionate response to our initial, contextually based questions.

WR: You've got to be kidding. I...

MH: Wally, let me speak.

WR: Sorry, Millie.

MH: Let me get this straight. You've had some sort of complaint, but you don't want to tell us what it is until you ask a bunch of questions.

DK: That's the sum of it, Ms. Hunt. I think Gordon spelled it out. Of course Wally should know what he is alleged to have done. And he will. And I suspect when he is told, he will spend no little time offering a full denial. That's a given. Before we get to that, we want his views on the client, on his role in her life. Without the complication of the accusation.

MH: Crap. Sounds like crap to me. We need a time out.

DK: If you must. But if you continue to abuse the process, we might have to take more definitive action. Shut the tape off, Marcia.

MD: The tape is stopped at…12:12.

Millie and I left the room and went to my office. "Jesus Wally, you need a maid?"

"I'll request one. This may not be the best time to do that, however."

We sat down. I offered her my comfy chair, but she demurred. "Your ass is on the firing line. Enjoy the comfort while you can."

"Millie, I'm not sure there is any big price to be paid by giving them a bit of palaver before they tell me what's cooking," I said about as innocently as I could.

"That's not the point, Wally. You can't let them steamroll you. They have a complaint; they should just get on with it. I don't know what they hope to gain by chatting you up first. Whatever that is, we need to exercise a little power. We can't make it easy for them."

"You're probably right," I admitted. "If they won't budge, let's let them ask a few questions. See where they're going."

"It's your ass in the frying pan," she said, using her favourite mixed metaphor. I was stymied trying to imagine a large enough cast iron frying pan to fit me. My sense of the process now was that they wanted me to talk about Angie, what brought her into care, my role etc. I felt comfortable doing that. I had to think, though, that they had got a hold of the complaint Ray Baker had spoken to me about. None of that had made it into the file.

"And Wally, the best advice I can give, and I know you know this, is just answer the question put to you. Keep it as brief as possible."

This was sound advice. People who didn't know how to keep their traps shut often fell into one of their own making.

We re-entered the interrogation chamber.

We nodded that we were ready.

MD: Mr. Rose and Union Rep Millie Hunt have re-entered the room and nodded their agreement to continue. It is November 20 at 12:20p.m.

DK: Wally, I'll be leading the questioning for the next while.

WR: I would expect nothing less, Dylan. Fire away.

DK: Can you recount for us the circumstances that brought Angie Gravelle into care?

WR: She was in care when I first met her. I think she'd been brought into care about a year before I started at the office. I was bumping another worker, and she was on his caseload, which I inherited. As I recall I think her mother had just run out of steam with her. May have hit her in frustration. One of those typical scuffles families get into. A dance of despair. Mostly, Angie was in care because she was just too tough to manage.

DK: Manage in what way?

WR: Most ways, I guess. Angie had temper tantrums. She ran away at the drop of a hat. Stealing from home and the community. Explosive.

DK: Would these behaviours bring her into care today?

MH: Don't answer that, Wally. Dylan, what has that got to do with anything?

DK: Millie, what can be the harm in hearing Wally's answer?

MH: Dylan, I don't know what the harm would be. But I'll tell you this; you should stick to your script. You are following a script, aren't you?

DK: Look Millie, if you want to be an obstructionist, well, I suppose there is little we can do about that. But I think it a shame that you waste our time, and belittle your well-known credibility, by putting up roadblocks everywhere. Wally is perfectly capable of delineating his scope of practice…clarifying what might have been.

MH: Fine! That's your position. Mine is… it's a pointless question, a management apples and oranges question.

WR: Look Dylan, I'm okay about giving you a hypothetical answer to your—what-would-you-have-done-today-all-things-being-equal—lottery.

DK: I…I suppose you're telling me, Wally, that…that Millie's right and it's a pointless question? My misstep.

WR: I don't know what this whole thing is about, Dylan, but what I might have done on a particular case years ago, seems…a trifle specious. And pointless.

DK: Like I said…my misstep. But let's be clear, we'll decide what is or is not pointless.

WR: I bow to management's right to determine the pointlessness of it all at every turn, Dylan.

DK: With that backhanded concession, we'll continue. As you noted, Ms. Gravelle had been in care about a year when you became her case worker.

WR: Correct.

DK: How old was she at that time?

WR: Fourteen. Almost fifteen.

DK: What kind of kid was she, Wally? I mean, we know she was a tough kid, but, well, how was she with you. Your personnel file constantly emphasizes the good rapport you have had, have been perceived to have had, with your youth clients. Did you have rapport with Ms. Gravelle?

WR: Rapport? No Dyl, we had little rapport.

DK: Why was that Wally? Why couldn't you bond with her?

WR: Don't know. Tried, but she had big signs that said "stay away, keep out."

DK: So, without rapport, without any kind of positive relationship, why, after she had been gone for two years, why were you the one to go to the airport the night she was flown back to the province? Why was that, Wally?

WR: I…

MH: We may need to conference, Wally.

WR: Good idea, Millie.

DK: Am I asking tough questions? I thought the last one was fairly easy. Why not send someone who has a good relationship with a youth to meet her? Or, at least, someone neutral.

WR: Look Dylan, Mr. Kirk, the real world that I work in, then and now, the one you seem to have conveniently forgotten about, doesn't have spare people lounging about waiting to step up and do little chores, like milk old Bessie or drive to the airport. Just doesn't happen. Wish it did. Anyway, I don't like to work nights. Never did. The plane was coming in …I can't quite remember… maybe it was seven at night. Who the fuck am I going to ask?

DK: After-hours. You could have asked them.

WR: Oh yeah, right. Sure, I could have. I just thought they might like to be investigating abuse cases rather than picking up some lazy worker's kid.

DK: You seem to have some easy excuses for placing yourself in harm's way. Not thinking through your steps. Exhibiting questionable judgment; compromising clients' well-being. And the hostility and the swearing are not appropriate.

MH: Mr. Kirk. You're setting an unacceptable tone. You're getting a reciprocal response. This whole inquisition seems futile. We need a break.

MD: Ms. Hunt and Mr. Rose are leaving the room at 12:27. The tape is turned off.

We bailed for a second time. At this rate we'd be there all day, sparring with Dylan and his coterie, yo-yoing in and out like a goddamn, discordant bungee…and looking resistant…non-compliant. I knew Millie was giving me sage advice, but this whole episode had been a simmering burden for years, and I wanted to purge it. I had done nothing wrong except keep a stupid event secret.

"Where we going with this, Millie? This is stupid."

"They're after your head, Wally. That's their agenda. And it won't take much. They have some kind of sexual abuse, sexual transgression suspicion. Who knows where it came from?"

"I don't think it matters. But, if I had to guess, it came from police files or maybe Angie or maybe the drunk on the plane. Regardless, their suspicions are driving this."

"We have two choices." Millie looked ferocious. "Either we just let them meander around till they get to the point, or we walk. No other options. None."

I wanted to be doing something more useful than rehashing an unpleasant incident. If I was advising me, if I had the sense to pay attention to myself, I'd walk. Straight out the door and wait until they coughed up their complaint. But Dylan Kirk was a singularly slippery guy. Had to be to stay on top of the heap in the corporate cesspool headquarters was. I knew that you had to be cunning to survive that hotbed of intrigue and political black ice.

"What'll it be, tiger?" Millie asked. "We can't go in again without a game plan we stick to."

"I want to know the complaint. No more side-stepping. They lay it out, or we walk and they do what they do."

"They could suspend you."

"They might anyway. I want them to tell me what itch they want me to scratch."

"Okay tiger. That's our position." With that, we returned to the hot seat.

MD: Ms Hunt and Mr. Rose returned at 12:35. Tape commences.

DK: Do we resume?

MH: We believe we have been patient and cooperative. However, we need to know the substance of your concern. Consider your fishing license revoked, Dylan.

DK: Fair enough, Millie. We weren't catching our quota anyway. Here's the nub of it. Recently, the RCMP was looking into any contact police services may have had with Ms. Gravelle. The reason isn't relevant to this. What popped up was an inquiry done some years ago by a retired sexual assault investigator, Ray Baker. You know him, Wally?

WR: I knew him.

DK: For the sake of the tape, and others in the room, Cpl. Baker was the child sexual assault expert for the Richmond RCMP for a dozen years at least. Anyway, he interviewed Ms. Gravelle after receiving an anonymous call that alleged that you, Wally, had known Ms Gravelle intimately when she was a child in your care. You recall?

WR: Hmmm.

DK: For clarity, Mr. Rose murmurs and nods his head. Anyway, a review of Ms. Gravelle's closed CIC (child in care) files found no reference to the allegation. That's primarily why we are here, Wally. Can you enlighten us? Why the omission?

WR: Why? I was embarrassed. Embarrassed, and the whole episode left me nauseated. And, in case you had any doubts, Dylan, the allegation was bogus. It didn't benefit me, Angie, or...what, posterity, to have it documented in her file.

DK: Wally, I would think that an allegation of sexual misconduct would be noteworthy, would be brought to the attention of your supervisor. Just in case it had legs. In case...well, just in case, Wally.

MH: You've been belatedly kind to state the reason for this inquisition. What's your next step, Dylan?

DK: You mean, what's next for Mr. Rose?

MH: What do you intend to do, Dylan?

DK: We'll be following up with Cpl. Baker as well as two airport Mounties, Stark and Wallender. We'll interview Ms. Gravelle, if possible. Depending on the results of those interviews, we'll possibly have to interview other youth who have been clients of Mr. Rose. Until then, we think Mr. Rose should be off the job. Some vacation seems in order.

WR: I'm not in the mood for a vacation. If you're going to suspend me, then get on with it. If not, I've got an active caseload and I would like to keep at it.

DK: Would you and Ms. Hunt mind giving us a few minutes?

WR: Of course.

DK: Good of you. Marcia?

MD: Ms. Hunt and Mr. Rose have left the room. The tape is turned off at 12:47.

It took them ten minutes to call us back in, to determine my interim sentence.

MD: Mr. Rose and Ms. Hunt have re-entered the room. The tape is turned on at 12:59.

DK: We struggled with the best course of action. We recognize the questionable source of the allegation, but your failure to document the incident, to apparently fail to bring it to the attention of your supervisor, was a significant omission. Still, at this time, we feel it would be unfairly pre-emptive to institute a remedial or punitive course of action. We will continue to fact-find. Until we re-convene, we will request that you not meet with female clients alone. That may be a hardship, possibly embarrassing, but that is a mandatory stipulation. We'll speak with your supervisor to apprise her of the concern and the interim measures. Any questions?

MH: Aside from asking why it's necessary to humiliate a long-time employee by shackling him to a babysitter, no.

DK: Good. Marcia, that wraps it up.

MD: This meeting concludes at 1:03.

Millie and I left them behind and went to my office. "Thanks, Millie. It could have been worse."

"Right. You've got to play it safe for the next while, Wally. Do you have any stewarding assignments that I'm unaware of?"

"No. None."

"What if one comes your way?"

"I don't know. Deal with it, I suppose. I'm feeling a little tarnished. Compromised. Stupid. I've never felt…immune from repercussion, but, after a time, I guess I got complacent."

"Natural to get that way," she offered. "Look, if you get a request to steward, touch base with me. I know that's a little mother-hen like but it may help any decisions that you have to make. I don't think you need to sequester your union activism, but you need to exercise some caution. Reputations are fragile. You've got a good one, and you want to keep it. Anyway," and she put a comforting hand on my shoulder, "you're okay?"

"As right as rain."

"Good. I'll head out. Talk to you later."

"Thanks, Millie. Appreciate the support."

After Millie left, I collapsed in my padded, $100 ergonomically-correct chair, exhausted and fearful. It felt like a Friday, even though it was only halfway through the second day of the week..

Chapter 17

Acceptance
Tuesday, November 20

After Millie headed out, I sat for quite a while in my office doing nothing more than being paid to be idle, coasting on the government dime. I felt less than guilty, more than convicted. The phone rang a few times, but it remained abandoned on the cradle. Someone would take a message. And if they didn't, well, if I had agreed to an employer-urged vacation, or been suspended, I wouldn't have been available to pick up the receiver anyways. Self-pity is unsightly, and that, more than anything, kept me burrowed in my cave.

I had been careless in the way I had managed the original incident with Angie and even more lax in my earnest but invasive monitoring of her subsequent life. There are actions we take that can be both justified and juvenile. If the system wanted to really get its hooks into me, they'd find a record of my electronic searches of Angie's welfare file. In the days when I first had done those sorts of searches, the rationale had been that I was just being efficient, sussing out information that would allow me and others to better protect kids. It wasn't an action I talked about with anyone. Occasionally I would assist younger workers to access the confidential screens, as we became more familiar with the technology. I barely gave it a second thought until a police officer with an evangelistic leaning was caught running plates of cars parked outside an abortion clinic. Though I felt more justified than the conniving Christian cop, the invasion of privacy issue, and my casual complicity in something not totally dissimilar, was not lost on me.

After I had ruminated in my self-imposed isolation chamber for about an hour, Kate knocked and entered.

"Gord brought me up to speed just now, Wally. How are you doing?"

I looked at her and shrugged. "I don't know. When you're in the wringer, I guess you feel squashed. Sooooo…squashed. There," I added, "that felt good."

"I don't know what to say, Wally. If what I've been told about your editing of events is anywhere near the truth, well, it doesn't inspire confidence."

Straight to my heart. If I was going to survive this string of debilitating events, rise above my own stupid omissions, I had to get Kate on my side. Up to now, I would have had little doubt that she trusted me, trusted my opinions, my observations, my work. The essential nature of child protection work—like most work, it is not often examined by its practitioners as they go about their tasks— requires that the chain of command has, if not faith, something approximating an assurance that positive, genuine, and dutiful conduct is occurring.

Kate was now cognizant that at least on this one file, I had selectively omitted details that should have been there, that should have been held up to the light. I wanted to posit that we all edit our activities. Journalists and others who document their observations have to be selective. Though selectively parsing problematic information was, to my mind, a natural process, once edited-out material finds unexpected illumination, it runs the risk of shining neon-brighter; radiating with an aggressive, uncomfortable intensity it might not have had if it had simply been unveiled earlier.

"I'm sorry, Kate. I may be guilty of hiding awkward stuff, embarrassing accusations…Silly me, perhaps I was desperately avoiding criticism…I certainly wasn't used to being in the cross-hairs of a drunk's bullshit gossip…but I haven't crossed the line in terms of Angie, or any kid. Never. I hope you believe that."

She looked away. Not a good sign. She then looked back at me.

"I hope that's true, Wally. I hope you can prove it. Or, that nothing is provable against you. But we still have to deal with the whole slimy mess. How do you think we should go about doing that?"

If I was to stay on the job, I had been directed not to be alone with female clients. Unless we were given an additional staffer, this would cause extreme pressure on the team. I doubted it was workable. At the same time, I needed to be at work, needed to serve the kids I felt responsible for, was responsible for. Part of that duty of service, that responsibility, involved those intimate one-to-one interactions, the chats, the planning, the anger, and the resolution.

Having a chaperone would neutralize some of that, perhaps too much to make it worthwhile.

"Let me lead the way at team meeting tomorrow, Kate. I'm the one who has to explain himself. I owe it to you and to our team. Let me do it there. And we can conscript volunteers to ride in my sidecar. Assuming anyone still wants me around. Make a list, check it twice…"

"I'm okay with that," she said. "And they will support you. I'm sure they will. But Wally, I think you need to be careful about what you say. The system has a hate on for you at the moment. You're vulnerable. Be careful that you don't say the wrong thing."

I had spent a lifetime saying the wrong thing. I doubted that would change.

"Do you want to take the rest of the day off?"

"I don't know," I replied. "Look, let me check my messages, scope out demands. I might cut out a bit early."

She rested her hand on my shoulder. "Call me if you need to talk."

Kate left and I went to the coffee room, poured a much too old cuppa and gave it a microwave minute. Then I went to the front to examine the message situation. There was a fistful waiting.

I felt someone approach from behind and place her hand on my shoulder. Roberta left it there for a moment and then said, "A machine would eliminate that unsightly bundle, Wally. Voice mail would be invisible, and you wouldn't feel so overwhelmed."

I must be looking like some dejected sad sack, I figured.

"Good point, Ro. Right on the money. I'll think about it."

"In a pig's eye you will," she said smilingly and moved on.

I walked back to my office sorting through the sheaf of 10 messages. Dru had called about Erin. Because Erin was a brand new client, I gave Dru the first call back.

I got her on the second ring. "You're hard to reach today," she commented.

"Past sins catching up! Anyway, you've met Erin?"

"We're set to boogie. Contract is ready to go. Do we need to talk about her roomies?"

"You mean Rock?"

"No, I mean Gina, for one. And bugger me if Ryan Conway isn't part of the equation."

"Housing young folk is a complex activity, Dru. If Ryan can, by some miracle, manage to live with Erin and Gina and the shepherd, well, we need to bless that union."

"How many limbs are you out on, Wally?"

"Enough. Why?"

"Just asking. Anyway, I'm with Erin now. If we swung by, do you suppose we could sign off? They're down to crumbs and a few secondhand tea bags. And Rock's tasty morsels."

I told her to come on by and we'd skate through the paperwork. I hoped I could get Kate to quickly sign off and forget that I was a risky proposition.

Monica had left a terse message: I don't want to talk with my mother— let the whole thing drop. I called her back, but she didn't answer.

I wanted to focus on Monica, prepare for Erin's agreement, do what I am supposed to do. I fully understood the stupidity of shackling me to another worker, wasting their time as well as mine, as well as whoever was receiving the benefit of our service. That didn't help. Understanding stupidity, and your part in it, doesn't make it go away. More than 50 percent of my youth clients were female. Much of my interaction with them was in conjunction with another worker, a support or outreach worker, usually female, and it was those women who really did the bulk of the meaningful work. I was simply the pencil pusher.

I called Monica again. Still no answer. I then started an electronic cheque request for some emergency funds for Erin.

Once that was done, I gave Monica one more dingle. I let it ring for much longer than proper etiquette endorsed. On another day, I would have jumped in the Batmobile and sped to her door. Today, my energy was drained.

Some minutes later, Dru and Erin arrived. We squeezed into my office and signed the youth agreement contract. For her the deal was to stick to school. We slid by the issue of her connubial roommate. It was not unlike the American military's "don't ask—don't tell" policy.

I could live with that.

Chapter 18

Day time-My culpa
Wednesday, November 21

I had 20-year-old scotch waiting for me at home, a gift from my ex when we parted. I didn't drink scotch then. I still don't. Even ancient, well-aged scotch. That made it the perfect divorce gesture. That sort of bitter humour was one of the reasons I had been attracted to her in the first place. The scotch had been sitting in my booze cellar for a long time, wrapped and untapped, a completely armed and outfitted soldier right next to a speck of rum and a dribble of rye. I had anticipated that the scotch would continue to sit there, untouched. But as I drove home, I felt a commuter funk creep up on me, grab me in my wounded heart, and drag me into old patterns of hard drinking, boozy solutions to problems. By the time I arrived home, I had reconsidered. There was some comfort in just knowing it was there.

I ordered a pizza and left the liquor alone. Forty minutes later, the disk of cheese and anchovies arrived. I opened a bottle of Barbera and sat down to wine, cholesterol, and one of my favourite old flicks, *The Last Picture Show*. The pizza and wine lasted the whole two hours. By the end of the film, I was so full of someone else's bittersweet nostalgia that my troubles were able to inch back into my brain, curl up, and go to sleep.

There is a dusty windswept desolation in the Texas town portrayed in Bogdanovich's film. The soft black-and-white cinematography, the intimacy of the lives of the characters, the quiet guidance of Sam the Lion, all served to soothe me a bit. That was darkly balanced by the shrill hunger demonstrated by Cybill Shepherd's gloriously conniving Jacy. Her fierce portrayal reminded me again, as it always had, that, towards the end of my marriage, Jeanne most resembled, in my admittedly biased view, an adult Jacy, a screaming Mimi, a poisoned and unredeemable casualty of me. I had picked the wrong film to watch. I should have watched Nine to Five.

I crawled off to bed at about nine and slept straight through to morning.

The drive to work was smooth. It was earlier than usual so the franticness which often permeated the drive was less. It seemed that way, anyway.

I'd had a good breakfast and a sound, if dreamless, sleep. I awoke at three and wrote out a few words of contrition that I might deliver to my workmates. Would they forgive my fast and loose ways with the computer, my obsessive habit of trying to possess some continuity of care for clients long departed from my administrative grasp?

I had gone back to sleep, my penitent's declaration still shapeless.

I was the first at work. As usual I made coffee and huddled in my office for two hours, writing my confession, aimlessly scribbling a few case notes that seemed to squirm their way into my thoughts. No one knocked. The phone didn't ring. The meeting time arrived and I crossed the hall, without my notes, and joined the group. There was a hubbub when I entered the room, quickly dashed by awkward silence. Kate, being the leader she is, put me into context.

"Morning, Wally. You're the top of our agenda. How are you?"

"Restless, Kate. Restless." There were about 10 of my co-workers sitting around our meeting table. They looked like what they were, a very tolerant group.

"I won't keep you in suspense. Kate has been directed to ensure that for the time being, I am not alone with any clients, females primarily. Given my alleged cover-up, my secret inclinations, who knows what I might do that involves any member of the human family."

I was getting hyperbolic, off-message and sarcastic.

"There has been an allegation…which is just an allegation…that I have been inappropriate with a client. To be as frank as I can, they think…at least I think they think…or may soon think…that I've been electronically stalking her. That part is not untrue. I have been obsessed with her, not to wish her harm but…to find some way to serve her, to be available for her in a way I was unable to be when she was a kid. Guilt I suppose."

Remember the path, I told myself. I was also aware that I was confessing sins not yet on the table. This was bound to confuse the hell out of my team.

"As I got older, and partially wiser, I realized that perhaps I could have helped her differently. Maybe not, maybe that was wishful thinking, but there you go. But to the crux of my sin…"

It was not going well. I should have written it out. My confession, my failure to keep at a safe and confidential distance led to my misguided insistence that I had some primary right to still be involved in a former client's life. Was it akin to the ownership notions of a slave owner? I bloody well hoped not. Too extreme. Still, there was a proprietary thread that wove itself through the core of the work. The healthier you were, the better able you were to unravel the spool.

My lapsing reverie reminded me that I hadn't actually used Angie's name. It was as if I had had it drawn to my attention in no uncertain terms that I should never utter her name again, that I'd gone so beyond the pale that I had no right to use her name, dredge it up, voice it in polite company. I almost bought into that. I knew I had stalked her, sniffed her out electronically, and that, by most standards, had abused what little privacy the world saw fit to bequeath her.

Here, before my real judges, the people with whom I plied my trade and shared similar aims and objectives, using each other's tools, those invisible chisels, hammers, and wrenches of listening, of narrative, of glances and guidance, I had become an emotional and extremist thief, a paternalistic and aloof terrorist. I had ventured into her last refuge, Angie's last catacomb of information; I had snuck into her cyber life, taken something of hers she needed to prize, didn't know was even being poached, wasn't even aware I was prying from her grip, her weakened grasp, her life.

It was the guilt talking. I felt like I was chewing away at myself as if I were a cob of corn.

There are moments when you need to just step aside. I wasn't sure if this was one of those, but as I scanned the faces of my professional partners, the ones I slogged away with day in and day out, I determined that I needed to regroup…away from work, away from my guilt.

"Look, guys, I thought this would work. I fucked up. I didn't think I was as bothered by my inquisition as I am. It's too tough, too freaking over the top."

I looked at Kate and she looked as if she'd bet on the horse that went lame just short of the finish line. "Kate, I need some personal time."

I walked out as she nodded her agreement.

Chapter 19

Carla Prentice

She had slaved for her wages for 10 hours on Friday, and was released half an hour past nine p.m., permitted, at last, to haul her self home. The shift included an expected but unpaid half-hour of cleaning up, chattering and schmoozing with her co-workers about how the shift had gone, what the sales were, what the weekend would bring. They also included the bus ride to and from work. This was her slave-mentality means of calculation. Her perfect world, on those infrequent occasions when she allowed herself to fantasize, would include, if not a Zellers limo that would pick her up, then at least mileage to and from home. Even one-way would be an improvement.

It always seemed odd to Carla that the way they concluded their Friday nights was so drawn out, as if some of the ladies didn't want to leave, as if work was a more attractive option then going home. Most of the workers, women except for Lance Drucker, the latest in an unending trail of male trainee managers, must be dead on their feet by closing, minds numbed by the boredom of the tasks they performed, the drone of the customers, the buzz of the bright unnatural fluorescent. She wanted to be out of there as fast as humanly possible, to be wherever she could put up her feet and rest.

Carla had seen a few hundred people during her shift. She kept staring through the line-ups, the blur of fidgety shoppers, beyond the customers she was serving, just praying for a glimpse of Skye.

Three days earlier, the two social workers had visited. She had given them tea. She was on her finest behaviour. The best they had to offer was counselling if and when…when (because there was no room for doubting) Skye returned. She had agreed to whatever would get her child back. She knew that it would never happen, the counselling. She saw no real worth to it, to hashing and rehashing the past, all of the hurtful behaviour, all of it so much contaminated water under the bridge. Even with the fear that circulated just under her skin, fear of whatever horror she had always expected would find her and strip the flesh off of her, tear her limb from emotional limb, even with that ominous sense of inevitability, she would do what was expected. If pretending to be open to talking with a counsellor would get people looking for her missing child, well, so be it.

She was upset with herself for allowing them to overhear her angry conversation with Brian when he had called. These days all he had to do was look at her and that would set her off. She knew he enjoyed watching her go ballistic but it didn't really make any sense. Didn't *seem* to make any sense. When it came down to it, it made all the perverse sense in the world. It was power. Unending power over her. She had never had any.

She stepped out into the liberating street. It was a cold night. The bus stop was one hundred yards away. The parking lot was still almost completely full. Theatre-goers, she guessed. Some people would park in the mall and catch a bus into Vancouver to see a film, or go clubbing. Dining in one of countless restaurants. There was little on-street parking uptown. The past few years had seen an explosion of new restaurants and night spots locally. Most catered to an Asian-Canadian clientele. Many of the local restaurants stayed open till one or two. Incredibly late hours, she thought. The city used to be such a sleepy burg, where, as they say about many places, they used to roll up the sidewalks at eight or nine or whatever time the city shut down. No longer. There was a nightlife happening here that she had no real awareness of. She just knew that it flourished, was supported by overseas money. So much money; so much life. She knew so little. She was afraid for Skye, afraid she had touched her toe in some putrid pool of life that would poison her, sicken her, take her away. Carla felt humbled by her exclusion from such a dangerous world.

Her bus was early, waiting for her, like her magical fantastical limo.

She showed the driver (someone new, a student perhaps, though it was November so probably not) her pass. The bus was mostly empty. She took a seat right at the front, a safer place in case undesirables boarded before she got home. She thought of something to say to the new driver. She closed her eyes to catch her thoughts. She drifted into a bus-hum, semi-sleep.

She'd made her break in her late teens, having left it way too long. She often berated herself for her tardy escape. Maybe if she'd run away earlier, she would have made different choices. Not that she believed she had ever had real authority over her decisions.

The actual running, well, leaving home, was ill-planned. Once out the door, she first went to a sort of a friend, Pat Lourdes. She'd stayed with Pat in her one bedroom apartment for three weeks until she'd devised some semblance of a plan. It was summer; she was so hungry for freedom, so stifled by Brian, by her mom's capitulation to him.

She got a job at a five and dime. With a small amount of savings and her pay, she rented a room in a boarding home near Pat's.

She'd met Cary on a bus early in the fall; he seemed invincible. The driver had gently challenged him, accused him of not paying. He had long blond hair, jeans that clung to him and a light-grey jacket with an American Eagle crest on the back. He took the drivers challenge and laughed it off. "No man, not me. I pay my way." He was so convincing that the driver put up his hands and said, "Okay kid, if that's the way it is." And Cary said back, "that's the way it is, buddy. You take care." He'd then sat down right in front of her. In a flash he'd spun around and stuck out his hand and said "I'm Cary Prentice. What do you like to do for fun?"

"Most anything," she had boastfully replied.

"Aren't you the fast one."

She smiled, unclear what he meant by "fast" but charged with a snap of excitement unfamiliar to her. It didn't matter what kind of fun. She had the sense that she needed to live life now, as quickly as possible, that her freedom was to be short-lived.

She had, however, successfully held him at bay; cooled his jets, or whatever it was that charged him up. But Cary had not left the bus empty-handed. He had borrowed a pen from the driver and written her phone number on his palm. The driver had grudgingly obliged. Cary wrote the seven numbers in the soft part of his palm. He then flashed the number to the driver and her. "Expect my call, girl," he had confidently assured her as he got off at his stop.

When she got off a few stops later, she had caught the driver smirking, saw him in the mirror that hung above the front of the bus. "Whatever amuses you, mister," she said to the driver, but only once she was safely on the street, and the bus was heading into the dark.

Cary called her a week later. By that time, she had written him off, any hope that he would call. She'd come to believe that the bus driver had jinxed them, put what her gram had called the "hoodoo" sign on her and Cary. When he called she almost dismissed his overture. "Took your time, fast mover," she had said.

He had called her bluff. "Them's the breaks, toots. Maybe another time."

This forced her to make a pass, a gesture. It came out as a sucky apology. "Sorry."

"You're a rude little girl, aren't you?" he said.

They agreed to meet at a local roller rink. She had never skated, on ice or on pavement. She took to it like she had always had wheels on her feet. Cary was an artist. He showed her how to keep her balance, how to start and stop. She fell a few times, but he always managed to catch her, to reach out and keep her from falling hard. They skated almost every song together. By the end of the evening he'd told her she was as sexy as a roller derby queen.

They'd then walked a few blocks to an A&W. She was famished but didn't want to spend money on fast food. She wondered as they walked if Cary would buy her something. She wanted him to make the gesture, to make the night a complete date. He'd already paid her way into the rink. She'd arrived first, had hung around outside, unsure if he would show. He was a few minutes late. He'd been running, and when he spotted her he gave a loud joyous laugh, infectious and exaggerated.

After they had grabbed something to eat, he escorted her home on the bus. He walked her to the boarding house. She assumed he'd make a move, grab or push his way onto her. Instead, he reached for her hand and kissed it in an elegant sweep, a silly and impressive gesture, old fashioned and captivating. He said he would be away for two weeks, working out of town. Could he see her when he returned? Of course she said.

He was away over a month. Five weeks. The work lasted longer than he had expected. Tree planting. Hard and hot. He was tired. He'd lost his place—his roommate had taken the rent he'd sent and flown the coop. "Asshole, always was. Christ, I'll beat his ass if I find him. He knows it."

Cary had a bit of money left but no place to stay. He was on the outs with his parents. He could make amends and crawl back home, but was that a way for a man to be, he pleaded, sucking up to parents who never had approved of him, never given him an inch? Could he stay with her? Keep his honour? Was that so much to ask? No, no it wasn't. Later she knew it should have been. It was a dangerous step for her. She wasn't supposed to have men stay over. Or women. Or dogs or cats or parents. She was still getting used to the routine of independence, the power of it. She was confused because there was an energy that bubbled out of Cary that unsettled her, that concerned her. If she kept him at a distance, not that she had too much say in that, given his propensity to stay away for weeks at a time, perhaps she could keep a little bit of control.

She could see the future clearly; a premonition, a fear. Mrs. Weeks, the boarding house proprietor was a large, snooty woman with a soft, whispery voice, the kind of voice that sounds like a quiet wind rattling a loose pane of glass somewhere at the back of the house. She would discover them. Cary had no concept of what it meant to be quiet. He didn't know how. His footsteps always fell heavy and constant, his voice carried up her spine.

Even in sleep, he could not be still. When Cary slept, he had a nasal rattle, usually soft and chirpy, but occasionally sounding like an electric saw. Lying next to him, she would imagine the sound magnified, sounding somewhat like the rumble of a freight train. It wasn't a sound easily muffled. She imagined Mrs. Weeks perched outside the door, preparing to burst in and catch her with her contraband lover.

Once, she tried to impress Cary with her concern; he started to vibrate, almost irritably. He caught himself. Then, he smiled and dismissed her with a stroke of his hand on her breast.

Cary was away more often than he was there. The times he stayed away increased. "Jobs," he said. "Gotta go where the work is, babe." By the next spring, he had been in her life for six months. He had actually stayed with her no more than a dozen days.

She didn't want to, but she began to miss her mother. Not Brian. But her mother, yes. The pull home was magnetic.

As she remembered those days, the innocence and the idiocy of them, her foolish imaginings and Cary's blatant failure to be a real part of her life, she thought again, had not stopped thinking, about Skye.

As her thoughts returned to the stress of the present, she realized that she needed to take some action, to prove to herself that she was capable, more than capable, of doing something meaningful.

As her stop approached, she was overwhelmed by the urge to find Skye, to suck up her whatever-it-was…her inertia…and look for her child, to bring Skye home.

Chapter 20

Night: Resistance
Wednesday, November 21

No matter which wall I looked at, the writing was on it. The implication of the writing wasn't crystal clear; rain or tears or spilt milk had dribbled down and smudged the ink, making decoding the message a bit of a task. No matter how murky the imaginary message was, I struggled to decipher it, like some war time intelligence clerk.

When an idea like this hatches in your brain, when a crazy germ-of-an-idea about just getting the hell out, starts careening around in your noggin like a psychotic ping pong ball, it's hard to catch your breath, slow the bugger down, weigh the implications.

I'd slipped through the balance of Wednesday feeling like a slug in an immaculate garden; trying not to take the bait, sensing that my slimy cover was exposed, that the salt was hunting me, ready to dissolve me and all my ragged parts.

I knew I had options. I could play this thing out, grieve any punishment the system imposed. I had spent half a life time butting heads with my superiors, chipping out a persona of someone who knew their job, did it well and didn't take much guff. Some guff, but not much.

I embraced the union grievance process. It was a little force of law, a buffer against the tyranny of a vindictive employer. Every time I had assisted a worker to seek this court of only resort because that's what a grievance often is, a last meaningful way to stand up for your rights, I felt just a tinge more secure.

So that was the public me. But I knew I was less cocksure and confident than the stalwart warrior I presented. I dreaded those elemental little personal dilemmas people get all tangled up in. I'd spent much of my adult life actively avoiding public expressions of "inner turmoil." My adolescence had run rampant with squeamish teen doubts, and I had vowed that, once I was an adult, I would stitch together a cloak of calm, of consistency, of quiet assurance.

This foolish declaration of invulnerability worked rather well early on. After my marriage crumbled, I had additional incentive to live a careful and shielded life. I could balance this personal quest for emotional immunity by extending the care and concern I had held in abeyance to the kids I ministered to. There was a monk's quality to it, even though I was habitually drawn into loving albeit brief interludes over the years. Nevertheless, I had remained irretrievably guarded.

Any life constructed around denial and asceticism, or in my case, emotional abstinence, is bound to unravel some at pivotal points. My undoing, my professional unravelling and the unthreading of my personal mask, had taken me by surprise. The signs were there, but I thought I could think my way out of them.

I hadn't always been a light sleeper. Until a few years ago, I had usually descended into a coma-like slumber. My sleep, typically, was akin to having a thick blanket cover me, shutting out any aspect of light, of sound, of disruption.

The only usual penetration of this cave-like sleeping method occurred when an especially complex child-welfare issue burrowed in. I imagine that anyone who has difficult and conflicting tasks to perform will suffer restless moments of sleep-deprivation from time to time. To manage these moments, I'd had a bundle of stress management workshops...though I was usually the smart-ass who declared that a few glasses of wine managed my stress well enough thank you very much.

A collage of departure scenarios began to trickle into my half-rested brain. I lay in bed, heard the clatter of rain, or perhaps it was one hundred River dancing neighbourhood cats, on the tin roof of my neighbour's garage across the way.

I have never liked long, drawn out farewells. By the same measure, sudden deaths, though they abruptly eradicate any chance of saying goodbye, are painfully, inappropriately efficient. As I lost my struggle for deep sleep, I began to sketch out the script I would use to say goodbye to the kids I served. Some would barely notice my absence. They would either be so bereft of meaningful connection that one more departure of some third-rate presence in their life would cause nary a ripple on their personal sea, or would shut down; deny that it meant anything to them. "Easy come, easy go. People do it all the time in my life."

I knew who these kids were and would try to find some way to not wound them any more than life already had. If I could finagle the system to fiscally assist them channel available funds their way, then I would do that. It was an ongoing struggle to make sure these undervalued kids had enough money to live on.

There were a number of youth on my caseload who were connected, had their own communities of support. I was nothing more than a bureaucrat who had some control over their lives; our relationships weren't particularly personal; they weren't especially hurting emotionally, at least no more than the rest of us. They would survive my departure with no ill effects.

That left the rest. Monica and her baby Sam, for example. Monica had a steel will and would survive, but I guessed I would miss. Somewhat unprofessionally, I hoped she would miss me too

Ryan was another one, though he was so bruised by the leave-taking of people in his world that my imminent exit wouldn't be something we could really discuss.

Some Hollywood films share a small conceit, a summary of the post-film lives of the characters we have met along the way. In *American Graffiti* we meet an ensemble of young characters at a pivotal time in their lives. After the film plays out their comedy/drama, we are given a synopsis of their life, or death, after the film. There is a full-circle quality to the summary, as if the characters were real, and who would refute that they were?

In the lives of all of us, people are unendingly slipping from our grasp like nomadic grains of sand. We lose sight of them, lose the smell and the taste of them, often forever.

I glanced at the alarm clock. It seemed that it should be later than just past midnight. Restless and revved up, I got out of bed and took a hot shower. From experience, I knew I wasn't going to get back to sleep any time soon. I began to think about Cathy and her newest case, the misplaced child, Skye. If I couldn't do anything for myself, stuck as I was in career transition, perhaps I could make some progress on this missing kid. I dressed quickly, grabbed some fruit to munch on, and drove into east Vancouver. It was a cold night, the air dry and silent. The streets were mostly empty, save for the occasional cab. In 15 minutes, I was parked across from the abandoned house we had visited last week. I felt a shade out of my element, staking out a squat, having no idea if anyone would be out and about at this hour. The rest of the block was dark, except for a slight shimmering aurora of distant light, perhaps coming from a kitchen some houses away. It might be someone getting up, sleep-struggling, snatching a bit of food from the fridge, sitting at the kitchen table, staring out the window at the alley, thinking about all those small details of living that sometimes collide in our weaker moments.

As I conjured up my anonymous citizen snacker, I realized I was ill at ease loitering on this street. The last thing I wanted was to be rousted by a curious cop. Guys sitting in cars on residential streets deep into the night are often looked upon with suspicion. To readjust my plan, such as it was, I switched on the engine and went in search of an all-night diner and some palatable coffee.

A few minutes later I was leisurely driving down Broadway. Traffic was slight. Scattered groups of pedestrians were bunched in small pulsating jumbles. The main drag was brightly lit, cheaply sly like a carnival arcade. I gave a quick eyeball scan to the out and about strollers, looking for a modestly hygienic café, but also hoping to see someone familiar. I was bowled over to see someone who looked a lot like Carla Prentice, bundled in a plastic rain coat, hugging the shadows, moseying tentatively. Beside her was an older fellow, about the same height as her, dressed in a wool winter coat. The old guy was gesticulating with his hands, which reached out, seemingly intent on pulling Carla, or her double, along in a direction she didn't appear to want to go. She kept shunning his overtures. They maintained their parallel pace.

Street parking was permitted in the wee hours on the usually active street, especially after the trolleys stopped running. I pulled over up ahead of the fussing couple, parked, got out, and leaned against the passenger side of my car. In seconds, Carla and the elderly fellow walked up.

" Mrs. Prentice," I hailed. "Sorry," I said, realizing I had spoken too abruptly, "it's Wally Rose. We met at your home last week."

She halted and focused, finding a context for me here in the gloomy city.

"You startled me, Mr. Rose. Us. My stepfather, Brian Scraggs." She gestured towards her companion. Scraggs took me in, scowling as if my presence was the last thing on earth he needed. He was a medium-height guy, with a weary-looking face, skin sagging like a rumpled bed sheet and running to puffiness. He had one of those abused noses, not unlike the late W.C. Fields, or his doppelganger, Bill Clinton.

Scraggs recovered from his presumably instinctive scowl and squeezed out a quick half-hearted smile.

He then reached out to shake my hand, and I reciprocated. His hands were sheathed in thin, supple leather gloves. He got a good grip on my extended hand, pumped a couple of times, and then released his grasp.

We were all at a conversational standstill. I decided to enhance Scraggs's discomfort level by letting them either explain their late- hours prowl or ask why I was lollygagging on the street.

Scraggs looked like he was going to say something, but Carla stepped up.

"After your visit, Mr. Rose, I felt like I had to do more…to find Skye. Like what any other loving mother would do."

"Sort of my reason too," I offered. "Why here in particular?" I couldn't imagine that Cathy had told her about our penetration of the squat.

"I spoke to Mr. Cardenas…Manny. He said Jordan might be in this neighbourhood. No guarantees, he said. He really didn't seem to want to tell me much, but I kept asking. He told me it might be safer to look here rather than downtown. Downtown was no place for me, he said. I guess I agreed with him. He's an expert, right? Knows the ways of the street?"

I nodded my agreement, though I couldn't really imagine Manny encouraging her in any way to come out at night, especially in this less skuzzy neighbourhood. He must have let something slip and she glommed onto it.

"At least that's what I thought. About Manny," she said. "Anyway, Dad said the only way I could come is if he came with me. We've been walking for over an hour. It's ugly here. Children selling themselves…ugly people everywhere. I feel dirty even being here."

"Tell her to go home, Rose. This is not the place for normal people. Tell her!" Scraggs raised his voice and caught the attention of some of the loitering street people.

"We should sit in my car," I offered. "Might be safer. And certainly more private."

They agreed. Carla crawled in the back, and Scraggs took the shotgun seat.

"I was looking for a coffee place before I saw you. Should we go there and talk?" I asked.

"Bullshit. Don't need to talk," said Scraggs. "We should go home."

"I'd like to talk with you, Mr. Rose," Carla lightly but firmly said, and added, "You can go home if you want, Brian. It might be better if you do. I'll make my own way home."

She turned to me. "Dad's parked a couple of blocks away. My car's off the road...the cost..."

That seemed to explain, in a roundabout way, why she had brought the openly hostile Scraggs.

Scraggs looked about to go nuclear. Some people just ooze control freak, every bit of their being demanding that they be in charge. Second fiddle is just not in their nature. They are the most awkward people to be around. They are constantly seething, like some cauldron of fanatical stew.

I could see the wheels turning in Scraggs' brain. If he couldn't get Carla to abandon her search, he'd be damned if he was going to leave himself. Yet he had read the situation correctly. Being here would serve no purpose unless we got incredibly lucky.

As well, I got the distinct impression that he didn't want her to spend any time with me.

"There are a couple of Italian coffee shops a few blocks away," I finally said. "That's where I'm going."

"I guess we'll both go," said Scraggs.

I I nodded, the three of us climbed in my car, and I drove down Commercial Drive. I parked next to an open coffee joint and we went in. I hadn't really expected any place to be open, but there were a couple of old Italian guys playing chess, and the waiter gave us a thumbs up as if to say, "I'd like to go home, but these old buzzards are good customers,..."

We ordered three coffees and took a table by a window that looked out on the street.

The whole thing was awkward, but I was getting a perverse kick in keeping silent. The tension between Carla Prentice and Brian Scraggs was palpable. Scraggs sat across from me; my back was to the corner window and Carla was to my left. Our knees crossed swords and we both retracted.

It was quite late into the morning, and I expected they were as tired as I was. Conversation would not come easily.

Finally, just after the steamed coffees arrived, Carla broke the tension with a small conversational lob.

"Are you often out this late, Mr. Rose?"

"No," I confessed effortlessly, "I'm usually curled up in bed getting my beauty sleep...which I clearly need a lot of."

She smiled, happy to have a less serious comment to respond to.

"I haven't been getting much sleep since Skye left. It doesn't seem proper to sleep."

"Nonsense, Carly," jumped in Brian Scraggs. "What crap are you spouting? Your daughter is off on a toot. She's not losing any sleep over you. Are you trying to impress this civil servant flunky with what a great mother you are?"

Carla looked at Scraggs, at his little verbal uppercut to me, his angry denunciation of her. She stared at him for a moment and then looked away.

"I musta been out of my mind coming here," Scraggs said. "Giant waste of my time. I'm leaving. If you don't want to be stuck in this den of iniquity, girl, you'd better come with me."

Carla Prentice looked like she might give in to her stepfather's power play. I decided to give her at least one option.

"I'll give you a lift if you want to stay and talk, Mrs. Prentice."

Scraggs gave me a glare with eyes like two flaming blow torches. Before she answered, he made his move.

"Fine, missy. See you around." With that dismissive flourish, he was gone.

Once he had left, the fresh night air seemed to return. I was convinced Carla had had a crushing weight lifted. It wasn't my place to comment on Scraggs's departure, tempting as it was, so I offered to get a refill for her.

"No, I'm fine. But thank you."

We sipped what coffee we had left. I went and got a couple of aging Italian pastries to enhance the experience.

We chewed and crumbled them, holding our tongues and wondering how long the cafe would remain open. The old chess players had departed, and I knew we were a sorry excuse for economic prosperity.

"I should apologize for Brian."

"No you shouldn't. At least, not on my account." I wanted to add, but didn't, that I've had my own incredibly boorish moments from time to time, and try not to hold it against others who cut loose.

"I'd like to say that he's not often like that…rude and blustery and so incredibly angry…I'd be lying though…he's always been like that. Not early on. He was almost kind then. But later"

"When was that? When did he become part of your family?"

"Oh, I guess since I was seven…maybe eight years old."

"Your mother still alive?"

"Yes. She's not well, though. I try and see her every couple of weeks. She and Brian helped raise Jordan…at least until I got myself better situated." She paused, thinking about those early days, I suppose. "It took me a while to grow up."

"I'm still working on it," I confessed. Typically I wouldn't be this candid with clients or near-clients. I was concerned about Scraggs, the kind of impact people like him have on families. At the same time I needed to get home and get some shut-eye.

I yawned, sending the obvious message.

"I'm keeping you?"

"Not really," I said. "However, I'm way past the age when staying up this late is smooth-sailing. I probably should head home. I'll give you the lift I promised."

I stuck a tape of Sarah Vaughn singing "Soulfully" in the tape deck as we sped through the night. "Round Midnight," the Thelonious Monk classic, was playing as I pulled into her driveway. I wished her goodnight and told her I would talk with Cathy to see what more we could do. She thanked me, and I drove home, exhausted and mildly pleased with myself for just being a good listener. I also decided I would see what I could dig up on Brian Scraggs.

Chapter 21

Night-Trust
Wednesday, November 21

Though she was young and comparatively healthy, Skye could feel the energy of her youth, of her usual good health, seeping slowly out of her body. She knew she needed a good nights' sleep, a commodity in short supply these past few days and certainly not often available to kids on the street. Jordan had told her that years ago when he had come back whimpering and beat, temporarily humbled, speaking to Brian in that fake-polite tone she knew so well, looking for all the world like a wet dog seeking permission to come into the house. He'd even smelled like a wet dog that first late afternoon he returned.

He also lavished grand praise on "sack time," especially the hours between dawn and noon. I missed those, he had told her more than once. But that was sometime after he returned from street exile.

He'd shown up late one wet Monday afternoon. The police had found him and returned him home. Skye had just returned from school, and their mother wouldn't get back from work for hours.

The police were in a hurry. They saw no reason to worry about leaving Jordan. They departed, but admonished him that they'd call in a couple of hours to talk to his mom. Jordan pushed pass Skye and walked right in as if it was his own house. He snorted "I'm back, little sister," and took a flying leap onto the couch. She cowered away from him those first few minutes. He sat, perched sullen and squirrel-like, hogging the TV remote, simmering in a dark bubbling pool of his own pissiness.

She grabbed the phone and retreated to the bathroom. She wanted to call her mother right away, but knew that calls at work were not encouraged. It had to be life or death. She wondered...is this life or death? It meant nothing to her then. Life and death. They were just one thing...the way it was. It wasn't life. Maybe it was death? It wasn't that stretched-out-cold-in-a-casket death she knew a little bit about. It was more like being stuck in some invisible block of ice, a glassy ice that you could see out of, but it kept you frozen but breathing, somehow still breathing.

When her mother returned home, the fireworks Skye expected to erupt didn't happen. Carla changed her clothes, made supper, spoke to a policeman who called like they said they would, and once done with that, served Jordan dinner. He had remained on the couch, staring at the tube, changing channels every few minutes, shovelling down the mac and cheese. She and her mother ate at the table, occasionally glancing over at him, waiting for something to happen the way it had when he had exploded and run away more than a year earlier.

He wolfed down the first mixture. Carla brought the pot to him and ladled out seconds. His only thanks was to dig in almost as soon as the food reached his plate.

Skye was 10 when Jordan had first left; 11 when the cops brought him back. He stayed home a year that time, a year of tiny tortures. Their mother simply couldn't deal with him. In the end, he left. Oddly, once he had gone a second time, they found ways to talk and see each other. All three of them learned how to get along a little better.

It was during this time, these past couple of years, that he became more like the brother she remembered: the kidder, the clever one, the occasionally intolerant but forgiving older brother. It's just that he wasn't there all that often. Because he wasn't at hand, and often was without a phone, much of the advice she sought from him was after the fact. By then his advice and her own sense of the repercussions of her already-made decisions were in accord. For example, though she knew about drugs, had seen and heard him and his friends smoking up in the house when she was younger, he had advised her to wait for a little while. She was willing to take her time . And then, last summer, she had left home for a few days after a spat with her mom. Cori Bailey had offered her a place to stay. Cori's dad was cool with that. Cori's mom had split a few years earlier, and she and her dad were tight. He was a roofer, worked long hours in good weather and wasn't around a lot, good weather or not. Something like her mom, except her mom was at home more. Both she and Cori had hard-working parents. She knew that. Cori's dad was a lot less uptight about things like dope and staying up late. Cori showed her where her dad kept his stash, and they borrowed a bit and smoked up on the balcony. Later that afternoon, Cori invited a couple of boys from the next floor up. They were a little older and had grabby hands, even after smoking the weed. Cori slapped Peter, the older one, when he patted her butt. This only egged him on, as the slap was pretty lightweight. His friend Gareth snuggled on the couch with Skye but kept his hands to himself. Sort of.

Skye stayed a few days, almost a week. Eventually she got tired of sleeping on the couch and just being in the way, not that Cori or Mr. Bailey had said anything directly. One day she just got up, went to the mall, saw her mom, and said, "I'm back. Okay?" Her mom nodded and she went home, and that was that. Her first runaway.

Until now. And this time she did it up in bows.

She stood in the shadows on the opposite side of the street from the streetlight. She couldn't believe her mom would come looking for her. It just wasn't what she expected. Her mom rarely took chances: life was too perilous. Her caution had made her ineffective when Jordan rebelled. And her grandfather walked all over her mother. Like she was a little kid. When her grandmother was there to witness the demeaning behaviour of the old man, the best she would do was sigh and tell her daughter to "Get a backbone, Carly."

Skye kept her eyes sharply and sadly on her mom. And Brian. She could barely look at him, yet it would be foolhardy not to watch his every move. Why would she bring him here? How did they know where she was? Mesmerized by her curiosity, Skye followed after her mother and step-grandfather, staying in the darkness, barely breathing, careful of where her feet landed, wanting to keep her surveillance secret.

Her mother and Brian made their way onto Broadway. Shadowing them would be more difficult in the glare of the busy thoroughfare. She could see Brian waving and whacking his arms in the air the way he liked to do to control the space around him, as if he was swatting a million flies away, a million ideas, bullying her mother, driving home point important only to him and his control over her.

She clung to the darkness, stepping in to a door well, peeking out just enough to see. She saw a car pull over just ahead of her mom and Brian. A man got out, older, tall, bearded, and leaned against his car on the sidewalk side. In a moment, all three of them were talking. They seemed to know each other. After a few moments, they got in the man's car and drove away. She tried to follow but could not keep up. Having nowhere to go, the Skytrain long shut down, and afraid to return to Bo's squat if Jordan wasn't there, she continued along Commercial Drive, following in the general direction of the stranger's car. It was cold, and she was underdressed for the weather. She wanted to weep. Why was she even walking this way? How could she keep up to a car? Her tired legs wanted to dissolve. She wanted to curl up on the cold concrete, burrow into a crevice in a wall and sleep. But she was scared. She kept walking.

And then she saw the car, although she'd walked only a few blocks. She came closer and saw the lights of a café. She cautiously looked in through the fogged-up window and saw the three of them sitting together. And then, before she could decide what to do, Brian got up and left. She panicked. She slipped back down the long wall of businesses. Brian came out into the night. He turned towards where she was and started walking in her direction. He was old and didn't move all that fast, but he was strong. She knew that. He looked like he shouldn't be strong. He had a fat chin and a soft belly, but he had strong hands. And in any case, she wasn't strong. She remembered the previous summer. She'd been sent over to clean her grandparents' house. She would earn $10 for helping her grandmother. That was the deal. Brian would be out. But when she got there, it went all cockeyed. Her grandmother had had to leave to help a friend just released from hospital and Brian had to postpone his bowling game. He was angry that he wouldn't get to do what he wanted. The house needed cleaning. No discussion, said her grandmother as she left. Moira needs me. I need you, thought Skye, more than your sick old friend. She wanted to go home but there was no way. She was trapped. She'd have to do all the cleaning. Brian didn't clean. That was his rule.

She started vacuuming the living room. Brian was downstairs in the basement repairing a chair. She finished the carpet and the furniture. She then had to dust. Brian had left a small step ladder for her to reach the ceiling and upper walls. She was on the ladder, stretching to reach distant cobwebs with the feather duster. All of a sudden Brian was behind her, touching the calf of her right leg, gripping it, releasing it, gripping it again. His right hand slowly slithered up her bare leg to her shorts. The hand planted itself on her rear. The fingers of the hand moved the softness of the fleshy cheek, and squeezed. Then his left hand went to the other cheek of her bottom. She froze, like a space ray had stunned her, like she was back in that invisible block of icy glass.

"Safety first, little Skye. You should have waited for me before climbing the ladder. I told you that, right? Just like your good-for-nothing mother. Useless as a turd."

He hadn't told her. She would have remembered. She remembered everything back then. At least, as much as she heard.

He caught up to her.

"Jesus H. Christ, you're a sneaky little bitch, aren't you?" Brian snarled as he grabbed her arm. She shook him loose and started running. Back towards Broadway and the safety of light. Brian chased after her. He was yelling and wheezing. Surely she could outrun a nasty, old, fat man. She was so tired, but she found the wind to run. As her feet were moving, as her heart was pumping, she couldn't stop the awful thought that he'd catch her, that no matter what she did, she couldn't get away. She shot over the bridge that crossed the steep ravine and the train tracks below. She glanced back and could not see Brian. But he must be there. He must be just behind her.

Momentarily out of his sight, she tried to get off the sidewalk. She jumped to the left, flew over a barricade, landed in space, her legs pedaling the air, hoping for any kind of traction, knowing it was not to be, not believing she had been so rash, tumbling through the swoosh of black air, crashing down onto the steep, trash-burdened slope of the deep ravine, smashing her head against a hunk of discarded concrete, her body slamming out of sight, into the sleeping, brutally sharp, blackberry jungle at the bottom.

Chapter 22

Old wounds
Thursday, November 22

Even with the consumption of strong, late-night coffee, I managed a solid four hours of sleep. When I got up I felt renewed, but hungry. I called Kate Morris at home and advised her that I was pretty much over feeling sorry for myself, that I was going to play by the stupid rules and would be in the office before her... as usual. She thanked me for the heads-up and said she'd beat me in so I had better hit the road right away. I said, oh yeah, you and whose commute?

I am not a jogger by nature but I have never been particularly averse to working up a bit of a sweat from time to time, and I imagine getting the old heart pumping at a gallop has some intrinsic health value. Still, I have never seen that there was any pleasure to be had in running, unless it is the sheer ecstatic panic to be found in outrunning a bear, escaping a burning building, or, in a rare case, an outraged husband.

However, the rain had stopped; there was a hint of winter-morning sun somewhere off in the east. Perhaps a bear had woken early from its hiber-nap and wandered into the city. I strapped on my running shoes, draped my aging body in sweats, and plodded off at 6:30 for a token 15-minute run. I was home in ten, having found a shortcut. Ten minutes and I was exhausted and dripping wet. I showered, had a slice of toast and some fresh coffee, and was in the office at 7:35 a.m. Kate beat me by a minute.

We met in her office, and I filled her in on my recovery from self-pity and my interesting stakeout.

"You are nuts," she said emphatically.

"Maybe. I'll let Cathy know that I've been poaching her case...and that step-grandfather may be a *player*. Sinister guy."

"Contact the Records Management Unit. Maybe there is some history we don't know about. Ask them to do a quick search. We'd like to know today." Kate was in boss mode and her clipped delivery made me grin. She was revved up by my recovery. As a rule she was rather slow-speaking, deliberate, and thoughtful, and preferred to have her minions come up with the ideas. She seemed content to create the conditions that would allow us to think things through.

It was too early to pester RMU, and I knew I'd have to present myself in person to emphasize that I wanted some action. I spent half an hour doing some draft recording. I heard Cathy come in the building and decided I would pigeonhole her and confess my poaching.

I steered her into my office and sat her down.

"You're a little pushy this morning, Wally. Feeling the pressure of the leash?"

"Naw. Look." And I began my evening's tale. In 15 minutes I had shared the whole futile, sleepless mess with her.

"Stakeout? You poor, deluded, wannabe dick."

I cracked a smile, pleased that she knew the language of noir.

"A bit of fantasy, I grant. Still, I think I made a connection with Carla Prentice. I'm off to RMU to see what, if anything, they have on Scraggs. There has gotta be some history...pre-electronic history."

I wanted to tell her more, not words of concern for missing children and hobbled parents and men of uncertain reliability, particularly. Something else, something really best left unsaid...that I am in need of some love, some refreshment of intimacy as I sense time drizzling away from me. That I also fear seeming the middle-aged fool. That I have no experience with growing old. And who does?

In my twenties I often wondered what time would do to me. In the Woodward's shopping center I would look upon the wrinkled and leathery faces, gathered about in small pockets near the deli, gazing out on the salami buyers, wanting a look, a nod, some recognition that their lives were at least as interesting as a Cornish pasty. Some may have found some small comfort watching the world rush by. Would I die a player, someone involved in the oomph of his life? Or would I end up in some urban mall watching the purveyors of sliced sandwich meat hawk their wares?

While I silently imagined verboten workplace love trysts, Cathy patted me on the shoulder and exited my office.

I called RMU, said I was desperate for a file that might not exist and would be there in two shakes of a bureaucrat's tail.

The city is full of little business malls, rolling out into the countryside, like a never-ending, concrete freight train. These storage communities, that harbour fly-by-night, small-scale manufacturing depots, pop-up more and more along and inside of major arteries of transport.

I parked and entered the shadowy hall of mouldy old records. It was just 9:30.

I explained my quest to the clerk, Vicky I-can't-remember-her-last-name. She was young, 30 or so, but with that inside, cloistered pallor that comes from hiding away from the wink of the sun. I had a brief Bogie moment, that scene from *The Big Sleep* when Bogart steps inside a bookstore to escape a sudden downpour and comes face to face with a four-eyed, professionally glossed Dorothy Malone, book store proprietress and budding party girl. Her transformation worked for the old Hump if only because he had a flask of flame juice in his car. I was without my flask.

Unaware of my irrepressible cinematic imaginings, Vicky didn't veer from her own business-like script and explained the self-evident fact that "people don't just drop in here." I explained that I respected the rules perhaps more than anyone else I had ever met, and that it was causing me an astonishing amount of torment to be a party to my own disrespect for the exquisitely honed file request system. I apologized for circumventing decades of practice but, in this case, I needed to see what was what ASAP. And worse, I didn't actually know what I was looking for or if indeed it actually existed.

And then I offered the clincher. I had called. I was not unexpected.

After disappearing briefly back among the shelves, likely to consult with a superior, Vicky returned and explained their system of file storage. More importantly, she made it clear that they couldn't allow me to roam harum-scarum amid the boxes. I would have to offer up names and let them look.

Many years of files were manually recorded. It was a labour-intensive thing I was asking.

Aside from not having many names, and no sure geography, I was as prepared as a boy scout in the Himalayas. I gratefully accepted Vicky's non-negotiable offer of help and gave her the names I had. I gave her the two most likely names. "The first name is Jane Baynes. She married Brian Scraggs in the early to mid-seventies. Don't know for sure though." I paused. "I think they lived in Burnaby."

The previous evening I had used my offer to drive Carla back home to wheedle tidbits of information from her. The wheedling was incidental to the offer of a ride. From the sleepy, rambling recitation of her life, I extracted the nitty-gritty: that Burnaby had been her home base most of her life, that she had never strayed far from home, even to the point of not going with her husband when he shuffled off to live with the buffalo in Alberta. Ultimately, she raised her two kids on her own. Yes, her mother and stepdad helped out some…too much, if the truth be known…but families were like that, weren't they…too much of one thing, not enough of other stuff.

I was having some trouble staying awake and on the road, so I grunted and nodded and let her talk as if I was a full party to the conversation.

Eventually, we rolled onto her street, and I pulled up to her door.

As she had started to exit, she turned to me and tentatively reached out to touch my right hand, which was glued to the steering wheel. "I appreciate you looking for Skye…it seems above and beyond." Her hand had rested on mine for less than a second-an appreciative gesture, a kindness. "And…about Brian," she added, "…I'm sorry about him."

"A hard man to like…" I had said, more candid than I wanted to be.

She gestured that she agreed with my observation and got out of the car. Before closing the door, she leaned in and asked if I was all right to drive home. I said I might wait here a few minutes just to make sure. She invited me in. I thanked her but said I would be off in a couple of minutes. She closed the car door and walked away.

I rubbed my eyes, slapped my face lightly, and drove home.

My RMU reverie was jostled by Vicky declaring that "that's not all that helpful." I must have looked lost. "Burnaby," she continued, "well, I'm afraid we don't cross reference by city."

Looking somewhat perturbed by my obvious inadequacies, and by what she clearly felt would be a big waste of her time. She reluctantly agreed to have a look for files under the names Scraggs and Baynes. She advised me to sit. I sat.

It wasn't like RMU was a dentist's office. There were no popular magazines to help pass time. Stark would have been too elaborate a description of their alleged waiting room. Forced to fall back on my meagre inner resources, I sat and closed my eyes...just for a moment. I am often willing to confess that at least 10 percent of my work day is unproductive. I plan for it. This is my think time really, time when I sort and clarify and come to terms with the work that I do, the absolutely mandated things that have to be done and all those extraneous little details that flesh out the body of work, that furnish the job with its esoteric rewards.

In my heavy-lidded reverie I listed the youth I needed to see, tallied them in order of both their existing crises and my bureaucratic requirements. Without bothering to resort to pen and paper, I was having difficulty jotting down my thoughts. The exercise may seem modest; how careful could one be creating an imaginary to-do list?

As I visualized the list, created my set piece of names and tasks, I prioritized the coming few days. No matter what I planned, other demands were sure to surface. I could see that now, had always known it, the sad fact that the peak pleasure of my job was in its unpredictability. I couldn't be responsible if I failed to do something, because I had no real control. Emerging events ruled my pathetic roost.

I was not unaware that this was the anniversary of JFK's assassination. In times to come, would I remember that I honoured the day of his death one year by sitting in a totally unfriendly waiting room, wasting the time of a clerk or two looking up files which might not exist? I certainly knew how to grieve. And show respect.

As the minutes slipped by, I regained my professional composure a bit. I had loafed long enough. I sent word to the beleaguered Vicky that I was expected elsewhere and would check back with her towards the end of the day to see if she had found anything. She countered my offer and said she would call *me* if there were any results. We exchanged out respective informational vitals, and I drove back to the office.

The traffic was thin for a weekday. The air was cold, but I kept the driver's window down just to enjoy the sting of a winter breeze against my face. The few hours' sleep I had managed were quickly proving insufficient for my needs. How quickly we age into naptime. I'd be sawing logs before lunch at the rate I was going.

The refreshing breeze and my active mind kept me awake and I was back at the office at 11:15. In those 15 minutes on the road, I had reached a life-changing decision.

You can always tell when a pall has been cast over a familiar place; you live with the emotional temperature of your work place, or home, or wherever you intimately go. It's not necessarily the gloomy darkness suddenly descending into a room, or that the curtains have been tenderly shut to shield sorrowful eyes from the light, or any other appreciable thing that you'd notice right away as you entered. It might even take a few moments as yours senses adjust to the false and brittle quiet. The eyes of others don't necessarily suddenly avert from yours; they may, of course, human nature being what it is; but likely they will glance quickly up at you and then tear away, as if those who know an as yet undisclosed agony, are regrettably privy to it, are shattered by the fullness of the information, and it is too much for them to share. They desperately avoid being the one to reveal it. But they know, everyone knows that someone will tell. Everyone wants you to know; they just don't want to be the one to tell.

It wouldn't have been fair to extract it from the first person in my line of fire. I would have to make entry slowly, with an appropriate office pace, craft my way to my office. Someone might intercept me and clue me in.

The intensity of my cluttered office almost overwhelmed me. Fortunately, no matter where I chucked my valuable work tools and documents, I always left the chair free. It welcomed me, and I took a load off.

I looked up, and Cathy was in the doorway. She was the messenger.

"Some early morning bottle collectors were scavenging along Commercial Drive…below it actually…the part that runs over the train track gully." I nodded. I knew that spot, had driven over it twice last night.

"They found a young girl. Dead. There was a police patrol car driving by. They tentatively identified her pretty quickly. It's Skylark Prentice, I'm afraid."

She burst into tears. Welled up, anyway. I got up and approached her, gestured as if to comfort her. She silently consented. I reached out and embraced her. Other staff assembled in the hallway outside my office. Just to be there. To support us and offer what little anyone can when this happens. I continued to hold Cathy. How long? How does one end an embrace of consolation? Was it more than that? I was clearly overthinking the moment. We simultaneously released each other. She had been holding me as well, supporting me in a way I hadn't thought to need.

How painfully odd. Neither of us had known the girl. On our team, Dru Janes was the only one who had ever met Skye. Did it matter? Cathy and I knew the mom and knew her grief would be insurmountable.

We had stepped back from our supportive embrace. Then, with that breath of relaxed space between us, Cathy said she needed to contact Carla. I understood that and said that it sounded like a good plan.

"You'll come with me, right?"

Did I have a choice? Of course. Would I make the right one? Hopefully, I would find some way to offer what modest support I could, knowing that nothing would soothe the pain that Carla Prentice would be feeling, knowing that I didn't want to add to her suffering by any foolish, pre-emptive misstep.

Social Work is a profession, by no means the only one, which often finds itself buried in the mire of loss. I hadn't given this luminous truth more than cursory thought until a few years into the work. I'm not saying I hadn't tossed it around somewhere in the darker regions of my brain, just that I hadn't worked at it. Loss was just one more big-ticket emotional item which I hadn't actively shopped for. I suppose you don't have to actually shop for it. Loss seems to find you no matter where you are hiding.

Most of the kids I had dealt with over the years were past masters at being tripped up by their losses. These losses were rarely subtle. Memories of everything that had been ripped out of their lives were always smacking them about. Many didn't deal with the blows all that graciously. Who could? Violence… towards themselves or others, prostitution, often after the traumatic loss of their innocence, drugged and drunken crazy behaviour, mutilation, of themselves or animals, suicide, a murder here or there—all of the troubles in their lives made my occasional emotional shortfalls seem petty. Even "petty" seems too strong a term.

When Jeanne had given me the old heave ho, packed up Jake and her other belongings, and hightailed it to a more rewarding domestic arrangement, I wanted to weep. I tried to… but I couldn't. Didn't! For a time I felt like a kid who has moseyed away in a mall and wondered where Mommy might be. Jeanne's flight left me rootless but I had been somewhat numb even before she departed. I spent a bit of time being angry, as if it was expected. Ultimately, I did not want to be one of those cranky aggressive ex-spouses who haemorrhaged all over the place when wife and child moved away. Jake had never asked me why I hadn't raised him, fought for him, and I certainly hadn't brought up the subject. I had always been included in his life, like some distant relative who came by every couple of years if the wind was blowing in the right direction.

I was never an overly intimate, always-there-no-matter-what dad. Jeanne and I had made sure that Jake and I had visits and I took advantage of most of those opportunities. But I had missed much of his life. I was clearly an underachieving parent, stuck in the doldrums of my failed choices.

My fallback position was always that I had my work. I always felt good about that. That's where my success as a human being was going to be noted. Not on my collapsed home front.

Once I was a cog in the system, I started to accumulate a host of experiences, other people's experiences. They burrowed under my skin. They were always there, leaving little room for anything else. Back in the early eighties, I worked with a mom and her two little daughters. Charlene Hutton was a strong-willed young woman in her late twenties who believed that her daughters, Casey, who was eight, and Melissa, a year younger, were old enough to look after themselves while she was out enjoying a healthy social life. The girls *were* fairly independent for their age and seemed to appreciate their mother's confidence in them. Of course, the local school and the neighbours in the apartment complex they lived in had a slightly different analysis. In time, the kids were apprehended. Charlene was perceived to be a fairly competent mother apart from the forceful and potentially dangerous avowal about their capacity to manage without adult supervision during her occasional absence. State intervention in her life and our requirement that she modify her extreme views eventually began to have a positive impression on her. It was beginning to seem that our high-quality work was going to be blessed with an all around happy outcome. Unfortunately, fate, fickle and frenzied, intruded. Days before the kids were to be returned, Charlene went on a date with some anonymous devil. We never discovered who that was. They came back to her place and, at some point in the evening, she was raped and murdered. Strangely enough, it was a quiet death. None of her neighbours apparently heard a thing.

Her kids never got to say goodbye, always an irreparable facet of sudden death. In due course, they went to live with relatives in Kamloops.

In all my life, none of my losses would or could match theirs.

But if I was being honest with myself, not that I was 100 percent comfortable with unbridled self-examination, I knew that I still had time to make a few amends. I had a son who was beginning the intricate journey of marriage. While I had no advice to offer from the success column, maybe my experience of profound failure might have a nugget worth sharing.

And maybe, just maybe, I could even squeeze out a bit of grandfatherly steadfastness should the opportunity arise.

I drew my thoughts back to Carla Prentice and her insurmountable loss.

I knew that we were jumping the gun by rushing right out. Cathy had told me that the police had advised after-hours that they had found the body of a young girl and that the description matched the missing person's circular for Skye Prentice. I could understand Cathy's desire to reach out to Carla, but these sorts of entanglements required tact and timing. We were aware that the body was very likely Skye's, but probably there had been no formal identification.

I followed Cathy to her office and suggested we go to talk to Kate. Even as I said it, Kate was in Cathy's office, and the three of us strategized. Cathy would speak directly to the police, get their take on the death, and find out what their next steps would be. Kate would reach up the ladder of our ministry and see what our wiser, more removed and level-headed talking heads had to offer in the way of advice. I would advise Skye's school, once we had some assurance that it was indeed Skye. I would also try and contact her brother through Manny.

As we parceled out our small administrative tasks, I was uncomfortably aware that Skye, if it indeed was her, had died within inches of where I had been less than a dozen hours earlier. It was also where Carla and Brian Scraggs had also spent some time together and apart in the wee hours of this morning. All of us, mere minutes and feet away from where this sad little girl had died.

That suggestive shadow of time and happenstance did not sit well with me. Was it Billy Burroughs who said there are no coincidences? I couldn't remember. Maybe others have said it. It sounds like something *anyone* could have said. As if it mattered. The police would make their determinations, all I could do was give information. If there were dots to be connected, that was their bailiwick.

Chapter 23

Jordan Prentice and the whole ball of wax

It seemed to Jordan that his bones had been pulverized, turned to salt, as if he had looked back at some cataclysm of his own making. He could not escape believing that he had been the cause of Skye's slip into eternal darkness. His body sagged onto the pavement. He saw nothing recognizable, heard nothing but Bo's nattering voice.

Bo had tracked him down to give him the news. Bo was a notorious bullshitter.

"Quit fucking with me, Bo. I'm in no mood." But Bo had that look, that classic cat-swallowed-the-canary look.

Bo persisted. He had heard the EMT vehicles wailing in the night, startling him out of an unusually deep sleep. Sirens were commonplace and he couldn't explain why this one jarred him awake. Against his usual practice, he had slipped out of the squat in the early morning darkness and skulked his way the couple of blocks to the source of the action. The body was still where it fell, though it was now covered by a police tent. The entire area was cordoned off and there was no way to tell who it was, who was dead, which mattered little to Bo at that point aside from the excitement and the chaos and the chance to poke around someone else's grungy little tragedy.

Street scuttlebutt told him that a couple of binners had found the girl. The police had taken them away to interrogate. Without much effort, Bo discovered that there had been three of them. Calgary Al had decided to slip away from his two buddies because of a small matter of an outstanding warrant. He couldn't believe his two buddies actually wanted to get involved. He had said,

"Do what the fuck ya want. Just leave me out of it. I got enough misery." It wasn't a threat, but they knew better than to cross him.

Calgary Al was pretty sure he could hang around the edges of the crowd and sneak a peek at the outcome of his shared discovery without risking detection. Even though he also had an inkling that the two screwed-up good citizens he'd been hanging with would eventually spill their guts, he felt confident. To them he was just old Calgary Al. The joke would be on the cops. He hated Calgary, avoided it whenever he could. And besides, he was from Winnipeg. Anyway, Al was his old man's name, not his.

As street smart as he was, Calgary Al couldn't help mentioning to others that it was sad to see such a little girl snuffed out.

Eventually, Bo caught wind that there was a third person who had found the body. When braced by Bo, Al readily gave a description of the body that they'd found.

Jordan had little choice but to believe the news, as difficult as it was to accept.

Still overwhelmed by grief and guilt, he made his way to a phone at the Clearing House. He called his mother. It was close to noon. She was usually only in one of two places…home or work. There was no answer.

He needed to be with her, but going to where she worked would be hopeless. Stupid. He hit up a Clearing House staff for a return bus ticket and in moments was on a bus for the slow ride to his mother's home.

Two busses later he was dropped about four blocks from his mother's street. It wasn't a neighbourhood he knew well and he'd missed it by one stop. They had moved often when he was growing up; sometimes every couple of months. There had been a period of dubious stability when he had stayed with his grandparents, and his mother and father attempted to live together in Calgary. That had lasted as long as it took to conceive Skye. Then there were a couple of years where they had all lived with Brian and Jane. Eventually, for everyone's sanity, Carla and her two children set up shop on their own and began the slow escalation to limited success.

He couldn't remember a time when he'd felt grounded. His mom *tried* to bring balance into their lives; she worked hard, was honest and a pretty straight shooter. But she had so many doubts about herself. And whenever the events of her day swelled up like a giant wave had rolled in on her, coming close to crushing her, she would invariably retreat to her parents, to the punitive, but available Jane and Brian. They sucked much of the remaining life from her. That was how he saw both Brian and Jane, as aging, energy-sucking vampires.

Jordan tried to walk with firmness and intensity towards his mother's house. But he sensed that he didn't have sufficient resolve. He could barely concentrate on the act of walking. His feet should move, more naturally, he thought. He shouldn't have to think about moving his legs. He knew how to walk. But there was a pressure on either side of his head, just above his ears, a pressure that was not unfamiliar. He was about a block away. His legs were taking charge. They slowed down, almost began to lock in place. He thought it strange that his legs were in control of him…skinny, tired limbs controlling his brain. How fucked was that?

He jerked to a dead stop. Up ahead he saw Brian's car. It had pulled into the carport. He shifted off the sidewalk and shrunk behind a tree. It should have been obvious to him that they would leap to his mom's side. The tree had long branches with scaly bark. He peered through the undulating branches.

He remained motionless. Brian and Jane had got out of the car and walked through the carport to his mom's door. He could hear them knock. Brian always knocked and buzzed. Both. Never just one. Knock and buzz. He wanted to leave no doubt that *he* was at the door, that everyone knew that the Great Brian, had arrived and was seeking immediate entry.

Another car was coming down the street from behind him. He shifted position so that he wouldn't be seen. This confused him. He knew why he wanted to avoid Brian and his grandmother. What was odd to him was why he didn't want to be seen by strangers. The car passed by. There were two people in the vehicle, an older fellow and a somewhat younger woman. The driver, the woman, looked at him…looked his way, looked through him. The car drove on.

He clung to the tree. As his head rested on the hard wood, he replayed the steps he had taken to get there. Today, he had lost a third of his world. Skye had been his hope, their hope for some small redirection. Even as he thought that, he knew he had put too much weight on Skye's shoulders. Not that it mattered. She was immune to the pressure he was now bearing down on her.

He'd never thought of it before. It was only now, now that she was gone, that it was safe to acknowledge not only how much he loved her, but also how pivotal she had been to their survival.

He wanted to weep. If ever there was a time to, this was it. He clutched tighter to the tree, to the cold trunk of the aging eucalyptus. The name had come to him; he recalled a small lullaby Carla had once sung to them:

Weep Eucalyptus weep; against the swizzle-stick sea
Seep Eucalyptus seep; your sweet oils into the sea;
Sleep Eucalyptus sleep; let the whistling wind ever be
Sleep Eucalyptus sleep, in the arms of the wind, the mountains and me.

It was such a faint memory, so thread-like and distant, that he doubted it. And she may have made it up...he had a hazy recollection of her playfulness, humming tunes. He continued to cling to the tree, but aware that this extended hug had gone on a little too long, serving no purpose other than to root him in indecision. He released his grip, turned away from the tree and slipped down the trunk into a sitting position. An elderly face peered out of a window of the house on whose property he was trespassing. The old person, man or woman he could not tell, was holding the flimsy curtain to one side with their left hand and squinting out, staring at him as if he was the most curious creature ever.

The ground was too cold. The wet earth was beginning to chill him. He raised himself up and shivered. He'd been sniffling for days. Now it was the cold, his cold and his sorrow.

The wizened face continued to stare at him. If Jordan didn't move, he feared he might become as old, as caged as the ancient gawker.

Cathy had sharp eyes. She spotted Jordan Prentice as we drove by. We opted to have me walk back and see if it was him.

"Are you Jordan?" I asked the young man sitting trance-like on the lawn. He looked up and took me in. I had on my best, most accessible smile. He seemed to be in great distress. He had on a worn old winter jacket, dark blue and somewhat large for him. He continued to sit on the ground, resting against a tree. I approached him from directly in front, hopefully in a non-threatening manner.

He nodded. "Yeah, who are you?"

"I'm a social worker. Wally Rose. I extended my hand out to shake his. He followed suit.

"Ground must be cold," I suggested.

"Yeah. Cold. Wet too." He started to get up. I again offered my hand. He grabbed hold, and I gave him a slow tug.

Once elevated, he looked at the ground, brushed himself off, and said, "Thanks."

I nodded that it was okay. His demeanour suggested that he knew his sister's fate. Or it could also have been the dark acceptance of fate some people on the street have, a weary solemnity that verged on depression, an unrelenting melancholy.

"Did you know Skye?" he enquired. "Is that why you're here on my mom's street?" He looked beyond me towards his mother's basement suite. "I guess she knows?"

I looked towards Carla's place. There were a few cars parked in front of the house. Cathy would have entered the sad home by now, offered her condolences to Carla, all the time trying to gently display a bearing of care and concern.

"About your sister? Yeah, I'm pretty sure she does, Jordan. She probably could use you to be with her right now, I'd think. Are you up for that?"

I had come to recognize when my words were saccharine. I decided to clam up and let Jordan decide what he wanted to do, who he wanted to talk to. We were on someone's front lawn. I looked up at the house and saw an elderly mug staring out of a window. I saluted with a tip of my imaginary hat. The oldster nodded, or wobbled, its head, and cracked what I took to be a token look of relief.

"Look Jordan, you need to decide what you want to do. My partner is in with your mom, and I'm about to join her and pay my respects. Can I do anything for you?"

He wasn't thawing. I'd been there. When in doubt, freeze. Think. Try to make some sense of it. But there was no sense to be had. I was pretty sure that he needed help to make it as far as his mother's house. The home had started to fill up with a small cadre of compassionate people, all trying to comfort Carla. It was foolish to try, but it had to be done. There were things you just showed up for—christenings, weddings, funerals. And news of unexpected death. All of those rites of passage that need to be acknowledged. I had missed a bundle of them in my life. And once they were missed, there was no makeup test. The time had passed. Gone. This young man, his mother's only remaining child, needed to put in an appearance; he needed to hold his mother; to be held by her. He had already completed most of the journey. He was a featured player in this pointless tragedy, and, I also considered, might know something about the true cause of Skye's untimely exit.

"Come on," I said. "I'll walk there with you."

It was a silent stroll, that few hundred feet to the basement suite. There were a couple of cars other than Cathy's in the driveway. I knocked. I should have let Jordan do it, but he was close to automaton mode. We could hear muffled activity inside. I knocked a little louder. Jordan didn't seem to have the wherewithal to just open the door. Someone turned the knob. The door was opened by a middle-aged fellow, dark blue suit, wisp of grey hair strands reaching from the left side of his handsome head to the other side, paunch, but nicely tucked-in shirt, red face but not splotchy. He looked past me to Jordan, who had remained one step behind. "Come in, Jordan. Your mom could use you." He reached past me and tugged Jordan in. "Who are you?" he asked.

"Social Worker," I confessed. "My colleague's already here." I pointed into the suite in the general direction of Cathy, who was standing to one side, looking sad and supportive.

"Jack Wyden," he said and offered a hand to shake. "I'm a friend of Carla's. Actually, more a friend of Brian's…well, both Brian and Janie…" He stopped his extended explanation of who exactly he was friends' with and retreated into the suite.

I nodded a vague acknowledgement and followed him and Jordan into the claustrophobic suite. It had felt like a spacious phone booth when just the three of us had been in it a few days earlier. Now it seemed positively coffin sized, cramped, clammy, and hopeless. There were about a dozen people in the living room. Wyden made his way to the couch where Carla was sitting. He rested awkwardly on the arm of the couch, balancing himself by plunking his left arm on Carla's shoulder. She seemed to accept the gesture. Jordan stood in front of his mom. She reached out to him and drew him down next to her. He seemed to turn to putty. He surrendered into the seat next to her.

She held his hand; he burst into tears and they embraced each other. I moved closer to Cathy. She was talking to an older woman, the grandmother I guessed, but I wasn't sure. Scraggs came out of the washroom, looked around the room, saw me and shot me a scowl. The guy was wound tighter than a roll of duct tape. His grief, or his guilt, was getting to him, no doubt. I nodded back, held my middle finger in check, and offered him a weak smile.

The grief was getting to me too. I'd never done small emotional gatherings well. I start to sweat and look for the exit, reconsider if there was someone there I really want to get together with, reject the candidates available, and look again for the exit. Healthy families immerse themselves in ceremonial rituals. Perhaps something positive was going on in this room of caring people who'd gathered with a moment's notice to support the family of Skye Prentice.

Though there were a dozen people in the tight and solemn quarters, I noticed that the resonance of the voices had begun to lessen. Condolences had been offered, acquaintances renewed; it was time to be getting back to a cheerier life. I caught Cathy looking at me. I hoped it was a "well, we've done what we can" look, a fitting gambit prior to hitting the road. I suppose I'd been expecting the unfolding of a revelation of historical sexual abuse. That had been our secondary rationale in coming and staying a while longer than we had expected. I had an image of truth revealed, born perhaps from such set scenes as were found in films like *After the Thin Man*, where all the surviving suspects are corralled in one room while the detective whittled away at the facts of the case until the only obvious suspect left had to be the guilty party.

I had a tendency to let my imagination work overtime, and often fell victim to movie references to explain away human failings. And, worse than anything else, I occasionally took myself too seriously and wound up disappointing one and all.

As I dallied on the fringe, holding up a wall and trying to assess the tone of the room, I kept my eyes on Brian Scraggs as well as on Jordan and his mother. Scraggs was circling the small coterie, chit-chatting here and there, rotating around his stepdaughter and her son. His eyes were locked on them. Were they intentionally avoiding meeting his gaze? It seemed that way. In my cinematic universe, something would naturally pop. But that didn't seem to be happening. Scraggs did come closer but Carla stuck a hand out in the universal "stop right there, buddy" sign. He gave her an angry look that said "'how dare you?" Nevertheless, he reared to a halt and changed direction. This led him straight to Cathy. I doubted they had met. I was unsure what he knew about our part in the mix, other than that we were social workers.

They started talking and I moved closer. It was a short conversation. "She won't say...too damn soft...but the family wants you to leave. There's no need for the government to be here."

Cathy wouldn't be one to cause a fuss. She was a confident worker but knew this was no time for the state to exacerbate a family's woe.

Stating the obvious, I interjected with, "I see you met Mr. Scraggs." Cathy nodded, not wanting to protract the pleasure, I suspected.

"We should probably go." She nodded again and went over to Jordan and his mother. She placed her hand quietly on Carla's shoulder, shook hands with both mother and son, turned and joined me, and we left.

The course of my next few months was set; a laundry-list of mechanical steps in the unravelling of my obligations, the wrapping up of my duties of care. That this epochal personal moment fell within the demanding Christmas season only served to layer my leaving with a sense of grand gestures, ones I would probably be the only one to pay much attention to.

Once I'd made the decision to wind down, I had to give some serious thought to discharging my professional duties. In many ways, they had become very personal promises, not necessarily spoken, but issued freely to each youth with whom I had a compact; an exchange between official of the state and young person who was beneficiary of some guardianship service, or, if not guardianship, some similar benefit or weight. Each of the young people I was connected to had some portion of pressing business that needed completion. Each was in his own life's play; each had barely reached the end of the first act.

I would review their lives and determine the most appropriate gift I could give. Likely it would be some small bureaucratic gesture, some token to ease the present or the future or to mitigate some poignant piece of the past. High on my list of parting gestures was to support Kate to find the time to act as an emissary for Monica Maggin. I drafted an e-mail to Kate saying that I appreciated her covenant to intervene between mother and daughter and that I knew that she would not only make the effort to open some lines of communication, but would give it her all. I was laying it on thick, I suppose. Kate would see right through my pandering.

Over the next few weeks, as I arranged my parting gestures, I would lay out a personal campaign to meet with each of the youth.

For some, it would be a small agony to see me. Kevin would resist. There wasn't enough time in creation for me to begin to soften the blows life had pummelled him with.

Ryan would painfully voice the unending abandonment he had always struggled with.

For a new kid like Erin, I hoped my small token, the support already in place, would please her.

As befitted the occasion, my team would arrange something, a going away celebration, a ceremony of moving on, an observance for them as well as for me. I had been to plenty. They all smack of a wake with the body still slightly warm and right there in the room.

The employer squashed its vendetta against me. Why waste a bullet on a lame duck when he was likely going to waddle away anyways. Millie Hunt was somewhat perturbed because she felt we could win it. Having had some experience at winning, I could see her point.

Nevertheless, I imagine that Skye's death and the impact on my team influenced the decision to sidestep my indiscretion. We had gone the extra mile in trying to provide service to the Prentice family. Even in the cold light of a remote bureaucracy, this counted for something.

Chapter 24

Pasture
Spring the following year

It was a warm spring day. I had caught the morning ferry from Horseshoe Bay, landed in the old coal-mining town of Nanaimo, bypassed its sprawling clutter of strip malls excesses, and driven up Island. Once not much more than a trim little country town, with a cosy city core, Nanaimo had ballooned over the years. Its northern commercial district had swollen into a distended, compulsive-shoppers wet dream.

I couldn't get past the strand of malls and big-box emporiums fast enough.

20 minutes north of Nanaimo, the new Inland Island Highway reaches the Parksville turnoff. This is where the old highway picks up. If I had been in a hurry, I could have stayed on the efficient, four-lane speedway. But I wasn't in any particular rush. And I had a destination. And more, I had memories of countless holiday car trips up island when I was a kid, sitting in the back seat of my old man's Valiant, the summer breeze, dashed with sea spray, blowing in my mom's open window, whipping through the back seat, cooling my sister and me as our damp legs stuck to the plastic seats, drying the sweat and the tears from our laughter, our crying, our yelps of joy and contentment with the fullness of family life. Those frenzied camping trips, accented by an overnight stay in an auto court when summer rains poured down with too much abandon or when we couldn't find space in campgrounds. Those were my halcyon days, made all the more bittersweet by my inability to replicate them for my son, for my fragmented family, for my notion of how I had wanted my life to unfold.

Dave Waters, my social-worker friend, had invited me up to his home to spend a weekend and debrief my plans, pretty much finalized, to accept the government's recent buyout offer to all of their human bits of public service antiquity. As public policy, it flew in the face of the anticipated boomer meltdown. Thousand of aging children conceived in the wake of World War 2 would be abandoning careers in favour of retirement. However, their bumbled planning worked for me. Essentially it would allow me to retire at full pension at age 55, which was just around the corner. Otherwise, I'd be on tap to graduate from the work world in maybe five years. And I wouldn't have lasted.

The previous September 11, a Monday morning, I had been lounging on my couch at home around nine a.m...the TV was on mute... I was contemplating how best to manage my second week or so of stress leave...gaping into the wasteland of my aimless day...when...the image of a meandering airplane caught my eye...a television horror show...that terrible thrust of metal into the World Trade Centre. That cataclysmic event had sent most of the western world reeling; on a very selfish note it was a wrenching message that life was a crapshoot, and that I needed to engage in some long-term self-care. I was exhausted. My nights, up to then, had been an unsettled jumble of thoughts, fears and visions of small impending professional disasters... and there had been much lack of sleep...hours...days without sleep.

After September 11, the whole earth seemed on fire.

More stressful on the home front though, for me, was the lacklustre expectation that I engage with a psychologist. Surely talking about the pressure would relieve my stress. Odd premise, I thought. I didn't need to talk about my torment to understand it. I didn't want to understand it; to understand it, I thought, would only reinforce the gulf which was insinuating itself between me and the demands of working with damaged and courageous kids.

Nevertheless, my leave had given me the first real inkling that I could reformat my life, step away from the work, from the kids I was committed to. I began to see, somewhat surprisingly, that my life, my psychic life, my true life, was bordering on the verge of collapse. Ultimately, I had no choice; I needed an escape. That insight, coupled with a nonsensical government policy shift, set the stage.

I parked my car next to the small terminal and caught the next ferry to what Dave often called his "Oyster" Island. Dave was Johnny-on-the-spot to pick me up. "Why spend money when we're going to be so wasted you won't be driving anyway?" he had said, which, considering he was usually an abstainer, amused me a bit.

I jumped into his old pickup and we plodded up the ferry hill and the few kilometres to his woodland home.

Dave and Carolyn had bought their land, twenty acres, back in the '60s when it was (forgive me) dirt cheap. For years they simply camped on it. Eventually, as finances allowed, they built a home. Their property was in the middle of the island, and the house they built was positioned on a small knoll that gave them, when it was completed, a faint glimpse of the sea to the east.

Ten years earlier, they had packed in the city and their jobs and lit out to their island sanctuary. I had met Dave back in the late seventies, when I'd travelled to Victoria with Lindy Lavallee and her social worker, Pru Tait. Lindy was being placed in a specialized resource and I'd been asked to come along to make the transfer easier, to be an escort and a bit of influence in case Lindy got agitated. Dave was the local worker who would carry the case until Lindy returned to the Lower Mainland. We hit it off and had remained friends over the years.

After they retired, Dave and Carolyn had a few grand years. Their plans hit a rut in the road, however, and, in due course, Carolyn became irretrievably ill and had died two years ago. Dave had been shattered, and I had spent a week with him as he dealt with the loss. The experience of giving support was profound for me and, not that our friendship needed that time together, it had allowed our bond to strengthen.

This go-around, though my impending loss was of a different variety, Dave had offered to be a sounding board for my imminent escape. He showed me the spare room and poured us each a glass of red wine. We adjourned to the porch. The porch had been Carolyn's idea. One of her favourite movies was an old Richard Widmark thriller, *Panic in the Streets*. Although there was a lot to recommend the film, what entranced Carolyn the most was one of the story lines. While much of the film was bleak, violent, and foreboding, the scenes of the home where the public health officer hero lived, where he escaped to, entranced her. The movie was set in New Orleans where many homes had enclosed porches that screened out the bugs but allowed summer breezes to waft gently through. Carolyn insisted, once they got around to building, that a southeast-facing screened porch, with electric heating, extra insulation and double-glazed windows, was a must. In the summer, the room was somewhat cooler, with soft, random breezes flowing through. In the winter, if there was even a hint of winter sun, the room was almost comfortable, at least in the late morning. They had attached storm shutters for really inclement weather but on this day, in the early afternoon, the faint sun warmed the porch to shirt-sleeve comfort. We settled into the thickly upholstered old couch and chair and stared out into the sloping field.

"Thanks, Dave. This feels good."

He waved it away, as if the gesture of friendship was predestined. From time to time, in between sips of wine, I took him in. Dave was shorter than me, a few years older, and a lot skinnier, sort of a Jimmy Stewart body type. Skinny guys always look the same. Once they get sick, they waste away quickly, but it's hard to notice. Dave didn't look sick, which was a relief. He had a bit of a tan, but I knew he skied and hiked. Reflecting light from mountain snow and bright winter glare would give anyone colour.

I wanted to get into it, into dancing around my dilemma. Talking about myself was uncomfortable but I wanted to get on with it…get on with it so it would be over. But there were some preliminaries

"You still miss her I guess, eh?" I chipped in to the silence. Of course he still missed her, the scent of her, her deep laugh, her comfort, and her class. I'd spent much of my life on my own. You learn to manage, to get through the day and do the stuff that needs doing on your own. You may be lonely but you are independent and self-reliant. People like Dave and Carolyn were more complete, larger than their individual parts. Once death intervened and interrupted their partnership, the survivor suddenly became less than his or her part. That was how I romanticized their coupled existence, and the effects of loss.

"Always will," he said, "always."

"Yeah. It's not the same, I know. Not by a long shot. But sometimes, you know, I still feel married to Jeanne. How fucked is that? Divorced more than half my life and I still incorporate her into my aimless fantasies."

He questioned that. "I hope you're exaggerating a bit."

"A bit, maybe," I granted.

"Look Wally, I'm doing well. As good as I could be. Slow and easy. Everyday unearths a bit of recovered ground. Keeping busy when I want to, kicking back when I need to. What about you?"

I took a mouthful of the wine and gave his question a glib answer. "I made a choice a long time ago. Career. The fact that I fell into it aside, I lucked into my life's work. Loved doing it, even the shitty stuff. Now, it's withering up. And I can tell that I'm going to miss it."

"You loved it, eh? What, the tons of paper work? The bureaucratic anemia? No, what I mean is, the *bureaucratic constipation*. You couldn't have loved that? I know, for a fact, that you didn't. You loved being *useful*, that whole ball of wax, in spite of the bullshit. Which, even *I* haven't forgotten, was piled higher and deeper every blessed year."

"Yeah. The bullshit. Anyway, maybe I haven't said it right. I have a lot wrapped up in the job. Who I am...how I see myself. This is not a big mystery. I know I will miss all of it. And I'm...I know this sounds demented...I'm afraid I'll get bored. I'm not a hobby guy...not like you." Dave was a woodworker, an artisan. He made furniture, and had done so for years, way before he had left the city.

A long silence followed...10 minutes, 12. I don't know what Dave was being silent about except I assumed he had come to embrace the quiet of a widower's life. I had no idea what people were actively in his life now. The week I had spent with him two years earlier, after Carolyn died, had been filled with people, a few relatives, but mostly kindly, supportive neighbours, who brought food and comfort and all the things you might not necessarily experience in the city.

I was taking advantage of the intermittent silence to think about him and what on earth I had expected him to guide me to.

"What I found," Dave fractured our stillness, "what I found...what I had to learn later...months later, after I packed it in...was that the kids I missed the most were the ones I had been with at the end. You know how it is, Wally...the old ones, your piece of work with them is over...you've given them your best shot; your memories of them are as intact as they will ever be…a few may even keep in touch…on their terms, not yours. And then there are the ones you've never met; will never meet. Someone else will help them…it's the ones that are there now…right there, as needy, as available, as ready or not for whatever you bring to them…but they have a sort of shelf life too, and they will go to your successor, your replacement. It's covered, my friend."

The afternoon trickled effortlessly into the evening. We grazed on odds and sods in his fridge, and drank more than we should have, more than I should have, at any rate. The winter sun slipped from view and Dave and I drifted into our separate silences. Later, after snoozing for a time, we woke and he pointed me to my bed. I shuffled off to its comfort and dreamed…something, I'm sure.

In the morning he whipped up some asparagus and feta omelettes with a big side plate of fried oysters. It was a Sunday morning religious experience. After a couple of buckets of coffee, we went for a long walk through the woods, across the two-lane country road that traced the edge of sea. We strolled along the water's border for an hour or so until we hit a public campground.

By then a squall was forming. You could sense the storm taking shape; the water rippled; sea birds fluttered like Armageddon was nigh. The imagery suited me. But I was calm, thoughtful, a trace hung-over, and prepared for the next step. Dave had spotted the obvious—that the momentum of the lives of the kids I cared for would continue, that I could leave at any time and that, most of all, I should leave when I was on the ascent, not spiralling down. Now, the question was, what was my current direction? Could I ever pinpoint it?

We continued our trek away from the ocean. The tide was high. We rambled into the woods which adjoined the empty campground. It was a soft, meandering saunter with a gently sloping trail. The woods, Dave said, had once been a private estate, and was now a park.

The mainstay of the small park turned out to be a large clear grassy field, the home of the long composted, barely remembered bowling green. I could scarcely imagine what it must have once looked like. The field seemed like a high mountain meadow, hidden from view; untouched; unseen. Yet Dave told me that, 100 years earlier, there had been a vibrant, hearty, rural community culture; neighbours from nearby islands would have rowed over to spend the day and then braved the unforgiving, often unsettled sea to journey home. Even with that courageous ocean-going adventure under their belts, perhaps still woozy from some homemade island brew, they would have to journey inland any number of miles from their shore to reach the primitive safety of their home.

Time was different in those days. Lives were lived rough, they were full and complete, though likely shorter than now, but still, it would have all made sense to those living their hard lives. Their world was more basic. I could see that this search for simplicity was a factor for Dave in how he planned to spend his concluding years. When, I wondered, did you accept that you were on that final stretch, the back nine, the last leg? I had reached the stage where these were meaningful, if uncomfortable, questions. Given that I was unschooled in permitting these cerebral guests to land on my shallow mental shore, I suppose I was hoping for Dave to impart a definitive, somewhat painless drop-kick of wisdom. I was close.

We found an old bench and parked our aching fannies. Dave had a thermos of coffee and poured two cups. These country guys were very prepared. I was succumbing to the magic of the meadow, the melancholy of past times, the familiar comfort of hot coffee, the blissful aroma of it, steaming in a ceramic cup on a sun-chilled morning. In the city, on the job, similar moments, moments of brief reflection, of thought catching, of wiser contemplation, would flicker low and summarily flare out with any one of a hundred interruptions. The city was chock full of interruptions. They were avoidable, of course. City parks are large acreages and one can easily get lost in them. But I had found that I often manufactured my own distraction, as if too much contemplative solace would undermine my determination, my forward thrust. Years earlier I went for long, early-morning spring bike rides and was amazed to discover one particular morning, an army of silent tai chi disciples deep in the woods of Burnaby's Central Park. Their grace, their undulating beauty was an image of urban tranquility that stayed with me, even though I continued to race through my frantic days unabated.

Dave pulled out a joint and lit it. We had never discussed marijuana, except in the context of the sixties, and of course, Canada's unforgivably long failure to address, in any meaningful way at least, decriminalization. "A local product," he said, offering me a toke. "Certified organic!"

It had been years since I'd last smoked. The opportunity had cropped up from time to time, but professional jitters directed me to exercise restraint with any urge to indulge my diminishing list of pleasurable vices. In the sanctuary of these angelic woods, I accepted his gesture, drawing the smoke in and holding it in my lungs. The smoke was bittersweet, almost spicy. Hot to the tongue. The wind from the sea was whipping through the tops of the trees that sheltered the meadow. Dave topped up our cups of coffee and I rested, relaxed and unruffled, as if I had reached the end of some long journey and need go no further.

THE END

About Bill Engleson

Bill Engleson worked in the child welfare arena for more than 25 years, most of them as a front-line, journeyman, government protection social worker and a dedicated union activist. He surprised himself by taking his leave in March 2002 after a timely early retirement offer.

Shortly thereafter, he began an exhilarating eighteen months journey as a program manager for an eclectic urban social service agency, The Lower Mainland Purpose Society.

He completed that adventure in December 2003 and moved from the Lower Mainland to Denman Island. His key activities since then have been writing in a number of genres, community volunteering in the arts and social services, a lengthy stint as a marriage commissioner, and chopping wood when required.

He has written Like a Child to Home principally to depict, in fictional form, aspects of the demanding child welfare world he encountered, experiences not often explored in literature. Like a Child to Home is also very much meant to be a means of paying tribute to the amazingly resilient young people that he met along the way as well as to the hard working adults who shared that journey.

Printed in Canada